MURDER IN THE VICARAGE

MURDER IN THE VICARAGE

Classic Tales of Clerical Crime

Edited & Introduced by
Rex Collings

BELLEW PUBLISHING
London

This collection first published in Great Britain
in 1991 by Bellew Publishing Company Limited
7 Southampton Place, London WC1A 2DR

This collection © Rex Collings 1991

ISBN 0 947792 70 8

Phototypeset by Input Typesetting Ltd, London

Printed and bound in Great Britain by
Billings & Sons Ltd

CONTENTS

Acknowledgements

Grateful acknowledgement is made to the following for permission to reprint the material in this volume:

Mr Leggat Leaves his Card by J S Fletcher reprinted by permission of Faber and Faber Ltd from *Best Detective Stories 2* edited by Edmund Crispin.

Aitken and Stone Ltd for the story *Sanctuary* taken from *Miss Marple's Final Cases* copyright © Agatha Christie Limited 1979.

A P Watt Ltd on behalf of Jean Bell for *The Lion's Tooth* taken from *Fenn Country* by Edmund Crispin.

Whilst all reasonable attempts have been made to contact the original copyright holders, the Publishers would be happy to hear from those they have been unable to trace, and due acknowledgements will be made in future editions.

INTRODUCTION

'*While the knights kill him we hear the*

CHORUS:

Clear the air! Clean the sky! Watch the wind! take stone from stone and wash them

. . .

The knights, having completed the murder advance to the front of the stage and address the audience.

From *Murder in the Cathedral* T. S. Eliot

THERE is a sense in which in the majority of detective stories their authors like the knights in Eliot's play address the audience, the reader; and to the extent to which the reader, having suspended reality, accepts, or partially accepts, the proffered unravelling of the case, is the author deemed to have succeeded. Becket's murder, fact not fiction, is one of the most famous of clerical crimes, it captured the attention and the imagination of the medieval world, and the potency of the martyrdom is even today undiminished, although the present pilgrims to Canterbury may lack the time and endurance of their Chaucerian predecessors, preferring the motor-car or char-a-banc to the horse; and the afternoon or day's outing to days and nights of uncomfortable travelling.

The Church has provided not only victims but perpetrators and executioners too – and this is, as one would expect, reflected in literature as well as in life. When Kipling wrote:

Brandy for the Parson
'Baccy for the Clerk
Laces for a lady, and letters for a spy,
Watch the wall, my darling, while the Gentleman go by.

he was recording the fact that in the eighteenth century in many coastal areas, in the villages and hamlets, the Parson, if not an active participant (which often he was) was a passive beneficiary of the crime. Smuggling then even as it does today bred crime and led to death if not to damnation: and spying was as prevalent then as it is now.

In the novels of the period that began at the end of the eighteenth century, the clergy of the Established Church lacked heroic stature; those in Miss Austen's works – Mr Elton and Mr Collins for example – would today qualify for the description 'wimp'; and in Dickens's early novels written as the old world was being cleansed by the hurricane engendered by the accession of the young Virgin Queen, the curates in *Sketches by Boz* were still not men of bottom but were wan and usually palely loitering; and the Dissenters, exemplified by Stiggins in *The Pickwick Papers* – a man much addicted to Pineapple rum – are often figures of contempt set up to be ridiculed, men lacking prestige, integrity, and influence.

Trollope, the Reynolds of the Established Church writing rather later, in the high noon of the Victorian era, reflected the change that had by then taken place in the general standing of the Clergy, now comfortable, worldly, cultivated, secure in their place in society. But this picture neglects, is largely unrepresentative of that other but also real Victorian world that included the slums in which that saint of ritualism Father Dolling actually ministered, the world from which the unworldly but pigheaded Mr Crawley is rescued when his daughter marries the Archdeacon's son. He, Mr Crawley is brushed, reclothed, and rehoused, and inducted into a richer more comfortable living, not left to minister to the poor and dispossessed of the Barchester brickfields.

It is true that there is, in Trollope, at least one wicked criminal clergyman; a liar, a thief, a bigamist and a murderer: Mr Emilius, husband to Lady Eustace, the notorious 'Lizzie', but as Trollope clearly and with some chauvinism points out Mr Emilius was not native born.

> '. . . by name Yosef Mealyus – as everyone was very careful to call him, – had come to England, had got himself ordained as a clergyman, had married a rich wife with a title, although he had a wife still living . . .
>   Could they have succeeded in discovering where he had bought the weapon, his years of penal servitude would have affected him but a little. They did not succeed; and though it can not be said that any mystery was attached to the Bonteen murder, it has remained one of the crimes which are unavenged by the flagging law. And so the Rev. Mr Emilius will pass away from our story.'

Phineas Finn who had been wrongly accused of the Bonteen murder, is released, he marries the enigmatic and very rich Madame Goesler, the heroine (who also acted as a detective), and eventually returns to office as a minister of the Crown.

It was however Dickens who in his last and unfinished work *The Mystery of Edwin Drood* (1870) unmasks the other, the hidden side of clerical life. There is a strange compelling fascination about unfinished work, whether it is music, poetry, the novel, or architecture. Building sites, empty roofless houses, have for many an irresistible attraction. There is a drive, a desire to finish, to complete, to know what comes next, however banal or disappointing it may turn out to be – hence perhaps the fascination today exercised by soap operas.

So with *Edwin Drood*, perhaps the darkest of all Dickens's works, a book in which it never seems to be fully daylight, so much seems enveloped in a noisome fog – physical, mental, and spiritual. Years ago I attended the ordination of a friend in Rochester Cathedral (the Cloisterham of *Edwin Drood*): it was a cold, damp, grey day, the trees dripped, and the greasy puddles on the pavement, as thick as spots on a leopard's skin were difficult to avoid. The Cathedral lit within by electricity, unlike the days of Edwin Drood, from the outside blazed in the dark like a huge coloured lantern; but there were when we went in dark, unlit menacing corners, and the umbrellas and the wetness of our clothes gave the cathedral a damp sour smell.

I have chosen parts of Edwin Drood: The first chapter set in the opium den in which the Revd Mr Jasper makes his appearance;

Shaking from head to foot, the man whose scattered consciousness has thus fantastically pieced itself together, at length rises, supports his trembling frame upon his arms, and looks around. He is in the meanest and closest of small rooms. Through the ragged window-curtain, the light of early day steals in from a miserable court. He lies, dressed across a large unseemly bed, upon a bedstead that has indeed given way under the weight upon it. Lying, also dressed and also across the bed, not longwise, are a Chinaman, a Lascar, and a haggard woman. The two first are in a sleep or stupor; the last is blowing at a kind of pipe, to kindle it. And as she blows, and shading it with her lean hand, concentrates its red spark of light, it serves in the dim morning as a lamp to show him what he sees of her.

'Another?' says this woman, in a querulous, rattling whisper. 'Have another?'

He looks about him, with his hand to his forehead.

'Ye've smoked as many as five since ye come in at midnight,' . . .

and the two later chapters which deal with Drood's inexplicable disappearance and Jasper's reaction. I have also included an article from *The Cornhill* of March 1884 which I find is one of the most convincing of the attempts to solve the mystery; to answer those two questions: Was Drood killed? and if so, Who killed him?

There have been many attempts not only to unravel and resolve the mystery but to finish the book. In each generation there seems to be someone who feels the urge to proffer a definite, final solution. The only certainty is that unless some hitherto undiscovered letter or manuscript appears in which Dickens himself provides a solution, the mystery will remain forever unsolved. If the reader does not know the novel perhaps the extracts and essay here published will provide a sufficient reason and incentive for undertaking what will surely prove to be a rewarding and frustrating exercise.

The period from late Victorian times until the Second World War was one of the golden ages of the Anglican clergy, secure in their place in society, usually with adequate means, well educated, in many cases erudite; rectories and vicarages occupied often by eccentrics and scholars, in the early years by men exemplified by the parson in that marvellous but neglected poem of Masefield: *The Everlasting Mercy* and by the old absent-minded scholar-rector in

Dream Days, as well as by the clergymen who play so important a rôle in M R James's stories.

The Nonconformists flourished too, especially in the West and North where the wealthy industrialists built and endowed chapels, and, largely self-educated, lay readers thundered against the Establishment's wickedness in social as well as in moral matters. This was the time, the heyday of the nonconformist conscience when Gladstonian morals ruled – and he was a high churchman.

The most famous of all clergy detectives was born near the beginning of this age. Father Brown, the dumpy self-effacing Roman Catholic Priest, the creation of G K Chesterton bestrides the period like a colossus. Chesterton mastered the art of the short detective story and was only rivalled by Conan Doyle. It is fascinating to compare their two creations: Father Brown and Sherlock Holmes. Conan Doyle was born in 1859 and Chesterton almost a generation later in 1873. Holmes leapt fully clad from his creator's pen in 1887, when he appeared in the short novel *A Study in Scarlet*; The *Strand* stories began in 1891 – Chesterton's first book of Father Brown stories *The Innocence of Father Brown* was published in 1913. Books by both authors were published in 1927. *The Case-Book of Sherlock Holmes* was the last time a new collection of Holmes's adventures appeared (Doyle died in 1930), *The Secret of Father Brown* was followed in 1935 by *The Scandal of Father Brown* (Chesterton died in 1936). Two passages from *The Secret of Father Brown* are I believe worth quoting for they illustrate the difference between the two men and their approach to detection, in the first Father Brown is talking to an American Professor.

'I'm afraid' said the American, in tones that were still doubtful, and keeping his eye on the priest rather as if he were a wild animal. 'that you'd have to explain a lot to me before I knew what you were talking about. The Science of detection..'

Father Brown snapped his fingers with the same animated annoyance. 'That's it' he cried; 'that's just where we part company. Science is a great thing when you can get it; in its real sense one of the greatest words in the world. But what do these men mean, when they use it nowadays? When they say detection is a science? When they say criminology is a science? They mean getting *outside* a man and studying him as if he were a gigantic insect; in what they would call a dim impartial light; in what I should call a dead and dehumanized light. . . . I don't try to get outside the man. I try to get inside the murderer . . . Indeed it's much more than that don't you see? I *am* inside a man. I am always inside a man, knowing his arms and legs; but I wait till I know I am inside a murderer, thinking his thoughts, wrestling with his passions till I have bent myself into the picture of the hunched and peering hatred; till I see the world with his bloodshot and squinty eyes, looking between the blinkers of his half-witted concentration; looking up the short and sharp perspective of a straight road to a pool of blood. Till I am really a murderer.'

The second extract actually refers to Sherlock Holmes, in it two men, one a professional policeman, Bagshaw, and the other an amateur detective are talking:

'Ours is the only trade.' said Bagshaw, 'in which the professional is always supposed to be wrong. After all, people don't write stories in which the hairdressers can't cut hair and have to be helped by a customer; or in which a cabman can't drive a cab until his fare explains to him the philosophy of cab-driving. I'd never deny that we often tend to get into a rut; or in other words, have the disadvantage of going by a rule.'

'Surely' said Underhill, 'Sherlock Holmes would say he went by a logical rule?'

'He may be right' answered the other 'but I mean a collective rule. It's like the staff work of an army. We pool our information.'

'And you don't think detective stories allow for that?' asked his friend.

'Well, let's take any imaginary case of Sherlock Holmes, and Lestrade, the official detective. Sherlock Holmes, let us say, can guess that a total stranger crossing the street is a foreigner, merely because he seems to look for the traffic to go to the right instead of the left. I'm quite ready to admit Holmes might guess that. I'm quite sure Lestrade wouldn't guess anything of the kind. But what they leave out is the fact that the policeman, who couldn't guess, might very probably know. Lestrade might know the man was a foreigner; merely because his department has to keep an eye on all foreigners, some would say on all natives too. As a policeman I'm glad the police know so much, for everyman wants to do his job well.'

It is Father Brown's ability to get inside the criminal or sinner's mind – an ability shared with Edgar Wallace's Mr J G Reeder – that enables him to solve many mysteries so convincingly. It is this, strengthened by the marriage of common sense to an understanding of the way people react, gained in the confessional, that was such a potent almost irresistible force.

There was, perhaps a generation later than Father Brown, a female detective created who by the same intuitive methods based on a thorough and detailed knowledge of human nature managed to solve mysteries that puzzled the most acute and brilliant minds of Scotland Yard and of the provincial police forces: Miss Jane Marple. But Miss Marple unlike Father Brown is at her best, her most convincing in the more involved full length novel; her essays into the short story lack the interest and distinction which the longer treatment provides, that for example are present in *Murder in the Vicarage* a between the wars work from the Marple's case-book.

There is a sense in which Miss Christie's creation, Miss Marple, is a secular and feminine Father Brown, although it is doubtful whether that formidable and loyal churchwoman would be one of those whinging feminists loudly demanding entry into the priesthood and the right to be called 'Father'.

That other Queen of the detective story, a contemporary of Agatha Christie – Dorothy L Sayers – was herself a child of the rectory. She produced in *The Nine Tailors* a novel of some merit and erudition which was set in a Fenland parish; although he was himself neither the criminal nor the detective, the rector (Mr Venables), and also his great East Anglian Church itself towering over the flat Fenland are central to the story; and its portrait of a country living and its comfortably off occupant is (heaven help me!) a valuable contemporary social document.

Since the Second World War there has been a noticeable change in peoples reaction to clergymen and to the Church. The accepted place in the scheme of things that was occupied by the man in the dog collar has vanished as completely as Boot's lending library and Fuller's tea shops. There is now no generally nor widely accepted and recognized central place for the Church and her clergy outside the surviving great state occasions of marriages, deaths, Coronations and Jubilees. This can be illustrated by a simple example. Shortly after the war ended a friend of mine became a curate of a London East End Parish; and often on a Saturday afternoon I would meet him and we would go out into the country beyond Epping Forest, to Ongar or Greensted – sometimes finishing our journey by 'bus.

If Robert (my friend) wore his dog collar – in those days priests often did, and he on many occasions would have come straight from a wedding or some other parish function – it was very seldom indeed that he would be charged a fare, the 'bus conductor would say a friendly word of greeting and pass on. This would be unlikely to happen today. But it was this kind of incident that needs to be remembered when reading these detective stories if their setting is to be fully appreciated.

Margery Allingham another of the notable and talented group of women writers of detective stories, in *Tiger in the Smoke*, brilliantly portrays post-war life in a London rectory. One of the book's central characters old Canon Avril carries into the present age the virtues, wisdom, and standards of the past. This book, or so I am prepared to maintain, is one of the finest of post-war crime stories, in plot, character delineation and writing, an extraordinary high standard has been reached, it merits that title so freely and often undeservedly awarded by publishers to many reprints: A Classic of Crime.

But Canon Avril is a survivor from a past period – a living dinosaur, since his time there has been a sea change. Gradually but with ever gathering momentum the once secure place of the clergyman in everyday life has been eroded or demolished and the clergy themselves have changed too, mostly for the worse. Young clergy today with their straggly beards and faded, stained jeans seem to prefer to call themselves social workers rather than priests and the shelves of their offices are occupied by computers and piles of discs rather than by books – which to them often seem as alien as split infinitives, unformed, unfinished sentences and expletives are familiar, and they tend too to come from a class and background different from that to which Mr Venables and Canon Avril belonged.

The contemporary fictional clergyman reflecting perhaps the real one is seldom more than a boring and unsexy figure, constantly straining to be progressive in a bitchy, *Guardian* fashion and the part they play in the story is little more, usually, than a walking on one.

In Mollie Hardwicke's series about the antique dealer Doran Fairweather, Doran's husband the Revd Rodney Chelmarsh is a reluctant priest with very loose ties to the formularies of his Church; and with apparently little affection or respect for it. In one of Jonathan Gash's Lovejoy novels – Lovejoy himself is a splendid figure – the criminal is a clergyman but in this case as in most of contemporary novels the clerical status of the criminal is not really an essential part of the story.

One very successful and brilliant post-war creation is 'religious', that is Brother Cadfael, but his cases are set in medieval England and his virtues are the old eternal ones; there is no contemporary equivalent no *fin de siécle*. The same is true of that universally successful medieval Whodunnit: *The Name of the Rose*, here the clerical detective is a Religious, cerebral rather than intuitive in his methods.

What is important, but what is sometime often forgotten is the readership. For whose entertainment were the stories written? The readership, the market for a detective story has over the years changed and changed fundamentally. Consider for example one of the stories in this present collection; *The Genuine Tabard*. This exemplifies very well the privileged world in which so many of the clergy lived and worked, a world which the reader was expected to know, to understand and to appreciate. This kind of story demanded knowledge of that world before it could be intelligently read. What I am I suppose trying to say is that one, if not the most important element of the pre-war attraction of the detective story was their 'snobbery', if one understands, then one belongs, class (and education) mattered, it was an essential ingredient. It was for a largely middle class leisured audience that the books were written, an audience which had been well brought up (itself a 'snob' phrase), readers who were well grounded in the Authorized Version, forced as children to read Dickens and Jane Austen – people to whom Nannies were Nannies and not Grandmothers. Essentially the ordinary detective story is and was little more than an expanded crossword puzzle – a tranquilizer for the élite.

Only the really great writer could and did ignore this – that is why I have included parts of *Edwin Drood*. For in *Drood* Dickens although dealing with fictional crime illuminates real life, it does not matter to him, nor to us, whether an 'h' is dropped or an infinitive split. It is not the fascination of the story nor even the challenge of the mystery that is important, it is that one learns a little more of human nature, that one's appreciation of life is enriched and extended and that one is enabled better to understand not only the people with whom one daily mixes but even oneself. In form it may be the same but when tested it is as different as a tomato picked from one's own garden is from a Canary. But to go back to the readership, since the War the readership, the market has changed and the contemporary raw and raunchy murder story has little appeal for the heirs to the audience for whom Dr Sayers wrote. The old stories are reprinted and new jackets designed, there may still be a market for Josephine Tey and Edmund Crispin, but it is I suspect a somewhat nostalgic one of middle-aged fogeys a little bored with and tired of the incessant 'bonking' and violence that distinguishes so many of those modern successors to Lord Peter and Miss Marple, who people the pages of books which now seem either to be designed for middle-aged failures in soiled macintoshes or for frustrated pimply youths – essentially masturbatory works, or books designed for the more pretentious sisters of the average Mills & Boon reader.

I know that there is a number of most excellent popular crime writers – one has even lately been enobled, a mystery in itself – who could perhaps justly claim that they maintain the 'true' detective tradition, that is not my point, here I am thinking of the clerical crime, the crime of the vicarage or the Chapter House, not the theological kind, for in a sense all crime has its basis in theology; fratricide the disposal of husbands by dangerous postings or, betrayal, all can be found in the Bible. Perhaps this is why Father Brown is so convincing for Chesterton was well versed in theology and this grounding enabled him to understand human beings and the strange and beautiful paradoxes of their lives; he knew why the dog did not bark.

MURDER IN THE VICARAGE

THE MYSTERY OF
EDWIN DROOD

Charles Dickens

Chapter I

THE DAWN

AN ancient English Cathedral Tower? How can the ancient English Cathedral tower be here! The well-known massive grey square tower of its old Cathedral? How can that be here! There is no spike of rusty iron in the air, between the eye and it, from any point of the real prospect. What is the spike that intervenes, and who has set it up? Maybe it is set up by the Sultan's orders for the impaling of a horde of Turkish robbers, one by one. It is so, for cymbals clash, and the Sultan goes by to his palace in long procession. Ten thousand scimitars flash in the sunlight, and thrice ten thousand dancing-girls strew flowers. Then, follow white elephants caparisoned in countless gorgeous colours, and infinite in number and attendants. Still the Cathedral Tower rises in the background, where it cannot be, and still no writhing figure is on the grim spike. Stay! Is the spike so low a thing as the rusty spike on the top of a post of an old bedstead that has tumbled all awry? Some vague period of drowsy laughter must be devoted to the consideration of this possibility.

Shaking from head to foot, the man whose scattered consciousness has thus fantastically pieced itself together, at length rises, supports his trembling frame upon his arms, and looks around. He is in the meanest and closest of small rooms. Through the ragged window-curtain, the light of early day steals in from a miserable court. He lies, dressed, across a large unseemly bed, upon a bedstead that has indeed given way under the weight upon it. Lying, also dressed and also across the bed, not longwise, are a Chinaman, a Lascar, and a haggard woman. The two first are in a sleep or stupor; the last is blowing at a kind of pipe, to kindle it. And as she blows, and shading it with her lean hand, concentrates its red spark of light, it serves in the dim morning as a lamp to show him what he sees of her.

'Another?' says this woman, in a querulous, rattling whisper. 'Have another?'

He looks about him, with his hand to his forehead.

'Ye've smoked as many as five since ye come in at midnight,' the woman goes on, as she chronically complains. 'Poor me, poor me, my head is so bad. Them two come in after ye. Ah, poor me, the business is slack, is slack! Few Chinamen about the Docks, and fewer Lascars, and no ships coming in, these say! Here's another ready for ye, deary. Ye'll remember like a good soul, won't ye, that the market price is dreffle high just now? More nor three shillings and sixpence for a thimbleful! And ye'll remember that nobody but me (and Jack Chinaman t'other side the court; but he can't do it as well as me) has the true secret of mixing it? Ye'll pay up according, deary, won't ye?'

She blows at the pipe as she speaks, and, occasionally bubbling at it, inhales much of its contents.

'O me, O me, my lungs is weak, my lungs is bad! It's nearly ready for ye, deary. Ah, poor me, poor me, my poor hand shakes like to drop off! I see ye coming-to, and I ses to my poor self, "I'll have another ready for him, and he'll bear in mind the market price of opium, and pay according." O my poor head! I makes my pipes of old penny ink-bottles, ye see, deary – this is one – and I fits in a mouthpiece, this way, and I takes my mixer out of this thimble with this little horn spoon; and so I fills, deary. Ah, my poor nerves! I got Heavens-hard drunk for sixteen year afore I took to this; but this don't hurt me, not to speak of. And it takes away the hunger as well as wittles, deary.'

She hands him the nearly-emptied pipe, and sinks back, turning over on her face.

He rises unsteadily from the bed, lays the pipe upon the hearth-stone, draws back the ragged curtain, and looks with repugnance at his three companions. He notices that the woman has opium-smoked herself into a strange likeness of the Chinaman. His form of cheek, eye, and temple, and his colour, are repeated in her. Said Chinaman convulsively wrestles with one of his many Gods or Devils, perhaps, and snarls horribly. The Lascar laughs and dribbles at the mouth. The hostess is still.

'What visions can *she* have?' the waking man muses, as he turns her face towards him, and stands looking down at it. 'Visions of many butchers' shops, and public-houses, and much credit? Of an increase of hideous customers, and this horrible bedstead set upright again, and this horrible court swept clean? What can she rise to, under any quantity of opium, higher than that! – Eh?'

He bends down his ear, to listen to her mutterings.

'Unintelligible!'

As he watches the spasmodic shoots and darts that break out of her face and limbs, like fitful lightning out of a dark sky, some contagion in them seizes upon him: insomuch that he has to with-draw himself to a lean arm-chair by the hearth – placed there, perhaps, for such emergencies – and to sit in it, holding tight, until he has got the better of this unclean spirit of imitation.

Then he comes back, pounces on the Chinaman, and seizing him with both hands by the throat, turns him violently on the bed. The Chinaman clutches the aggressive hands, resists, gasps and protests.

'What do you say?'

A watchful pause.

'Unintelligible!'

Slowly loosening his grasp as he listens to the incoherent jargon with an attentive frown, he turns to the Lascar and fairly drags him forth upon the floor. As he falls, the Lascar starts into a half-risen attitude, glares with his eyes, lashes about him fiercely with his arms, and draws a phantom knife. It then becomes apparent that the woman has taken possession of this knife, for safety's sake; for she too starting up, and restraining and expostulating with him, the knife is visible in her dress, not in his, when they drowsily drop back, side by side.

There has been chattering and clattering enough between them, but to no purpose. When any distinct word has been flung into the air, it has had no sense or sequence. Wherefore 'unintelligible!' is again the comment of the watcher, made with some reassured nodding of his head, and a gloomy smile. He then lays certain silver money on the table, finds his hat, gropes his way down the broken stairs, gives a good morning to some rat-ridden doorkeeper, in bed in a black hutch beneath the stairs, and passes out.

That same afternoon, the massive grey square tower of an old Cathedral rises before the sight of a jaded traveller. The bells are going for daily vesper service, and he must needs attend it, one would say, from his haste to reach the open Cathedral door. The choir are getting on their sullied white robes, in a hurry, when he arrives among them, gets on his own robe, and falls into the procession filing in to service. Then, the Sacristan locks the iron-barred gates that divide the sanctuary from the channel, and all of the procession having scuttled into their places, hide their faces; and then the intoned words, 'WHEN THE WICKED MAN –' rise among groins of arches and beams, awakening muttered thunder.

Chapter XV

IMPEACHED

NEVILLE LANDLESS had started so early and walked at so good a pace, that when the church-bells began to ring in Cloisterham for morning service, he was eight miles away. As he wanted his breakfast by that time, having set forth on a crust of bread, he stopped at the next roadside tavern to refresh.

Visitors in want of breakfast – unless they were horses or cattle, for which class of guests there was preparation enough in the way of water-trough and hay – were so unusual at the sign of 'The Tilted

Wagon', that it took a long time to get the wagon into the track of tea and toast and bacon. Neville in the interval, sitting in a sanded parlour, wondering in how long a time after he had gone, the sneezy fire of damp fagots would begin to make somebody else warm.

Indeed, 'The Tilted Wagon', as a cool establishment on the top of a hill, where the ground before the door was puddled with damp hoofs and trodden straw; where a scolding landlady slapped a moist baby (with one red sock on and one wanting) in the bar; where the cheese was cast aground upon a shelf, in company with a mouldy tablecloth and a green-handled knife, in a sort of cast-iron canoe; where the pale-faced bread shed tears of crumb over its shipwreck in another canoe; where the family linen, half washed and half dried, led a public life of lying about; where everything to drink was drunk out of mugs, and everything else was suggestive of a rhyme to mugs; 'The Tilted Wagon', all these things considered, hardly kept its painted promise of providing good entertainment for Man and Beast. However, Man, in the present case, was not critical, but took what entertainment he could get, and went on again after a longer rest than he needed.

He stopped at some quarter of a mile from the house, hesitating whether to pursue the road, or to follow a cart track between two high hedgerows, which led across the slope of a breezy heath, and evidently struck into the road again by and by. He decided in favour of this latter track, and pursued it with some toil; the rise being steep, and the way worn into deep ruts.

He was labouring along, when he became aware of some other pedestrians behind him. As they were coming up at a faster pace than his, he stood aside, against one of the high banks, to let them pass. But their manner was very curious. Only four of them passed. Other four slackened speed, and loitered as intending to follow him when he should go on. The remainder of the party (half-a-dozen perhaps) turned, and went back at a great rate.

He looked at the four behind him, and he looked at the four before him. They all returned his look. He resumed his way. The four in advance went on, constantly looking back; the four in the rear came closing up.

When they all ranged out from the narrow track upon the open slope of the heath, and this order was maintained, let him diverge as he would to either side, there was no longer room to doubt that he was beset by these fellows. He stopped, as a last test; and they all stopped.

'Why do you attend me in this way?' he asked the whole body. 'Are you a pack of thieves?'

'Don't answer him,' said one of the number; he did not see which. 'Better be quiet.'

'Better be quiet?' repeated Neville. 'Who said so?'

Nobody replied.

'It's good advice, whichever of you skullers gave it,' he went on angrily. 'I will not submit to be penned in between four men there, and four men there. I wish to pass, and I mean to pass, those four in front.'

They were all standing still; himself included.

'If eight men, or four men, or two men, set upon one,' he proceeded, growing more enraged, 'the one has no chance but to set his mark upon some of them. And, by the Lord, I'll do it, if I am interrupted any farther!'

Shouldering his heavy stick, and quickening his pace, he shot on to pass the four ahead. The largest and strongest man of the number changed swiftly to the side on which he came up, and dexterously closed with him and went down with him; but not before the heavy stick had descended smartly.

'Let him be!' said this man in a suppressed voice, as they struggled together on the grass. 'Fair play! His is the build of a girl to mine, and he's got a weight strapped to his back besides. Let him alone. I'll manage him.'

After a little rolling about, in a close scuffle which caused the faces of both to be besmeared with blood, the man took his knee from Neville's chest, and rose, saying: 'There! Now take him arm-in-arm, any two of you!'

It was immediately done.

'As to our being a pack of thieves, Mr Landless,' said the man, as he spat out some blood, and wiped more from his face; 'you know better than that at midday. We wouldn't have touched you if you hadn't forced us. We're going to take you round to the high road, anyhow, and you'll find help enough against thieves there, if you want it. – Wipe his face somebody; see how it's a trickling down him!'

When his face was cleansed, Neville recognised in the speaker, Joe, the driver of the Cloisterham omnibus, whom he had seen but once, and that on the day of his arrival.

'And what I recommend you for the present, is, don't talk, Mr Landless. You'll find a friend waiting for you, at the high road – gone ahead by the other way when we split into two parties – and you had much better say nothing till you come up with him. Bring that stick along, somebody else, and let's be moving!'

Utterly bewildered, Neville stared around him and said not a word. Walking between his two conductors, who held his arms in theirs, he went on, as in a dream, until they came again into the high road, and into the midst of a little group of people. The men who had turned back were among the group; and its central figures were Mr Jasper and Mr Crisparkle. Neville's conductors took him up to the Minor Canon, and there released him, as an act of deference to that gentleman.

'What is all this, sir? What is the matter? I feel as if I had lost my senses!' cried Neville, the group closing in around him.

'Where is my nephew?' asked Mr Jasper, wildly.

'Where is your nephew?' repeated Neville. 'Why do you ask me?'

'I ask you,' retorted Jasper, 'because you were the last person in his company, and he is not to be found.'

'Not to be found!' cried Neville, aghast.

'Stay, stay,' said Mr Crisparkle. 'Permit me, Jasper. Mr Neville, you are confounded; collect your thoughts; it is of great importance that you should collect your thoughts; attend to me.'

'I will try, sir, but I seem mad.'

'You left Mr Jasper last night with Edwin Drood?'

'Yes.'

'At what hour?'

'Was it at twelve o'clock?' asked Neville, with his hand to his confused head, and appealing to Jasper.

'Quite right,' said Mr Crisparkle; 'the hour Mr Jasper has already named to me. You went down to the river together?'

'Undoubtedly! To see the action of the wind there.'

'What followed? How long did you stay there?'

'About ten minutes; I should say not more. We then walked together to your house, and he took leave of me at the door.'

'Did he say that he was going down to the river again?'

'No. He said that he was going straight back.'

The bystanders looked at one another, and at Mr Crisparkle. To whom Mr Jasper, who had been intensely watching Neville, said, in a low, distinct, suspicious voice: 'What are those stains upon his dress?'

All eyes were turned towards the blood upon his clothes.

'And here are the same stains upon this stick!' said Jasper, taking it from the hand of the man who held it. 'I know the stick to be his, and he carried it last night. What does this mean?'

'In the name of God, say what it means, Neville!' urged Mr Crisparkle.

'That man and I,' said Neville, pointing out his late adversary, 'had a struggle for the stick just now, and you may see the same marks on him, sir. What was I to suppose, when I found myself molested by eight people? Could I dream of the true reason when they would give me none at all?'

They admitted that they had thought it discreet to be silent, and that the struggle had taken place. And yet the very men who had seen it looked darkly at the smears which the bright cold air had already dried.

'We must return, Neville,' said Mr Crisparkle; 'of course you will be glad to come back to clear yourself?'

'Of course, sir.'

'Mr Landless will walk at my side,' the Minor Canon continued, looking around him. 'Come, Neville!'

They set forth on the walk back; and the others, with one exception, straggled after them at various distances. Jasper walked on the other side of Neville, and never quitted that position. He was silent, while Mr Crisparkle more than once repeated his former questions, and while Neville repeated his former answers; also, while they both hazarded some explanatory conjectures. He was obstinately silent, because Mr Crisparkle's manner directly appealed to him to take some part in the discussion, and no appeal would move his fixed face. When they drew near to the city, and it was suggested by the Minor Canon that they might do well in calling on the Mayor at once, he assented with a stern nod; but he spake no word until they stood in Mr Sapsea's parlour.

Mr Sapsea being informed by Mr Crisparkle of the circumstances under which they desired to make a voluntary statement before him, Mr Jasper broke silence by declaring that he placed his whole reliance, humanly speaking, on Mr Sapsea's penetration. There was no conceivable reason why his nephew should have suddenly absconded, unless Mr Sapsea could suggest one, and then he would defer. There was no intelligible likelihood of his having returned to the river, and been accidentally drowned in the dark, unless it should appear likely to Mr Sapsea, and then again he would defer. He washed his hands as clean as he could of all horrible suspicions, unless it should appear to Mr Sapsea that some such were inseparable from his last companion before his disappearance (not on good terms with previously), and then, once more, he would defer. His own state of mind, he being distracted with doubts, and labouring under dismal apprehensions, was not to be safely trusted; but Mr Sapsea's was.

Mr Sapsea expressed his opinion that the case had a dark look; in short (and here his eyes rested full on Neville's countenance), an un-English complexion. Having made this grand point, he wandered into a denser haze and maze of nonsense than even a mayor might have been expected to disport himself in, and came out of it with the brilliant discovery that to take the life of a fellow-creature was to take something that didn't belong to you. He wavered whether or no he should at once issue his warrant for the committal of Neville Landless to jail, under circumstances of grave suspicion; and he might have gone so far as to do it but for the indignant protest of the Minor Canon: who undertook for the young man's remaining in his own house, and being produced by his own hands, whenever demanded. Mr Jasper then understood Mr Sapsea to suggest that the river should be dragged, that its banks should be rigidly examined, that particulars of the disappearance should be sent to all outlying places and to London, and that placards and advertisements should be widely circulated imploring Edwin Drood, if for any unknown reason he had withdrawn himself from his uncle's home and society, to take pity on that loving kinsman's sore bereavement and distress, and somehow inform him that he was yet alive. Mr

Sapsea was perfectly understood, for this was exactly his meaning (though he had said nothing about it); and measures were taken towards all these ends immediately.

It would be difficult to determine which was the more oppressed with horror and amazement: Neville Landless, or John Jasper. But that Jasper's position forced him to be active, while Neville's forced him to be passive, there would have been nothing to choose between them. Each was bowed down and broken.

With the earliest light of the next morning, men were at work upon the river, and other men – most of whom volunteered for the service – were examining the banks. All the live-long day the search went on; upon the river, with barge and pole, and drag and net; upon the muddy and rushy shore, with jack-boots, hatchet, spade, rope, dogs, and all imaginable appliances. Even at night, the river was specked with lanterns, and lurid with fires; far-off creeks, into which the tide washed as it changed, had their knots of watchers, listening to the lapping of the stream, and looking out for any burden it might bear; remote shingly causeways near the sea, and lonely points off which there was a race of water, had their unwonted flaring cressets and rough-coated figures when the next day dawned; but no trace of Edwin Drood revisited the light of the sun.

All that day, again, the search went on. Now, in barge and boat; and now ashore among the osiers, or tramping amidst mud and stakes and jagged stones in low-lying places, where solitary water-marks and signals of strange shapes showed like spectres, John Jasper worked and toiled. But to no purpose; for still no trace of Edwin Drood revisited the light of the sun.

Setting his watches for that night again, so that vigilant eyes should be kept on every change of tide, he went home exhausted. Unkempt and disordered, bedaubed with mud that had dried upon him, and with much of his clothing torn to rags, he had but just dropped into his easy-chair, when Mr Grewgious stood before him.

'This is strange news,' said Mr Grewgious.

'Strange and fearful news.'

Jasper had merely lifted up his heavy eyes to say it, and now dropped them again as he drooped, worn out, over one side of his easy-chair.

Mr Grewgious smoothed his head and face, and stood looking at the fire.

'How is your ward?' asked Jasper, after a time, in a faint, fatigued voice.

'Poor little thing! You may imagine her condition.'

'Have you seen his sister?' inquired Jasper, as before.

'Whose?'

The curtness of the counter-question, and the cool slow manner in which, as he put it, Mr Grewgious moved his eyes from the fire to his companion's face, might at any other time have been exasperating. In his depression and exhaustion, Jasper merely opened his eyes to say: 'The suspected young man's.'

'Do you suspect him?' asked Mr Grewgious.

'I don't know what to think. I cannot make up my mind.'

'Nor I,' said Mr Grewgious. 'But as you spoke of him as the suspected young man, I thought you *had* made up your mind. – I have just left Miss Landless.'

'What is her state?'

'Defiance of all suspicion, and unbounded faith in her brother.'

'Poor thing!'

'However,' pursued Mr Grewgious, 'it is not of her that I came to speak. It is of my ward. I have a communication to make that will surprise you. At least, it has surprised me.'

Jasper, with a groaning sigh, turned wearily in his chair.

'Shall I put it off till to-morrow?' said Mr Grewgious. 'Mind, I warn you, that I think it will surprise you!'

More attention and concentration came into John Jasper's eyes as they caught sight of Mr Grewgious smoothing his head again, and again looking at the fire; but now, with a compressed and determined mouth.

'What is it?' demanded Jasper, becoming upright in his chair.

'To be sure,' said Mr Grewgious, provokingly slowly and internally, as he kept his eyes on the fire: 'I might have known it sooner; she gave me the opening; but I am such an exceedingly Angular man, that it never occurred to me; I took all for granted.'

'What is it?' demanded Jasper once more.

Mr Grewgious alternately opening and shutting the palms of his hands as he warmed them at the fire, and looking fixedly at him sideways, and never changing either his action or his look in all that followed, went on to reply.

'This young couple, the lost youth and Miss Rosa, my ward, though so long betrothed, and so recognising their betrothal, and so near being married – '

Mr Grewgious saw a staring white face, and two quivering white lips, in the easy-chair, and saw two muddy hands gripping its sides. But for the hands, he might have thought he had never seen the face.

' – This young couple came gradually to the discovery (made on both sides pretty equally, I think), that they would be happier and better, both in their present and their future lives, as affectionate friends, or say rather as brother and sister, than as husband and wife.'

Mr Grewgious saw a lead-coloured face in the easy-chair, and on its surface dreadful starting drops or bubbles, as if of steel.

'This young couple formed at length the healthy resolution of interchanging their discoveries, openly, sensibly, and tenderly. They met for that purpose. After some innocent and generous talk, they agreed to dissolve their existing, and their intended, relations, for ever and ever.'

Mr Grewgious saw a ghastly figure rise, open-mouthed, from the easy-chair, and lift its outspread hands towards its head.

'One of this young couple, and that one your nephew, fearful, however, that in the tenderness of your affection for him you would be bitterly disappointed by so wide a departure from his projected life, forbore to tell you the secret, for a few days, and left it to be disclosed by me, when I should come down to speak to you, and he would be gone. I speak to you, and he is gone.'

Mr Grewgious saw the ghastly figure throw back its head, clutch its hair with its hands, and turn with a writhing action from him.

'I have now said all I have to say: except that this young couple parted, firmly, though not without tears and sorrow, on the evening when you last saw them together.'

Mr Grewgious heard a terrible shriek, and saw no ghastly figure, sitting or standing; saw nothing but a heap of torn and miry clothes upon the floor.

Not changing his action even then, he opened and shut the palms of his hands as he warmed them, and looked down at it.

Chapter XVI

DEVOTED

WHEN John Jasper recovered from his fit or swoon, he found himself being tended by Mr and Mrs Tope, whom his visitor had summoned for the purpose. His visitor, wooden of aspect, sat stiffly in a chair, with his hands upon his knees, watching his recovery.

'There! You've come to, nicely now, sir,' said the tearful Mrs Tope; 'you were thoroughly worn out, and no wonder!'

'A man,' said Mr Grewgious, with his usual air of repeating a lesson, 'cannot have his rest broken, and his mind cruelly tormented, and his body overtaxed by fatigue, without being thoroughly worn out.'

'I fear I have alarmed you?' Jasper apologised faintly, when he was helped into his easy-chair.

'Not at all, I thank you,' answered Mr Grewgious.

'You are too considerate.'

'Not at all, I thank you,' answered Grewgious again.

'You must take some wine, sir,' said Mr Tope, 'and the jelly that I had ready for you, and that you wouldn't put your lips to at noon, though I warned you what would come of it, you know, and you not breakfasted; and you must have a wing of the roast fowl that has been put back twenty times if it's been put back once. It shall all be on table in five minutes, and this good gentleman belike will stop and see you take it.'

This good gentleman replied with a snort, which might mean yes, or no, or anything or nothing, and which Mrs Tope would have found highly mystifying, but that her attention was divided by the service of the table.

'You will take something with me?' said Jasper, as the cloth was laid.

'I couldn't get a morsel down my throat, I thank you,' answered Mr Grewgious.

Jasper both ate and drank almost voraciously. Combined with the hurry in his mode of doing it, was an evident indifference to the taste of what he took, suggesting that he ate and drank to fortify himself against any other failure of the spirits, far more than to gratify his palate. Mr Grewgious in the meantime sat upright, with no expression in his face, and a hard kind of imperturbably polite protest all over him: as though he would have said, in reply to some invitation to discourse: 'I couldn't originate the faintest approach to an observation on any subject whatever, I thank you.'

'Do you know,' said Jasper, when he had pushed away his plate and glass, and had sat meditating for a few minutes: 'do you know that I find some crumbs of comfort in the communication with which you have so much amazed me?'

'*Do* you?' returned Mr Grewgious, pretty plainly adding the unspoken clause: 'I don't, thank you!'

'After recovering from the shock of a piece of news of my dear boy, so entirely unexpected, and so destructive of all the castles I had built for him; and after having had time to think of it; yes.'

'I shall be glad to pick up your crumbs,' said Mr Grewgious, dryly.

'Is there not, or is there – if I deceive myself, tell me so, and shorten my pain – is there not, or is there, hope that, finding himself in this new position, and becoming sensitively alive to the awkward burden of explanation, in this quarter, and that, and the other, with which it would load him, he avoided the awkwardness, and took to flight?'

'Such a thing might be,' said Mr Grewgious, pondering.

'Such a thing has been. I have read of cases in which people, rather than face a seven days' wonder, and have to account for themselves to the idle and impertinent, have taken themselves away, and been long unheard of.'

'I believe such things have happened,' said Mr Grewgious, pondering still.

'When I had, and could have, no suspicion,' pursued Jasper, eagerly following the new track, 'that the dear lost boy had withheld anything from me – most of all, such a leading matter as this – what gleam of light was there for me in the whole black sky? When I supposed that his intended wife was here, and his marriage close at hand, how could I entertain the possibility of his voluntarily leaving this place, in a manner that would be so unaccountable, capricious, and cruel? But now that I know what you have told me, is there no little chink through which day pierces? Supposing him to have disappeared of his own act, is not his disappearance more accountable and less cruel? The fact of his having just parted from your ward, is in itself a sort of reason for his going away. It does not make his mysterious departure the less cruel to me, it is true; but it relieves it of cruelty to her.'

Mr Grewgious could not but assent to this.

'And even as to me,' continued Jasper, still pursuing the new track, with ardour, and, as he did so, brightening with hope: 'he knew that you were coming to me; he knew that you were intrusted to tell me what you have told me; if your doing so has awakened a new train of thought in my perplexed mind, it reasonably follows that, from the same premises, he might have foreseen the inferences that I should draw. Grant that he did foresee them; and even the cruelty to me – and who am I! – John Jasper, Music Master, vanishes!' –

Once more, Mr Grewgious could not but assent to this.

'I have had my distrusts, and terrible distrusts they have been,' said Jasper; 'but your disclosure, overpowering as it was at first – showing me that my own dear boy had had a great disappointing reservation from me, who so fondly loved him, kindles hope within me. You do not extinguish it when I state it, but admit it to be a reasonable hope. I begin to believe is possible:' here he clasped his hands: 'that he may have disappeared from among us of his own accord, and that he may yet be alive and well.'

Mr Crisparkle came in at the moment. To whom Mr Jasper repeated:

'I begin to believe it possible that he may have disappeared of his own accord, and may yet be alive and well.'

Mr Crisparkle taking a seat, and inquiring: 'Why so?' Mr Jasper repeated the arguments he had just set forth. If they had been less plausible than they were, the good Minor Canon's mind would have been in a state of preparation to receive them, as exculpatory of his unfortunate pupil. But he, too, did really attach great importance to the lost young man's having been, so immediately before his disappearance, placed in a new and embarrassing relation towards every one acquainted with his projects and affairs; and the fact seemed to him to present the question in a new light.

'I stated to Mr Sapsea, when we waited on him,' said Jasper: as he really had done: 'that there was no quarrel or difference between the two young men at their last meeting. We all know that their first meeting was unfortunately very far from amicable; but all went smoothly and quietly when they were last together at my house. My dear boy was not in his usual spirits; he was depressed – I noticed that – and I am bound henceforth to dwell upon the circumstance the more, now that I know there was a special reason for his being depressed: a reason, moreover, which may possibly have induced him to absent himself.'

'I pray to Heaven it may turn out so!' exclaimed Mr Crisparkle.

'*I* pray to Heaven it may turn out so!' repeated Jasper. 'You know – and Mr Grewgious should now know likewise – that I took a great prepossession against Mr Neville Landless, arising out of his furious conduct on that first occasion. You know that I came to you, extremely apprehensive, on my dear boy's behalf, of his mad violence. You know that I even entered in my Diary, and showed the entry to you, that I had dark forebodings against him. Mr Grewgious ought to be possessed of the whole case. He shall not, through any suppression of mine, be informed of a part of it, and kept in ignorance of another part of it. I wish him to be good enough to understand that the communication he has made to me has hopefully influenced my mind, in spite of its having been, before this mysterious occurrence took place, profoundly impressed against young Landless.'

This fairness troubled the Minor Canon much. He felt that he was not as open in his own dealing. He charged against himself reproachfully that he had suppressed, so far, the two points of a second strong outbreak of temper against Edwin Drood on the part of Neville, and of the passion of jealousy having, to his own certain knowledge, flamed up in Neville's breast against him. He was convinced of Neville's innocence of any part in the ugly disappearance; and yet so many little circumstances combined so woefully against him, that he dreaded to add two more to their cumulative weight. He was among the truest of men; but he had been balancing in his mind, much to his distress, whether his volunteering to tell these two fragments of truth, at this time, would not be tantamount to a piecing together of falsehood in the place of truth.

However, here was a model before him. He hesitated no longer. Addressing Mr Grewgious, as one placed in authority by the revelation he had brought to bear on the mystery (and surpassingly Angular Mr Grewgious became when he found himself in that unexpected position), Mr Crisparkle bore his testimony to Mr Jasper's strict sense of justice, and, expressing his absolute confidence in the complete clearance of his pupil from the least taint of suspicion, sooner or later, avowed that his confidence in that young gentleman had been formed, in spite of his confidential knowledge that his temper was of the hottest and fiercest, and that it was directly incensed against Mr Jasper's nephew, by the circumstance of his romantically supposing himself to be enamoured of the same young lady. The sanguine reaction manifest in Mr Jasper was proof even against this unlooked-for declaration. It turned him paler; but he repeated that he would cling to the hope he had derived from Mr Grewgious; and that if no trace of his dear boy were found, leading to the dreadful inference that he had been made away with, he would cherish unto the last stretch of possibility the idea, that he might have absconded of his own wild will.

Now, it fell out that Mr Crisparkle, going away from this conference still very uneasy in his mind, and very much troubled on behalf of the young man whom he held as a kind of prisoner in his own house, took a memorable night walk.

He walked to Cloisterham Weir.

He often did so, and consequently there was nothing remarkable in his footsteps tending that way. But the pre-occupation of his mind so hindered him from planning any walk, or taking heed of the objects he passed, that his first consciousness of being near the Weir was derived from the sound of the falling water close at hand.

'How did I come here!' was his first thought, as he stopped.

'Why did I come here!' was his second.

Then he stood intently listening to the water. A familiar passage in his reading, about airy tongues that syllable men's names, rose so unbidden to his ear, that he put it from him with his hand, as if it were tangible.

It was starlight. The Weir was full two miles above the spot to which the young men had repaired to watch the storm. No search had been made up here, for the tide had been running strongly down, at that time of the night of Christmas Eve, and the likeliest place for the discovery of a body, if a fatal accident had happened under such circumstances, all lay – both when the tide ebbed, and when it flowed again – between that spot and the sea. The water came over the Weir, with its usual sound on a cold starlight night, and little could be seen of it; yet Mr Crisparkle had a strange idea that something unusual hung about the place.

He reasoned with himself: What was it? Where was it? Put it to the proof. Which sense did it address?

No sense reported anything unusual there. He listened again, and his sense of hearing again checked the water coming over the Weir, with its usual sound on a cold starlight night.

Knowing very well that the mystery with which his mind was occupied, might of itself give the place this haunted air, he strained those hawk's eyes of his for the correction of his sight. He got closer to the Weir, and peered at its well-known posts and timbers. Nothing in the least unusual was remotely shadowed forth. But he resolved that he would come back early in the morning.

The Weir ran through his broken sleep, all night, and he was back again at sunrise. It was a bright frosty morning. The whole composition before him, when he stood where he had stood last night, was clearly discernible in its minutest details. He had surveyed it closely for some minutes, and was about to withdraw his eyes, when they were attracted keenly to one spot.

He turned his back upon the Weir, and looked far away at the sky, and at the earth, and then looked again at that one spot. It caught his sight again immediately, and he concentrated his vision upon it. He could not lose it now, though it was but such a speck in the landscape. It fascinated his sight. His hands began plucking off his coat. For it struck him that at that spot – a corner of the

Weir – something glistened, which did not move and come over with the glistening water-drops, but remained stationary.

He assured himself of this, he threw off his clothes, he plunged into the icy water, and swam for the spot. Climbing the timbers, he took from them, caught among their interstices by its chain, a gold watch, bearing engraved upon its back E. D.

He brought the watch to the bank, swam to the Weir again, climbed it, and dived off. He knew every hole and corner of all the depths, and dived and dived and dived, until he could bear the cold no more. His notion was, that he would find the body; he only found a shirt-pin sticking in some mud and ooze.

With these discoveries he returned to Cloisterham, and, taking Neville Landless with him, went straight to the Mayor. Mr Jasper was sent for, the watch and shirt-pin were identified, Neville was detained, and the wildest frenzy and fatuity of evil report rose against him. He was of that vindictive and violent nature, that but for his poor sister, who alone had influence over him, and out of whose sight he was never to be trusted, he would be in the daily commission of murder. Before coming to England he had caused to be whipped to death sundry 'Natives' – nomadic persons, encamping now in Asia, now in Africa, now in the West Indies, and now at the North Pole – vaguely supposed in Cloisterham to be always black, always of great virtue, always calling themselves Me, and everybody else Massa or Missie (according to sex), and always reading tracts of the obscurest meaning, in broken English, but always accurately understanding them in the purest mother tongue. He had nearly brought Mrs Crisparkle's grey hairs with sorrow to the grave. (Those original expressions were Mr Sapsea's.) He had repeatedly said he would have Mr Crisparkle's life. He had repeatedly said he would have everybody's life, and become in effect the last man. He had been brought down to Cloisterham, from London, by an eminent Philanthropist, and why? Because that Philanthropist had expressly declared: 'I owe it to my fellow-creatures that he should be, in the words of BENTHAM, where he is the cause of the greatest danger to the smallest number.'

These dropping shots from the blunderbusses of blunderheadedness might not have hit him in a vital place. But he had to stand against a trained and well-directed fire of arms of precision too. He had notoriously threatened the lost young man, and had, according to the showing of his own faithful friend and tutor who strove so hard for him, a cause of bitter animosity (created by himself, and stated by himself), against that ill-starred fellow. He had armed himself with an offensive weapon for the fatal night, and he had gone off early in the morning, after making preparations for departure. He had been found with traces of blood on him; truly, they might have been wholly caused as he represented, but they might not, also. On a search-warrant being issued for the examination of his room, clothes, and so forth, it was discovered that he had destroyed all his papers, and rearranged all his possessions, on the very afternoon of the disappearance. The watch found at the Weir was challenged by the jeweller as one he had wound and set for Edwin Drood, at twenty minutes past two on that same afternoon; and it had run down, before being cast into the water; and it was the jeweller's positive opinion that it had never been re-wound. This would justify the hypothesis that the watch was taken from him not long after he left Mr Jasper's house at midnight, in company with the last person seen with him, and that it had been thrown away after being retained some hours. Why thrown away? If he had been murdered, and so artfully disfigured, or concealed, or both, as that the murderer hoped identification to be impossible, except from something that he wore, assuredly the murderer would seek to remove from the body the most lasting, the best known, and the most easily recognisable, things upon it. Those things would be the watch and shirt-pin. As to his opportunities of casting them into the river; if he were the object of these suspicions, they were easy. For, he had been seen by many persons, wandering about on that side of the city – indeed on all sides of it – in a miserable and seemingly half-distracted manner. As to the choice of the spot, obviously such criminating evidence had better take its chance of being found anywhere, rather than upon himself, or in his possession. Concerning the reconciliatory nature of the appointed meeting between the two young men, very little could be made of that in young Landless's favour; for it distinctly appeared that the meeting originated, not with him, but with Mr Crisparkle, and that it had been urged on by Mr Crisparkle; and who could say how unwillingly, or in what ill-conditioned mood, his enforced pupil had gone to it? The more his case was looked into, the weaker it became in every point. Even the broad suggestion that the lost young man had absconded, was rendered additionally improbable on the showing of the young lady from whom he had so lately parted; for, what did she say, with great earnestness and sorrow, when interrogated? That he had, expressly and enthusiastically, planned with her, that he would await the arrival of her guardian, Mr Grewgious. And yet, be it observed, he disappeared before that gentleman appeared.

On the suspicions thus urged and supported, Neville was detained, and re-detained, and the search was pressed on every hand, and Jasper laboured night and day. But nothing more was found. No discovery being made, which proved the lost man to be dead, it at length became necessary to release the person suspected of having made away with him. Neville was set at large. Then, a consequence ensued which Mr Crisparkle had too well foreseen. Neville must leave the place, for the place shunned him and cast him out. Even had it not been so, the dear old china shepherdess would have worried herself to death with fears for her son, and with general trepidation occasioned by their having such an inmate. Even had that not been so, the authority to which the Minor Canon deferred officially, would have settled the point.

'Mr Crisparkle,' quoth the Dean, 'human justice may err, but it must act according to its lights. The days of taking sanctuary are past. This young man must not take sanctuary with us.'

'You mean that he must leave my house, sir?'

'Mr Crisparkle,' returned the prudent Dean, 'I claim no authority in your house. I merely confer with you, on the painful necessity you find yourself under, of depriving this young man of the great advantages of your counsel and instruction.'

'It is very lamentable, sir,' Mr Crisparkle represented.

'Very much so,' the Dean assented.

'And if it be a necessity – ' Mr Crisparkle faltered.

'As you unfortunately find it to be,' returned the Dean.

Mr Crisparkle bowed submissively: 'It is hard to prejudge his case, sir, but I am sensible that – '

'Just so. Perfectly. As you say, Mr Crisparkle,' interposed the Dean, nodding his head smoothly, 'there is nothing else to be done.

No doubt, no doubt. There is no alternative, as your good sense has discovered.'

'I am entirely satisfied of his perfect innocence, sir, nevertheless.'

'We-e-ell!' said the Dean, in a more confidential tone, and slightly glancing around him, 'I would not say so, generally. Not generally. Enough of suspicion attaches to him to – no, I think I would not say so, generally.'

Mr Crisparkle bowed again.

'It does not become us, perhaps,' pursued the Dean, 'to be partisans. Not partisans. We clergy keep our hearts warm and our heads cool, and we hold a judicious middle course.'

'I hope you do not object, sir, to my having stated in public, emphatically, that he will reappear here, whenever any new suspicion may be awakened, or any new circumstance may come to light in this extraordinary matter?'

'Not at all,' returned the Dean. 'And yet, do you know, I don't think,' with a very nice and neat emphasis on those two words: 'I *don't think* I would state it emphatically. State it? Ye-e-es! But emphatically? No-o-o. I *think* not. In point of fact, Mr Crisparkle, keeping our hearts warm and our heads cool, we clergy need do nothing emphatically.'

So Minor Canon Row knew Neville Landless no more; and he went whithersoever he would, or could, with a blight upon his name and fame.

It was not until then that John Jasper silently resumed his place in the choir. Haggard and red-eyed, his hopes plainly had deserted him, his sanguine mood was gone, and all his worst misgivings had come back. A day or two afterwards, while unrobing, he took his Diary from a pocket of his coat, turned the leaves, and with an impressive look, and without one spoken word, handed this entry to Mr Crisparkle to read:

   My dear boy is murdered. The discovery of the watch and shirt-pin convinces me that he was murdered that night, and that his jewellery was taken from him to prevent identification by its means. All the delusive hopes I had founded on his separation from his betrothed wife, I give to the winds. They perish before this fatal discovery. I now swear, and record the oath on this page, That I nevermore will discuss this mystery with any human creature until I hold the clue to it in my hand. That I never will relax in my secrecy or in my search. That I will fasten the crime of the murder of my dear dead boy upon the murderer. And, That I devote myself to his destruction.

SUGGESTIONS FOR A CONCLUSION
(from *The Cornhill*, March 1884)

The Mystery of Edwin Drood

THIS article had been written from the point of view of a mere reader of this unfinished story, and the solution here suggested is based on *internal evidence only*. Indeed, the article itself is the result of the fascination the mystery had on the writer's mind, when he lately read it for the first time. He believes that this is the first attempt to solve the mystery that has contented itself simply and solely with the story as left by Charles Dickens, and the writer has merely endeavoured to do, in the form of a short article, what every reader of 'Edwin Drood' endeavours to do in his head, viz. to deduce a correct conclusion from somewhat incomplete premises.

An ordinary reader must come to the conclusion that John Jasper got rid of his nephew, Edwin Drood; and yet, if such be the case, the inevitable question arises, Where, then, is the mystery? The answer is, In the manner of the riddance. So forcibly does internal evidence point to this conclusion, that one feels suspicious of being entrapped into an enticing but nevertheless erroneous solution. However, the general impression left by the book is that Jasper is guilty, an impression formed from a touch here, an expression there, till the circumstantial evidence which in the story tells against Neville Landless is woven by the reader round Jasper. The question – what became of Edwin Drood? – will be answered anon; but, first, the appearances which point to Jasper as the murderer must be briefly sketched.

First of all, Jasper is found in an opium den. That a man should take opium thus is presumptive evidence that there is something in or about him different to other men: it is uncanny. But it may be objected, De Quincey took opium. True, but he did so privately, and even De Quincey, we fancy, would have foregone the pleasures – to say nothing of the pains – of opium, rather than enter an East-end den for their enjoyment. Nor did De Quincey smoke opium, but drank it; so that the cases are not exactly parallel.

Why does Jasper listen so attentively to the mutterings of his three companion smokers, the woman, Chinaman, and Lascar? and why does he say to each that one word 'Unintelligible'? This will be explained hereafter.

On the evening of that day Jasper and Edwin Drood, uncle and nephew, are together, and during their conversation the following dialogue ensues:–

Jasper – 'You won't be warned, then?'

Edwin – 'No, Jack.'

Jasper – 'You can't be warned, then?'

Edwin – 'No, Jack, not by you. Besides, I don't really consider myself in danger.'

Why should he? and why, having gone so far, could not Jasper confide in his nephew? He warns him against a danger without saying what the danger is. Is it a warning? Is it not a threat?

Mr Jasper is scarcely the man to be fascinated by Mr Sapsea's self-complacency, and his politeness to the future mayor has surely some object underlying it. Durdles, too, is a strange acquaintance to be so enthusiastically taken up, and Jasper seems strangely interested in his keys. There is something which prejudices a reader against Jasper, and when it is discovered from Rosa's conversation with Helena that he loves Rosa, we feel that his extraordinary affection for his nephew is rather at variance with what we should expect, seeing that there is so strong a reason for jealousy.

The quarrel between Edwin and Neville in the street is evidently overheard by Jasper, who, while pretending to be a peacemaker by inviting them to his hospitable gate-house, with truly diabolical skill turns the conversation anew on the betrothal, and the quarrel breaks out afresh. Not satisfied with an ordinary quarrel, Jasper aggravates it by drugging the wine, thereby causing Neville's passion to blaze out so furiously against Edwin. To make this result yet more certain, Jasper looks from one to the other in turn as they make irritating remarks, knowing well that the presence of a third person always aggravates a quarrel between two others.

Jasper takes advantage of the ill-feeling between the young men, so as to have at hand an acknowledged enemy to Edwin, should such be required, and in this spirit he makes the most of the quarrel to Mr Crisparkle that same night, and hastens next day to inform Mrs Crisparkle as well. The latter action admits of two interpretations, a polite and a cunning. Mr Crisparkle would have kept the affair secret from his mother, but Jasper was too quick for him. He wished every one round him to know of Neville's animosity against Edwin, aware how greatly prejudice governs opinion, whether it be public or private.

Had Rosa's interview with Mr Grewgious been only a trifle more confidential on Rosa's part, the whole course of events might have been altered. But, as it was, Mr Grewgious had no suspicion of any disagreement between the betrothed, and consequently assured the white-lipped and anxious Jasper that Rosa had hinted no wish to be released from Edwin. They separate with the full understanding that the marriage will take place. Is there any difference between the 'God bless them both!' of Mr Grewgious and the 'God save them both!' of Mr Jasper? We fear so.

Perhaps the strongest hint in the book as to the murderer is the passage describing Mr Crisparkle finding Jasper asleep on a couch, when he called at the gate-house one evening, viz.: 'Long afterwards he had cause to remember how Jasper sprang from the couch in a delirious state between sleeping and waking, and crying out: "What is the matter? Who did it?" ' The proposal that he shall make peace between Edwin and Neville perplexes Jasper at first, for it is what he scarcely desires; but he seems to consider that their meeting at his house may be to his own advantage, and agrees to it. He explains his brief perplexity by showing some entries in his diary – made on the night of the quarrel – which express his fear of Neville's resentment against Edwin in the strongest language, and Mr Crisparkle is satisfied.

The ring, that was to have been Rosa's engagement-ring, is a rose of diamonds and rubies delicately set in gold, and is contained in an ordinary ring-case made for a single ring. This Mr Grewgious delivers to Edwin, charging him solemnly to bring it back to him if anything should be amiss between him and Rosa. It is plain that this ring is to be an important element in the story, especially when come these significant words, 'Let them' (the jewels in the ring) be. Let them lie unspoken of in his breast. However distinctly or indistinctly he entertained these thoughts, he arrived at the conclusion, Let them be. Among the mighty store of wonderful chains that are for ever forging, day and night, in the vast iron-works of time and circumstance, there was one chain forged in the moment of that small conclusion, riveted to the foundations of heaven and earth, and gifted with invincible force to hold and drag.' The origin of this mysterious sentence is Edwin's act in putting the ring back in his breast, without mentioning it to Rosa, when they mutually break off the engagement between them. As they said 'Good-bye' – little knowing all it meant – they kissed each other fervently. To them it was a kiss that meant that thenceforth they were to be to one another as brother and sister only, but to the watchful Jasper's jealous eyes it seemed but a lovers' parting salutation, and from that moment Edwin Drood was doomed.

Just previous to this interview, Mr Jasper has had 'a night with Durdles.' The first thing to be noticed in a notable chapter is that they pass a mound by the yard-gate, and that Durdles warns Jasper to beware of it, as it is quicklime, adding grimly, 'with a little handy stirring quick enough to eat your bones,' which naturally makes an impression on Jasper. Entering the Cathedral they go down into the crypt, of which Durdles has the key. Jasper has brought with him a bottle, whose contents, whatever they may be, prove at last too strong for Durdles, for after ascending the great tower and descending into the crypt again, he sinks down by one of the pillars and falls asleep at once. In his sleep he dreams that something touches him, and that something falls from his hands, and when he wakes he finds Jasper walking up and down, and sees the key of the crypt door lying at his side. It is two o'clock, so that Durdles has had a long sleep – so long that we are inclined to believe that Jasper has tried his trick of drugging again. As they finally emerge from the Cathedral, Deputy appears, with his fire of stones and impish chant, whereat Jasper's rage is unaccountable – except on the supposition that the expedition was not so unaccountable after all, and that a witness of it was what John Jasper least expected or desired.

On the eventful Christmas Eve Edwin Drood and Neville Land-less are to meet at the gate-house, and what each does during the day is of some importance, in consequence of after events. Neville burns his stray papers, prepares for a walking excursion, and buys a heavy stick: all which circumstances will be used against him afterwards. Edwin goes into the jeweller's shop to have his watch set, and the jewellery tells him of Jasper's remark, that he (Jasper) knew all the jewellery his nephew wore, viz. watch, chain, and shirt-pin; a subject to be recurred to again. Edwin's subsequent conversation with the opium woman is, though he knows it not, a terrible warning. She tells him that Ned is a dangerous name, a threatened name, to which he lightly replies, 'The proverb says that threatened men live long.' 'Then Ned – so threatened is he – should live to all eternity,' retorts the woman, and Edwin resolves to mention it to Jack (who alone calls him Ned) to-morrow. Why not to-day; why not to-day?

Jasper spends the day to some purpose, making much of his affection for his nephew to the shopkeepers whom he deals with, and calling on Mr Sapsea to mention his dinner party of three that night, and to insidiously prejudice him still further against Neville. Quite different is his method with Mr Crisparkle. He assures him he had overcome his black humours and fears of Neville, and that he means to burn this year's diary at the year's end. After this, come what may, the Minor Canon cannot possibly suspect Jasper. To-day Jasper has been wearing a large black scarf of strong close-woven silk, and before entering his gate-house he pulls it off and hangs it in a loop on his arm. 'For that brief time, his face is knitted and stern. But it immediately clears as he resumes his singing and his way.' And the three meet.

There is a great storm that night, and next morning Edwin Drood has disappeared. Neville has started on his walking tour, but being suspected is brought back. His story is simply that he and Edwin went down to the river at about twelve o'clock to watch the storm, that they stayed for about ten minutes, and that Edwin finally left him at Mr Crisparkle's door, saying he was going straight back to the gate-house. However, Jasper's deference to Mr Sapsea now

meets with its reward, for the mayor by his conduct certainly prejudices opinion against Neville, and unconsciously assists Jasper's
plans.

But when Mr Grewgious coldly and dispassionately informs
Jasper that Edwin and Rosa's engagement was broken off before
that terrible Christmas Eve, and that Edwin had forborne to tell
him of it out of consideration for his uncle's feelings, Mr Jasper
breaks utterly down. To have committed murder is terrible enough
to a murderer's mind, but to learn that the murder was utterly
objectless and fruitless – to learn it suddenly and without a moment's
warning – is one of those stunning surprises which even the strongest
nature cannot endure, and hence it is that Jasper swoons away at
Mr Grewgious' news.

But a man of resource like Jasper soon recovers his wits, and,
after telling Mr Grewgious and Mr Crisparkle (who has joined
them) that no quarrel took place between Edwin and Neville in his
house that night, he starts the theory that Edwin may have gone
away to spare himself the pain of awkward explanations, fitting this
theory in cleverly with what Mr Grewgious had just previously told
him. That Neville loved Rosa is another piece of news to Jasper,
which, though scarcely likely to improve the latter's feelings towards
Neville, at once suggests a powerful motive for Edwin's destruction
by his old enemy. Jasper still clings to his new theory, till, as he
had foreseen, Edwin's watch, chain, and shirt-pin are found at the
weir by Mr Crisparkle, and everything points not to absconding
but to murder. The jeweller's opinion that the watch had not been
re-wound since Edwin's visit to his shop (it had certainly run down
before being cast into the water) justified the hypothesis that it was
taken from Edwin not long after he left Jasper's house at midnight
with Neville, and had been thrown away after being retained some
hours. Rosa's evidence, too, dismisses the theory of absconding,
and Jasper shows Mr Crisparkle an entry in his diary, which declares
his conviction that Edwin was murdered – a conviction that we can
hardly doubt.

Now comes the question, how did Jasper effect his awful purpose?
After parting with Neville at Mr Crisparkle's door, Edwin went
straight back to the gate-house. Whether Jasper drugged him there
under guise of hospitality (and we know him to be a proficient in

the art), or by a sudden attack rendered all resistance impossible, matters little. He must have strangled him with that great black scarf, and then – how was he to dispose of the body? Referring to the night expedition with Durdles, it will be remembered that Durdles slept for a long time – probably not far short of two hours – in the crypt, and that he dropped the key of the crypt-door from his hand. Thus Jasper had ample time to leave the crypt in order to select a place for the interment of his future victim. The crypt itself was out of the question, because not only was Durdles then present, but it was notoriously one of the places in which he took a delight in making discoveries. Hence any tampering with the walls or pavement would be almost certainly detected. But where else?

On this expedition – as indeed always – Durdles carried his dinner bundle, and on a former occasion that bundle contained the key of Mrs Sapsea's tomb. Presuming, as we fairly may, that it contained this key that night, Jasper, having the bundle, had it in his power either to take a cast of the key or to substitute another for it, so as to see for himself if there were room in the tomb for another body. He had carefully scrutinised the key before: consequently nothing would be easier than to procure a similar one and to appropriate the real key, while substituting the false one in Durdles' bundle. Indeed, if the substituted key were not *precisely* similar to the real, it would not open the tomb, which would be all the more advantageous to Jasper.

Mention was also made of a mound of quicklime they passed by, and it is our opinion that either then (while Durdles slept), or on the night of the murder, Jasper procured some of this quicklime, and put it in Mrs Sapsea's tomb, afterwards inserting the body of the hapless Edwin. The quicklime would speedily destroy the body, and long before the tomb was again opened – which would probably not be till Mr Sapsea's death – all traces would have disappeared. Jasper had but to carry the body from the gate-house to the tomb, apparently no great distance; and any risk he ran of being seen was much diminished by the wildness of the night. Having finally disposed of his victim, he must have gone to the weir, and cleverly arranged the watch-chain so that it caught in the interstices of the timbers, while he flung the shirt-pin into the water, lest the discovery of all these articles at once might arouse suspicion from the fact of their clumsy exposure.

To rid himself of the corpse, to get to the weir (some two miles off), to arrange the jewellery, and to be safely back in his gate-house again without being seen, make up a night's work from which the boldest criminal might well shrink; but the fury of the storm favoured the murderer, and but for his collapse at Mr Grewgious' news Jasper might never have been suspected. The scheme by which it falls to Mr Crisparkle to find the watch, so that he becomes one of the chief witnesses against Neville, is an admirable stroke on Jasper's part, but it is more than counter-balanced by what Mr Grewgious saw as he warmed his hands, 'a heap of torn and miry clothes upon the floor.'

Mr Datchery we take to be a detective, employed by Mr Grewgious to keep a watch on Jasper. Notice his look of interest when Deputy, pointing to part of the gate-house, says, 'That's Jarsper's;' also his excessive politeness to Mr Sapsea, and remember that Jasper's politeness to the same person was not without an object. His white hair, too, is unusually thick and ample, and he has black eyebrows, which is strange.

More than half a year has gone since Edwin's disappearance, and Jasper naturally considers himself safe, so safe indeed that, when he avows his love to Rosa, he tells her that had his affection for his nephew been one silken thread less strong he would have swept even him from his path. A faint suspicion of Jasper had before crossed Rosa's mind, and now recurs with redoubled force, but the only object for such a crime – to win her – seems altogether too slight to account for it; so she hides her suspicion. If Neville and his sister suspect him, they say nothing: Mr Crisparkle is too open and frank to suspect anyone, and Mr Grewgious acknowledges that he dislikes Jasper, but nothing more. How is the murderer to be brought to justice?

Old habits can seldom be relinquished altogether, and we cannot be much surprised at finding Jasper in the opium den once more. The vision he has, under the influence of opium, and the broken sentences extracted from him by the woman, speak for themselves. As he lies in stupor on the bed the woman exclaims, 'I heard ye say once, when I was lying where you're lying, and you were making your speculations on me, "Unintelligible!" I heard you say so, of two more than me. But don't be too sure always; don't ye be too sure, beauty!' From which we gather, that in the first scene of all, this woman had listened to his comment on herself and companions, and had from that time devoted herself to learn his secret. It explains, too, why she tracked him that Christmas Eve, when she unconsciously warned the generous Edwin of his danger, and explains her exclamation, now, when Jasper leaves her house, 'I'll not miss ye twice!'

She follows him to Cloisterham and falls in with Mr Datchery who extracts information from her that rather astonishes him. After bargaining with Deputy to find out where she lives in London, Mr Datchery in the Cathedral next morning sees the woman's threatening gestures at Jasper, and afterwards hears from her own lips that she recognises him. He returns home for breakfast, opens his cupboard door, 'takes his bit of chalk from its shelf, adds one thick line to the score, extending from the top of the cupboard door to the bottom, and then falls to with an appetite.'

Here the unfinished story breaks off at an exciting moment, and it only remains to consider how Jasper's detection was brought about. Mr Datchery doubtless confided all he had learnt to Mr Grewgious, and they probably prevailed on the opium woman to allow them, or one of them, to be present at Jasper's next visit, the time of which they could ascertain for themselves. Lieutenant Tartar, disguised as a sailor, might, in the most natural manner, be present at the same time in the den, and the woman's questions (suggested, maybe, by Mr Datchery) to Jasper, when under the influence of opium, might extract valuable hints as to the manner of the crime, the bestowal of the body, &c., hints which a clever detective like Datchery might well piece together with the evidence obtainable from Deputy and Durdles. Deputy, be it remembered, saw Jasper and Durdles leaving the Cathedral on the night – or rather the morning – of their 'unaccountable expedition,' and could testify to Jasper's explosion of anger at his sudden appearance. Any account given by Durdles of what took place that night would be none too clear, but even he could not have forgotten dropping the key of the crypt-door, and the fact of Jasper having carried the bundle.

But what then? Supposing Jasper to have let fall a hint as to the burial of the body, the crypt would naturally be first thought of as a likely spot. Baffled there, for Durdles could soon tell if anything had been disturbed, attention would be drawn to the two keys carried by Durdles, and finally to that which had been in his dinner bundle, viz. the key of Mrs Sapsea's tomb. But what could be discovered on opening it? Scarcely a body, for more than six months had elapsed since Edwin's disappearance. Scarcely even bones, for, if the hypothesis that quicklime was used be the correct one, no bones would remain. Indeed, what could remain? What could resist the destructive properties of quicklime?

The answer is – the stones of the ring given by Mr Grewgious to Edwin, and never seen since. We know that Jasper (so the jeweller told Edwin) had a precise knowledge of Edwin's jewellery, and, exactly in accordance with that knowledge, Edwin's watch, chain, and shirt-pin were found at the weir. But Jasper could have had no knowledge of this ring, kept as it was in a case in Edwin's breast, unless, indeed, he examined his pockets after despatching him; which is unlikely, as plunder was by no means his object. It is almost certain, then, that the ring was buried on the body, and even if the action of the quicklime could destroy the case and the gold setting of the stones, it could not possibly affect the stones themselves, which were diamonds and rubies. These, Mr Grewgious could readily identify, and Bazzard could prove that the ring was delivered to Edwin. The ring, or the stones, once found and identified, the accumulated evidence of Mr Grewgious, Mr Datchery, Durdles, Deputy, Mr Crisparkle, Rosa, and the opium woman, would, we think, assuredly convict Jasper of Edwin Drood's murder, while his conscience-stricken appearance at the prospect of detection, when the first breath of suspicion fastened on him, would at once popularly condemn him.

In conclusion, let us make a guess at the future of some of the other characters in the book. Mr Tartar and Rosa would ere long be husband and wife, and we fancy Helena Landless would become Mrs Crisparkle. Neville, cleared from all suspicion, would have to begin the world anew: Mr Datchery and Durdles must remain as they are: we would not have them alter one whit. And Deputy? We can, perhaps, imagine (but faintly) his delight at 'Jarsper's' downfall, and by using our eyes keenly may discern him indulging, as once before, 'in a slow and stately dance, perhaps supposed to be performed by the Dean,' to more fully express his ecstasy.

THE RESIDENCE AT WHITMINSTER

M. R. James

D R Ashton – Thomas Ashton, Doctor of Divinity – sat in his study, habited in a dressing-gown, and with a silk cap on his shaven head – his wig being for the time taken off and placed on its block on a side table. He was a man of some fifty-five years, strongly made, of a sanguine complexion, an angry eye, and a long upper lip. Face and eye were lighted up at the moment when I picture him by the level ray of an afternoon sun that shone in upon him through a tall sash window, giving on the west. The room into which it shone was also tall, lined with bookcases, and, where the wall showed between them, panelled. On the table near the doctor's elbow was a green cloth, and upon it what he would have called a silver standish – a tray with inkstands – quill pens, a calf-bound book or two, some papers, a church-warden pipe and brass tobacco-box, a flask cased in plaited straw, and a liqueur glass. The year was 1730, the month December, the hour somewhat past three in the afternoon.

I have described in these lines pretty much all that a superficial observer would have noted when he looked into the room. What met Dr Ashton's eye when he looked out of it, sitting in his leather armchair? Little more than the tops of the shrubs and fruit-trees of his garden could be seen from that point, but the red-brick wall of it was visible in almost all the length of its western side. In the middle of that was a gate – a double gate of rather elaborate iron scroll-work, which allowed something of a view beyond. Through it he could see that the ground sloped away almost at once to a bottom, along which a stream must run, and rose steeply from it on the other side, up to a field that was park-like in character, and thickly studded with oaks, now, of course, leafless. They did not stand so thick together but that some glimpse of sky and horizon could be seen between their stems. The sky was now golden and the horizon, a horizon of distant woods, it seemed, was purple.

But all that Dr Ashton could find to say, after contemplating this prospect for many minutes, was: 'Abominable!'

A listener would have been aware, immediately upon this, of the sound of footsteps coming somewhat hurriedly in the direction of the study: by the resonance he could have told that they were traversing a much larger room. Dr Ashton turned round in his chair as the door opened, and looked expectant. The incomer was a lady – a stout lady in the dress of the time: though I have made some attempt at indicating the doctor's costume, I will not enterprize that of his wife – for it was Mrs Ashton who now entered. She had an anxious, even a sorely distracted, look, and it was in a very disturbed voice that she almost whispered to Dr Ashton, putting her head close to his, 'He's in a very sad way, love, worse, I'm afraid.' 'Tt – tt, is he really?' and he leaned back and looked in her face. She nodded. Two solemn bells, high up, and not far away, rang out the half-hour at this moment. Mrs Ashton started. 'Oh, do you think you can give order that the minster clock be stopped chiming to-night? 'Tis just over his chamber, and will keep him from sleeping, and to sleep is the only chance for him, that's certain.' 'Why, to be sure, if there were need, real need, it could be done, but not upon any light occasion. This Frank, now, do you assure me that his recovery stands upon it?' said Dr Ashton: his voice was loud and rather hard. 'I do verily believe it,' said his wife. 'Then, if it must be, bid Molly run across to Simpkins and say on my authority that he is to stop the clock chimes at sunset: and – yes – she is after that to say to my Lord Saul that I wish to see him presently in this room.' Mrs Ashton hurried off.

Before any other visitor enters, it will be well to explain the situation.

Dr Ashton was the holder, among other preferments, of a prebend in the rich collegiate church of Whitminster, one of the foundations which, though not a cathedral, survived Dissolution and Reformation, and retained its constitution and endowments for a hundred years after the time of which I write. The great church, the residences of the dean and the two prebendaries, the choir and its appurtenances, were all intact and in working order. A dean who flourished soon after 1500 had been a great builder, and had erected a spacious quadrangle of red brick adjoining the church for the residence of the officials. Some of these persons were no longer required: their offices had dwindled down to mere titles, borne by clergy or lawyers in the town and neighbourhood; and so the houses that had been meant to accommodate eight or ten people were now shared among three – the dean and the two prebendaries. Dr Ashton's included what had been the common parlour and the dining-hall of the whole body. It occupied a whole side of the court, and at one end had a private door into the minster. The other end, as we have seen, looked out over the country.

So much for the house. As for the inmates, Dr Ashton was a wealthy man and childless, and he had adopted, or rather undertaken to bring up, the orphan son of his wife's sister. Frank Sydall was the lad's name: he had been a good many months in the house. Then one day came a letter from an Irish peer, the Earl of Kildonan (who had known Dr Ashton at college), putting it to the doctor whether he would consider taking into his family the Viscount Saul, the Earl's heir, and acting in some sort as his tutor. Lord Kildonan was shortly to take up a post in the Lisbon Embassy, and the boy was unfit to make the voyage: 'not that he is sickly,' the Earl wrote, 'though you'll find him whimsical, or of late I've thought him so, and to confirm this, 'twas only today his old nurse came expressly to tell me he was possess'd: but let that pass; I'll warrant you can find a spell to make all straight. Your arm was stout enough in the old days, and I give you plenary authority to use it as you see fit. The truth is, he has here no boys of his age or quality to consort with, and is given to moping about in our raths and graveyards: and he brings home romances that fright my servants out of their wits. So there are you and your lady forewarned.' It was perhaps with half an eye open to the possibility of an Irish bishopric (at which another sentence in the Earl's letter seemed to hint) that Dr Ashton accepted the charge of my Lord Viscount Saul and of the 200 guineas a year that were to come with him.

So he came, one night in September. When he got out of the chaise that brought him, he went first and spoke to the postboy and gave him some money, and patted the neck of his horse. Whether he made some movement that scared it or not, there was very nearly a nasty accident, for the beast started violently, and the postilion being unready was thrown and lost his fee, as he found afterwards, and the chaise lost some paint on the gateposts, and the wheel went over the man's foot who was taking out the baggage. When Lord Saul came up the steps into the light of the lamp in the porch to be greeted by Dr Ashton, he was seen to be a thin youth of, say sixteen years old, with straight black hair and the pale colouring that is common to such a figure. He took the accident and commotion calmly enough, and expressed a proper anxiety for the people who had been, or might have been, hurt: his voice was smooth and pleasant, and without any trace, curiously, of an Irish brogue.

Frank Sydall was a younger boy, perhaps of eleven or twelve, but Lord Saul did not for that reject his company. Frank was able to teach him various games he had not known in Ireland, and he was apt at learning them; apt, too, at his books, though he had had little or no regular teaching at home. It was not long before he was making a shift to puzzle out the inscriptions on the tombs in the minster, and he would often put a question to the doctor about the old books in the library that required some thought to answer. It is to be supposed that he made himself very agreeable to the servants, for within ten days of his coming they were almost falling over each other in their efforts to oblige him. At the same time, Mrs Ashton was rather put to it to find new maidservants; for there were several changes, and some of the families in the town from which she had been accustomed to draw seemed to have no one available. She was forced to go farther afield than was usual.

These generalities I gather from the doctor's notes in his diary and from letters. They are generalities, and we should like, in view of what has to be told, something sharper and more detailed. We get it in entries which begin late in the year, and, I think, were posted up all together after the final incident; but they cover so few days in all that there is no need to doubt that the writer could remember the course of things accurately.

On a Friday morning it was that a fox, or perhaps a cat, made

away with Mrs Ashton's most prized black cockerel, a bird without
a single white feather on its body. Her husband had told her often
enough that it would make a suitable sacrifice to Æsculapius; that
had discomfited her much, and now she would hardly be consoled.
The boys looked everywhere for traces of it: Lord Saul brought in
a few feathers, which seemed to have been partially burnt on the
garden rubbish-heap. It was on the same day that Dr Ashton, looking out of an upper window, saw the two boys playing in the corner
of the garden at a game he did not understand. Frank was looking
earnestly at something in the palm of his hand. Saul stood behind
him and seemed to be listening. After some minutes he very gently
laid his hand on Frank's head, and almost instantly thereupon, Frank
suddenly dropped whatever it was that he was holding, clapped his
hands to his eyes, and sank down on the grass. Saul, whose face
expressed great anger, hastily picked the object up, of which it could
only be seen that it was glittering, put it in his pocket, and turned
away, leaving Frank huddled up on the grass. Dr Ashton rapped on
the window to attract their attention, and Saul looked up as if in
alarm, and then springing to Frank, pulled him up by the arm and
led him away. When they came in to dinner, Saul explained that
they had been acting a part of the tragedy of Radamistus, in which
the heroine reads the future fate of her father's kingdom by means
of a glass ball held in her hand, and is overcome by the terrible
events she has seen. During this explanation Frank said nothing,
only looked rather bewilderedly at Saul. He must, Mrs Ashton
thought, have contracted a chill from the wet of the grass, for that
evening he was certainly feverish and disordered; and the disorder
was of the mind as well as the body, for he seemed to have something he wished to say to Mrs Ashton, only a press of household
affairs prevented her from paying attention to him; and when she
went, according to her habit, to see that the light in the boys'
chamber had been taken away and to bid them good night, he
seemed to be sleeping, though his face was unnaturally flushed, to
her thinking: Lord Saul, however, was pale and quiet, and smiling
in his slumber.

Next morning it happened that Dr Ashton was occupied in church
and other business, and unable to take the boys' lessons. He therefore
set them tasks to be written and brought to him. Three times, if

not oftener, Frank knocked at the study door, and each time the doctor chanced to be engaged with some visitor, and sent the boy off rather roughly, which he later regretted. Two clergymen were at dinner this day, and both remarked – being fathers of families – that the lad seemed sickening for a fever, in which they were too near the truth, and it had been better if he had been put to bed forthwith: for a couple of hours later in the afternoon he came running into the house, crying out in a way that was really terrifying, and rushing to Mrs Ashton, clung about her, begging her to protect him, and saying, 'Keep them off! Keep them off!' without intermission. And it was now evident that some sickness had taken strong hold of him. He was therefore got to bed in another chamber from that in which he commonly lay, and the physician brought to him: who pronounced the disorder to be grave and affecting the lad's brain, and prognosticated a fatal end to it if strict quiet were not observed, and those sedative remedies used which he should prescribe.

We are now come by another way to the point we had reached before. The minster clock has been stopped from striking, and Lord Saul is on the threshold of the study.

'What account can you give of this poor lad's state?' was Dr Ashton's first question. 'Why, sir, little more than you know already, I fancy. I must blame myself, though, for giving him a fright yesterday when we were acting that silly play you saw. I fear I made him take it more to heart than I meant.' 'How so?' 'Well, by telling him foolish tales I had picked up in Ireland of what we call the second sight.' '*Second* sight! What kind of sight might that be?' 'Why, you know our ignorant people pretend that some are able to foresee what is to come – sometimes in a glass, or in the air, maybe, and at Kildonan we had an old woman that pretended to such a power. And I dare say I coloured the matter more highly than I should: but I never dreamed Frank would take it so near as he did.' 'You were wrong, my lord, very wrong, in meddling with such superstitious matters at all, and you should have considered whose house you were in, and how little becoming such actions are to my character and person or to your own: but pray how came it that you, acting, as you say, a play, should fall upon anything that could so alarm Frank?' 'That is what I can hardly tell, sir: he passed all in a moment from rant about battles and lovers and Cleodora and Antigenes to something I could not follow at all, and then dropped down as you saw.' 'Yes: was that at the moment when you laid your hand on the top of his head?' Lord Saul gave a quick look at his questioner – quick and spiteful – and for the first time seemed unready with an answer. 'About that time it may have been,' he said. 'I have tried to recollect myself, but I am not sure. There was, at any rate, no significance in what I did then.' 'Ah!' said Dr Ashton, 'well, my lord, I should do wrong were I not to tell you that this fright of my poor nephew may have very ill consequences to him. The doctor speaks very despondingly of his state.' Lord Saul pressed his hands together and looked earnestly upon Dr Ashton. 'I am willing to believe you had no bad intention, as assuredly you could have no reason to bear the poor boy malice: but I cannot wholly free you from blame in the affair.' As he spoke, the hurrying steps were heard again, and Mrs Ashton came quickly into the room, carrying a candle, for the evening had by this time closed in. She was greatly agitated. 'O come!' she cried, 'come directly. I'm sure he is going.' 'Going? Frank? Is it possible? Already?' With some such incoherent words the doctor caught up a book of prayers from the table and ran out after his wife. Lord Saul stopped for a moment where he was. Molly, the maid, saw him bend over and put both hands to his face. If it were the last words she had to speak, she said afterwards, he was striving to keep back a fit of laughing. Then he went out softly, following the others.

Mrs Ashton was sadly right in her forecast. I have no inclination to imagine the last scene in detail. What Dr Ashton records is, or may be taken to be, important to the story. They asked Frank if he would like to see his companion, Lord Saul, once again. The boy was quite collected, it appears, in these moments. 'No,' he said, 'I do not want to see him; but you should tell him I am afraid he will be very cold.' 'What do you mean, my dear?' said Mrs Ashton. 'Only that,' said Frank; 'but say to him besides that I am free of them now, but he should take care. And I am sorry about your black cockerel, Aunt Ashton; but he said we must use it so, if we were to see all that could be seen.'

Not many minutes after, he was gone. Both the Ashtons were grieved, she naturally most; but the doctor, though not an emotional man, felt the pathos of the early death: and, besides, there was the growing suspicion that all had not been told him by Saul, and that there was something here which was out of his beaten track. When he left the chamber of death, it was to walk across the quadrangle of the residence to the sexton's house. A passing bell, the greatest of the minster bells, must be rung, a grave must he dug in the minster yard, and there was now no need to silence the chiming of the minster clock. As he came slowly back in the dark, he thought he must see Lord Saul again. That matter of the black cockerel – trifling as it might seem – would have to be cleared up. It might be merely a fancy of the sick boy, but if not, was there not a witch-trial he had read, in which some grim little rite of sacrifice had played a part? Yes, he must see Saul.

I rather guess these thoughts of his than find written authority for them. That there was another interview is certain: certain also that Saul would (or as he said, could) throw no light on Frank's words: though the message, or some part of it, appeared to affect him horribly. But there is no record of the talk in detail. It is only said that Saul sat all that evening in the study, and when he bid good night, which he did most reluctantly, asked for the doctor's prayers.

The month of January was near its end when Lord Kildonan, in the Embassy at Lisbon, received a letter that for once gravely disturbed that vain man and neglectful father. Saul was dead. The scene at Frank's burial had been very distressing. The day was awful in blackness and wind: the bearers, staggering blindly along under the flapping black pall, found it a hard job, when they emerged from the porch of the minster, to make their way to the grave. Mrs Ashton was in her room – women did not then go to their kinsfolk's funerals – but Saul was there, draped in the mourning cloak of the time, and his face was white and fixed as that of one dead, except when, as was noticed three or four times, he suddenly turned his head to the left and looked over his shoulder. It was then alive with a terrible expression of listening fear. No one saw him go away: and no one could find him that evening. All night the gale buffeted the high windows of the church, and howled over the upland and roared through the woodland. It was useless to search in the open: no voice of shouting or cry for help could possibly be heard. All that Dr Ashton could do was to warn the people about the college, and the town constables, and to sit up, on the alert for any news, and this he did. News came early next morning, brought by the sexton, whose business it was to open the church for early prayers at seven, and who sent the maid rushing upstairs with wild eyes and flying hair to summon her master. The two men dashed across to the south door of the minster, there to find Lord Saul clinging desperately to the great ring of the door, his head sunk between his shoulders, his stockings in rags, his shoes gone, his legs torn and bloody.

This was what had to be told to Lord Kildonan, and this really ends the first part of the story. The tomb of Frank Sydall and of the Lord Viscount Saul, only child and heir to William Earl of Kildonan, is one: a stone altar tomb in Whitminster churchyard.

Dr Ashton lived on for over thirty years in his prebendal house. I do not know how quietly, but without visible disturbance. His successor preferred a house he already owned in the town, and left that of the senior prebendary vacant. Between them these two men saw the eighteenth century out and the nineteenth in; for Mr Hindes, the successor of Ashton, became prebendary at nine-and-twenty and died at nine-and-eighty. So that it was not till 1823 or 1824 that anyone succeeded to the post who intended to make the house his home. The man who did so was Dr Henry Oldys, whose name may be known to some of my readers as that of the author of a row of volumes labelled *Oldys's Works*, which occupy a place that must be honoured, since it is so rarely touched, upon the shelves of many a substantial library.

Dr Oldys, his niece, and his servants took some months to transfer furniture and books from his Dorsetshire parsonage to the quadrangle of Whitminster, and to get everything into place. But eventually the work was done, and the house (which, though untenanted, had always been kept sound and weather-tight) woke up, and like Monte Cristo's mansion at Auteuil, lived, sang, and bloomed once more. On a certain morning in June it looked especially fair, as Dr Oldys strolled in his garden before breakfast and gazed over the red roof at the minster tower with its four gold vanes, backed by a very blue sky, and very white little clouds.

'Mary,' he said, as he seated himself at the breakfast-table and laid down something hard and shiny on the cloth, 'here's a find which the boy made just now. You'll be sharper than I if you can guess what it's meant for.' It was a round and perfectly smooth tablet – as much as an inch thick – of what seemed clear glass. 'It is rather attractive, at all events,' said Mary: she was a fair woman, with light hair and large eyes, rather a devotee to literature. 'Yes,' said her uncle, 'I thought you'd be pleased with it. I presume it came from the house: it turned up in the rubbish-heap in the corner.' 'I'm not sure that I do like it, after all,' said Mary, some minutes later. 'Why in the world not, my dear?' 'I don't know, I'm sure. Perhaps it's only fancy.' 'Yes, only fancy and romance, of course. What's that book, now – the name of that book, I mean, that you had your head in all yesterday?' '*The Talisman*, Uncle. Oh, if this should turn out to be a talisman, how enchanting it would be!' 'Yes, *The Talisman*: ah, well, you're welcome to it, whatever it is: I must be off about my business. Is all well in the house? Does it suit you? Any complaints from the servants' hall?' 'No, indeed, nothing could be more charming. The only *soupçon* of a complaint besides the lock of the linen closet, which I told you of, is that Mrs Maple says she cannot get rid of the sawflies out of that room you pass through at the other end of the hall. By the way, are you sure you like your bedroom? It is a long way off from anyone else, you know.'

'Like it? To be sure I do; the farther off from you, my dear, the better. There, don't think it necessary to beat me: accept my apologies. But what are sawflies? Will they eat my coats? If not, they may have the room to themselves for what I care. We are not likely to be using it.'

'No, of course not. Well, what she calls sawflies are those reddish things like a daddy-long-legs, but smaller, and there are a great many of them perching about that room, certainly. I don't like them, but I don't fancy they are mischievous.'

'There seem to several things you don't like this fine morning,' said her uncle, as he closed the door.

Miss Oldys remained in her chair looking at the tablet, which she was holding in the palm of her hand. The smile that had been on her face faded slowly from it and gave place to an expression of curiosity and almost strained attention. Her reverie was broken by the entrance of Mrs Maple, and her invariable opening, 'Oh, Miss, could I speak to you a minute?'

A letter from Miss Oldys to a friend in Lichfield, begun a day or two before, is the next source for this story. It is not devoid of traces of the influence of that leader of female thought in her day, Miss Anna Seward, known to some as the Swan of Lichfield.

'My sweetest Emily will be rejoiced to hear that we are at length – my beloved uncle and myself – settled in the house that now calls us master – nay, master and mistress – as in past ages it has called so many others. Here we taste a mingling of modern elegance and hoary antiquity, such as has never ere now graced life for either of us. The town, small as it is, affords us some reflection, pale indeed, but veritable, of the sweets of polite intercourse: the adjacent country numbers amid the occupants of its scattered mansions some whose polish is annually refreshed by contact with metropolitan splendour, and others whose robust and homely geniality is, at times, and by way of contrast, not less cheering and acceptable. Tired of the parlours and drawing-rooms of our friends, we have ready to hand a refuge from the clash of wits or the small talk of the day amid the solemn beauties of our venerable minster, whose silver chimes daily 'knoll us to prayer,' and in the shady walks of whose tranquil graveyard we amuse with softened heart, and ever and anon with moistened eye, upon the memorials of the young, the beautiful, the aged, the wise, and the good.'

Here there is an abrupt break both in the writing and the style.

'But my dearest Emily, I can no longer write with the care which you deserve, and in which we both take pleasure. What I have to tell you is wholly foreign to what has gone before. This morning my uncle brought in to breakfast an object which had been found in the garden; it was a glass or crystal tablet of this shape (a little sketch is given), which he handed to me, and which, after he left the room, remained on the table by me. I gazed at it, I know not why, for some minutes, till called away by the day's duties; and you will smile incredulously when I say that I seemed to myself to begin to descry reflected in it objects and scenes which were not in the room where I was. You will not, however, think it strange that after such an experience I took the first opportunity to seclude myself in my room with which I now half believed to be a talisman

of mickle might. I was not disappointed. I assure you, Emily, by
that memory which is dearest to both of us, that what I went
through this afternoon transcends the limits of what I had before
deemed credible. In brief, what I saw, seated in my bedroom, in
the broad daylight of summer, and looking into the crystal depth
of that small round tablet, was this. First, a prospect, strange to me,
of an enclosure of rough, and hillocky grass, with a grey stone ruin
in the midst, and a wall of rough stones about it. In this stood an
old, and very ugly, woman in a red cloak and ragged skirt, talking
to a boy dressed in the fashion of maybe a hundred years ago. She
put something which glittered into his hand, and he something into
hers, which I saw to be money, for a single coin fell from her
trembling hand into the grass. The scene passed: I should have
remarked, by the way, that on the rough walls of the enclosure I
could distinguish bones, and even a skull, lying in a disorderly
fashion. Next, I was looking upon two boys; one the figure of the
former vision, the other younger. They were in a plot of garden,
walled round, and this garden, in spite of the difference in arrangement, and the small size of the trees, I could clearly recognize as
being that upon which I now look from my window. The boys
were engaged in some curious play, it seemed. Something was
smouldering on the ground. The elder placed his hands upon it, and
then raised them in what I took to be an attitude of prayer: and I
saw, and started at seeing, that on them were deep stains of blood.
The sky above was overcast. The same boy now turned his face
towards the wall of the garden, and beckoned with both his raised
hands, and as he did so I was conscious that some moving objects
were becoming visible over the top of the wall – whether heads or
other parts of some animal or human forms I could not tell. Upon
the instant the elder boy turned sharply, seized the arm of the
younger (who all this time had been poring over what lay on the
ground), and both hurried off. I then saw blood upon the grass, a
little pile of bricks, and what I thought were black feathers scattered
about. That scene closed, and the next was so dark that perhaps the
full meaning of it escaped me. But what I seemed to see was a
form, at first crouching low among trees or bushes that were being
threshed by a violent wind, then running very swiftly, and constantly turning a pale face to look behind him, as if he feared a

pursuer: and, indeed, pursuers were following hard after him. Their shapes were but dimly seen, their number – three or four, perhaps – only guessed. I suppose they were on the whole more like dogs than anything else, but dogs such as we have seen they assuredly were not. Could I have closed my eyes to this horror, I would have done so at once, but I was helpless. The last I saw was the victim darting beneath an arch and clutching at some object to which he clung: and those that were pursuing him overtook him, and I seemed to hear the echo of a cry of despair. It may be that I became unconscious: certainly I had the sensation of awaking to the light of day after an interval of darkness. Such, in literal truth, Emily, was my vision – I can call it by no other name – of this afternoon. Tell me, have I not been the unwilling witness of some episode of a tragedy connected with this very house?'

The letter is continued next day. 'The tale of yesterday was not completed when I laid down my pen. I said nothing of my experiences to my uncle – you know, yourself, how little his robust common sense would be prepared to allow of them, and how in his eyes the specific remedy would be a black draught or a glass of port. After a silent evening, then – silent, not sullen – I retired to rest. Judge of my terror, when, not yet in bed, I heard what I can only describe as a distant bellow, and knew it for my uncle's voice, though never in my hearing so exerted before. His sleeping-room is at the farther extremity of this large house, and to gain access to it one must traverse an antique hall some eighty feet long, a lofty panelled chamber, and two unoccupied bedrooms. In the second of these – a room almost devoid of furniture – I found him, in the dark, his candle lying smashed on the floor. As I ran in, bearing a light, he clasped me in arms that trembled for the first time since I have known him, thanked God, and hurried me out of the room. He would say nothing of what had alarmed him. 'Tomorrow, tomorrow,' was all I could get from him. A bed was hastily improvised for him in the room next to my own. I doubt if his night was more restful than mine. I could only get to sleep in the small hours, when daylight was already strong, and then my dreams were of the grimmest – particularly one which stamped itself on my brain, and which I must set down on the chance of dispersing the impression it has made. It was that I came up to my room with a heavy foreboding of evil oppressing me, and went with a hesitation and reluctance I could not explain to my chest of drawers. I opened the top drawer, in which was nothing but ribbons and handkerchiefs, and then the second, where was as little to alarm, and then, O heavens, the third and last: and there was a mass of linen neatly folded: upon which, as I looked with a curiosity that began to be tinged with horror, I perceived a movement in it, and a pink hand was thrust out of the folds and began to grope feebly in the air. I could bear it no more, and rushed from the room, clapping the door after me, and strove with all my force to lock it. But the key would not turn in the wards, and from within the room came a sound of rustling and bumping, drawing nearer and nearer to the door. Why I did not flee down the stairs I know not. I continued grasping the handle, and mercifully, as the door was plucked from my hand with an irresistible force, I awoke. You may not think this very alarming, but I assure you it was so to me.

'At breakfast to-day my uncle was very uncommunicative, and I think ashamed of the fright he had given us; but afterwards he inquired of me whether Mr Spearman was still in town, adding that he thought that was a young man who had some sense left in his head. I think you know, my dear Emily, that I am not inclined to disagree with him there, and also that I was not unlikely to be able to answer his question. To Mr Spearman he accordingly went, and I have not seen him since. I must send this strange budget of news to you now, or it may have to wait over more than one post.'

The reader will not be far out if he guesses that Miss Mary and Mr Spearman made a match of it not very long after this month of June. Mr Spearman was a young spark, who had a good property in the neighbourhood of Whitminster, and not infrequently about this time spent a few days at the 'King's Head,' ostensibly on business. But he must have had some leisure, for his diary is copious, especially for the days of which I am telling the story. It is probable to me that he wrote this episode as fully as he could at the bidding of Miss Mary.

'Uncle Oldys (how I hope I may have the right to call him so before long!) called this morning. After throwing out a good many short remarks on indifferent topics, he said, "I wish, Spearman, you'd listen to an odd story and keep a close tongue about it just for a bit, till I get more light on it." "To be sure," said I, "you may count on me." "I don't know what to make of it," he said. "You know my bedroom. It is well away from everyone else's, and I pass through the great hall and two or three other rooms to get to it." "Is it at the end next the minster, then?" I asked. "Yes, it is: well, now, yesterday morning my Mary told me that the room next before it was infested with some sort of fly that the housekeeper couldn't get rid of. That may be the explanation, or it may not. What do you think?" "Why," said I, "you've not yet told me what has to be explained." "True enough, I don't believe I have; but by the by, what are these sawflies? What's the size of them?' I began to wonder if he was touched in the head. "What I call a sawfly," I said very patiently, "is a red animal, like a daddy-long-legs, but not so big, perhaps an inch long, perhaps less. It is very hard in the body, and to me" – I was going to say "particularly offensive," but he broke in, "Come, come; an inch or less. That won't do." "I can only tell you," I said, "what I know. Would it not be better if you told me from first to last what it is that has puzzled you, and then I may be able to give you some kind of an opinion." He gazed at me meditatively. "Perhaps it would," he said. "I told Mary only to-day that I thought you had some vestiges of sense in your head." (I bowed my acknowledgments.) "The thing is, I've an odd kind of shyness about talking of it. Nothing of the sort has happened to me before. Well, about eleven o'clock last night, or after, I took my candle and set out for my room. I had a book in my other hand – I always read something for a few minutes before I drop off to sleep. A dangerous habit: I don't recommend it: but *I* know how to manage my light and my bed curtains. Now then, first, as I stepped out of my study into the great hall that's next to it, and shut the door, my candle went out. I supposed I had clapped the door behind me too quick, and made a draught, and I was annoyed, for I'd no tinder-box nearer than my bedroom. But I knew my way well enough, and went on. The next thing was that my book was struck out of my hand in the dark: if I said twitched out of my hand it would better express the sensation. It fell on the floor. I picked it up, and went on, more annoyed than before, and a little startled. But as you know, that hall has many windows without curtains, and in summer nights like these it's easy to see not only where the furniture is, but whether there's anyone or anything moving: and there was no one – nothing of the kind. So on I went through the hall and through the audit chamber next to it, which also has big windows, and then into the bedrooms which lead to my own, where the curtains were drawn, and I had to go slower because of steps here and there. It was in the second of those rooms that I nearly got my *quietus*. The moment I opened the door of it I felt there was something wrong. I thought twice, I confess, whether I shouldn't turn back and find another way there is to my room rather than go through that one. Then I was ashamed of myself, and thought what people call better of it, though I don't know about 'better' in this case. If I was to describe my experience exactly, I should say this: there was a dry, light, rustling sound all over the room as I went in, and then (you remember it was perfectly dark) something seemed to rush at me, and there was – I don't know how to put it – a sensation of long thin arms, or legs, or feelers, all about my face, and neck and body. Very little strength in them, there seemed to be, but, Spearman, I don't think I was ever more horrified or disgusted in all my life, that I remember: and it does take something to put me out. I roared out as loud as I could, and flung away my candle at random, and knowing I was near the window, I tore at the curtain and somehow let in enough light to be able to see something waving which I knew was an insect's leg, by the shape of it: but, Lord, what a size! Why, the beast must have been as tall as I am. And now you tell me sawflies are an inch long or less. What do you make of it, Spearman?"

' "For goodness' sake finish your story first," I said. "I never heard anything like it." "Oh," said he, "there's no more to tell. Mary ran in with a light, and there was nothing there. I didn't tell her what was the matter. I changed my room for last night, and I expect for good." "Have you searched this odd room of yours?" I said. "What do you keep in it?" "We don't use it," he answered. "There's an old press there, and some little other furniture." "And in the press?" said I. "I don't know; I never saw it opened, but I do know that it's locked." "Well, I should have it looked into, and, if you had time, I own to having some curiosity to see the place myself." "I didn't exactly like to ask you, but that's rather what I hoped you'd say. Name your time and I'll take you there." "No time like the present," I said at once, for I saw he would never settle down to anything while this affair was in suspense. He got up with great alacrity, and looked at me, I am tempted to think, with marked approval. "Come along," was all he said, however; and was pretty silent all the way to his house. My Mary (as he calls her in public, and I in private) was summoned, and we proceeded to the room. The Doctor had gone so far as to tell her that he had had something of a fright there last night, of what nature he had not yet divulged; but now he pointed out and described, very briefly, the incidents of his progress. When we were near the important spot, he pulled up, and allowed me to pass on. "There's the room," he said. "Go on, Spearman, and tell us what you find." Whatever I might have felt at midnight, noonday I was sure would keep back anything sinister, and I flung the door open with an air and stepped in. It was a well-lighted room, with its large window on the right, though not, I thought, a very airy one. The principal piece of furniture was the gaunt old press of dark wood. There was too, a four-post bedstead, a mere skeleton which could hide nothing, and there was a chest of drawers. On the window-sill and the floor near it were the dead bodies of many hundred sawflies, and one torpid one which I had some satisfaction in killing. I tried the door of the press, but could not open it: the drawers, too, were locked. Somewhere, I was conscious, there was a faint rustling sound, but I could not locate it, and when I made my report to those outside, I said nothing of it. But, I said, clearly the next thing was to see what was in those locked receptacles. Uncle Oldys turned to Mary. "Mrs Maple," he said, and Mary ran off – no one, I am sure, steps like her – and soon came back at a soberer pace, with an elderly lady of discreet aspect.

' "Have you the keys of these things, Mrs Maple?" said Uncle Oldys. His simple words let loose a torrent (not violent, but copious) of speech: had she been a shade or two higher in the social scale, Mrs Maple might have stood as the model for Miss Bates.

' "Oh, Doctor, and Miss, and you too, sir," she said, acknowledging my presence with a bend, "them keys! who was that again that come when first we took over things in this house – a gentleman in business it was, and I gave him his luncheon in the small parlour on account of us not having everything as we should like to see it in the large one – chicken, and apple-pie, and a glass of madeira – dear, dear, you'll say I'm running on, Miss Mary; but I only mention it to bring back my recollection; and there it comes – Gardner, just the same as it did last week with the artichokes and the text of the sermon. Now that Mr Gardner, every key I got from him were labelled to itself, and each and every one was a key of some door or another in this house, and sometimes two; and when I say door, my meaning is door of a room, not like such a press as this is. Yes, Miss Mary, I know full well, and I'm just making it clear to your uncle and you too, sir. But now there *was* a box which this same gentleman he give over into my charge and thinking no harm after he was gone I took the liberty, knowing it was your uncle's property, to rattle it: and unless I'm most surprisingly deceived, in that box there was keys, but what keys, that, Doctor, is known Elsewhere, for open the box, no that I would not do."

'I wondered that Uncle Oldys remained as quiet as he did under this address. Mary, I knew, was amused by it, and he probably had been taught by experience that it was useless to break in upon it. At any rate he did not, but merely said at the end, "Have you that box handy, Mrs Maple? If so, you might bring it here." Mrs Maple pointed her finger at him, either in accusation or in gloomy triumph. "There," she said, "was I to choose out the very words out of your mouth, Doctor, them would be the ones. And if I've took it to my own rebuke one half a dozen times, it's been nearer fifty. Laid awake I have in my bed, sat down in my chair I have, the same you and Miss Mary gave me the day I was twenty year in your service, and no person could desire a better – yes, Miss Mary, but it *is* the truth, and well we know who it is would have it different if he could. 'All very well,' says I to myself, 'but pray, when the Doctor calls you to account for that box, what are you going to say?' No, Doctor, if you was some masters I've heard of and I was some servants I could name, I should have an easy task before me, but things being, humanly speaking, what they are, the one course open to me is just to say to you that without Miss Mary comes to my room and helps me to my recollection, which her wits *may* manage what's slipped beyond mine, no such box as that, small though it be, will cross your eyes this many a day to come."

' "Why, dear Mrs Maple, why didn't you tell me before that you wanted me to help you to find it?' said my Mary. 'No, never mind telling me why it was: let us come at once and look for it.' They hastened off together. I could hear Mrs Maple beginning an explanation which, I doubt not, lasted into the farthest recesses of the housekeeper's department. Uncle Oldys and I were left alone. "A valuable servant," he said, nodding towards the door. "Nothing goes wrong under her: the speeches are seldom over three minutes." "How will Miss Oldys manage to make her remember about the box?" I asked.

' "Mary? Oh, she'll make her sit down and ask her about her aunt's last illness, or who gave her the china dog on the mantelpiece – something quite off the point. Then, as Maple says, one thing brings up another, and the right one will come round sooner than you could suppose. There! I believe I hear them coming back already."

'It was indeed so, and Mrs Maple was hurrying on ahead of Mary with the box in her outstretched hand, and a beaming face. "What was it," she cried as she drew near, "what was it as I said, before ever I come out of Dorsetshire to this place? Not that I'm a Dorset woman myself, nor had need to be. 'Safe bind, safe find,' and there it was in the place where I'd put it – what? – two months back, I dare say." She handed it to Uncle Oldys, and he and I examined it with some interest, so that I ceased to pay attention to Mrs Ann Maple for the moment, though I know that she went on to expound exactly where the box had been, and in what way Mary had helped to refresh her memory on the subject.

'It was an oldish box, tied with pink tape and sealed, and on the lid was pasted a label inscribed in old ink, "The Senior Prebendary's House, Whitminster." On being opened it was found to contain two keys of moderate size, and a paper, on which, in the same hand as the label, was "Keys of the Press and Box of Drawers standing in the disused Chamber." Also this: "The Effects in this Press and Box are held by me, and to be held by my successors in the Residence, in trust for the noble Family of Kildonan, if claim be made by any survivor of it. I having made all the Enquiry possible to myself am of the opinion that that noble House is wholly extinct: the last Earl having been, as is notorious, cast away at sea, and his only Child and Heire deceas'd in my House (the Papers as to which melancholy Casualty were by me repos'd in the same Press in this year of our Lord 1753, 21 March). I am further of opinion that unless grave discomfort arise, such persons, not being of the Family of Kildonan, as shall become possess'd of these keys, will be well advised to leave matters as they are: which opinion I do not express without weighty and sufficient reason; and am Happy to have my Judgment confirm'd by the other Members of this College and Church who are conversant with the Events referr'd to in this Paper. Tho. Ashton, S. T. P., *Præb. senr.* Will. Blake, S. T. P., *Decanus.* Hen. Goodman, S. T. B., *Præb. junr.*"

' "Ah!" said Uncle Oldys, "grave discomfort! So he thought there might be something. I suspect it was that young man," he went on, pointing with the key to the line about the "only Child and Heire." "Eh Mary? The viscounty of Kildonan was Saul." "How *do* you know that, Uncle?" said Mary. "Oh, why not? it's all in Debrett – two little fat books. But I meant the tomb by the lime walk. He's there. What's the story, I wonder? Do you know it, Mrs Maple? and, by the way, look at your sawflies by the window there."

'Mrs Maple, thus confronted with two subjects at once, was a little put to it to do justice to both. It was no doubt rash in Uncle Oldys to give her the opportunity. I could only guess that he had some slight hesitation about using the key he held in his hand.

' "Oh them flies, how bad they was, Doctor and Miss, this three of four days: and you, too, sir, you wouldn't guess, none of you! And how they come, too! First we took the room in hand, the shutters was up, and had been, I dare say, years upon years, and not a fly to be seen. Then we got the shutter bars down with a deal of trouble and left it so for the day, and next day I sent Susan in with the broom to sweep about, and not two minutes hadn't passed when out she come into the hall like a blind thing, and we had regular to beat them off her. Why, her cap and her hair, you couldn't see the colour of it, I do assure you, and all clustering round her eyes, too. Fortunate enough she's not a girl with fancies, else if it had been me, why only the tickling of the nasty things would have drove me out of my wits. And now there they lay like so many dead things. Well, they was lively enough on the Monday, and now here's Thursday, is it, or no, Friday. Only to come near the door and you'd hear them pattering up against it, and once you opened it, dash at you, they would, as if they'd eat you. I couldn't help thinking to myself, 'If you was bats, where should we be this night?' Nor you can't cresh 'em, not like a usual kind of fly. Well, there's something to be thankful for, if we could but learn by it. And then this tomb, too," she said, hastening on to her second point to elude any chance of interruption, "of them two poor young lads. I say poor, and yet when I recollect myself, I was at tea with Mrs Simpkins, the sexton's wife, before you come, Doctor and Miss Mary, and that's a family has been in the place, what? I dare say a hundred years in that very house, and could put their hand on any tomb or yet grave in all the yard and give you name and age. And his account of that young man, Mr Simpkins's I mean to say – *well!*" She compressed her lips and nodded several times. "Tell us, Mrs Maple," said Mary. "Go on," said Uncle Oldys. "What about him?" said I. "Never was such a thing seen in this place, not since Queen Mary's times and the Pope and all," said Mrs Maple. "Why, do you know he lived in this very house, him and them that was with him, and for all I can tell in this identical room" (she shifted her feet uneasily on the floor). "Who was with him? Do you mean the people of the house?" said Uncle Oldys suspiciously. "Not to call people, Doctor, dear no," was the answer; "more what he brought with him from Ireland, I believe it was. No, the people in the house was the last to hear anything of his goings-on. But in the town not a family but knew how he stopped out at night: and them that was with him, why, they were such as would strip the skin from the child in its grave; and a withered heart makes an ugly thin ghost, says Mr Simpkins. But they turned on him at the last, he says, and there's the mark still to be seen on the minster door where they run him down. And that's no more than the truth, for I got him to show it to myself, and that's what he said. A lord he was, with a Bible name of a wicked king, whatever his godfathers could have been thinking of." "Saul was the name," said Uncle Oldys. "To be sure it was Saul, Doctor, and thank you; and now isn't it King Saul that we read of raising up the dead ghost that was slumbering in its tomb till he disturbed it, and isn't that a strange thing, this young lord to have such a name, and Mr Simpkins's grandfather to see him out of his window of a dark night going about from one grave to another in the yard with a candle, and them that was with him following through the grass at his heels: and one night him to come right up to old Mr Simpkins's window that gives on the yard and press his face up against it to find out if there was anyone in the room that could see him: and only just time there was for old Mr Simpkins to drop down like, quiet, just under the window and hold his breath, and not stir till he heard him stepping away again, and this rustling-like in the grass after him as he went, and then when he looked out of his window in the morning there was treadings in the grass and a dead man's bone. Oh, he was a cruel child for certain, but he had to pay in the end, and after." "After?" said Uncle Oldys, with a frown. "Oh yes, Doctor, night after night in old Mr Simpkins's time, and his son, that's our Mr Simpkins's father, yes, and our own Mr Simpkins too. Up against that same window, particular when they've had a fire of a chilly evening, with his face right on the panes, and his hands fluttering out, and his mouth open and shut, open and shut, for a minute or more, and then gone off in the dark yard. But open the window at such times, no, that they dare not do, though they could find it in their heart to pity the poor thing, that pinched up with the cold, and seemingly fading away to a nothink as the years passed on. Well, indeed, I believe it is no more than the truth what our Mr Simpkins says on his own grandfather's word, 'A withered heart makes an ugly thin ghost.' " "I dare say," said Uncle Oldys suddenly: so suddenly that Mrs Maple stopped short. "Thank you. Come away, all of you." "Why, *Uncle*," said Mary, "are you not going to open the press after all?" Uncle Oldys blushed, actually blushed. "My dear," he said, "you are at liberty to call me a coward, or applaud me as a prudent man, whichever you please. But I am neither going to open that press not that chest of drawers myself, nor am I going to hand over the keys to you or to any other person. Mrs Maple, will you kindly see about getting a man or two to move those pieces of furniture into the garret?" "And when they do it, Mrs Maple," said Mary, who seemed to me — I did not then know why — more relieved than disappointed by her uncle's decision, "I have something that I want put with the rest; only quite a small packet."

'We left that curious room not unwillingly, I think. Uncle Oldys's orders were carried out that same day. And so,' concludes Mr inclined to suspect, a Jack-in-the-box, awaiting some future occupant of the residence of the senior prebendary.'

THE HAMMER OF GOD

G. K. Chesterton

THE little village of Bohun Beacon was perched on a hill so steep that the tall spire of its church seemed only like a peak of a small mountain. At the foot of the church stood a smithy, generally red with fires and always littered with hammers and scraps of iron; opposite to this, over a rude cross of cobbled paths, was 'The Blue Boar,' the only inn of the place. It was upon this crossway, in the lifting of a leaden and silver daybreak, that two brothers met in the street and spoke; though one was beginning the day and the other finishing it. The Rev. and Hon. Wilfred Bohun was very devout, and was making his way to some austere exercises of prayer or contemplation at dawn. Colonel the Hon. Norman Bohun, his elder brother, was by no means devout, and was sitting in evening dress on the bench outside 'The Blue Boar,' drinking what the philosophic observer was free to regard either as his last glass on Tuesday or his first on Wednesday. The colonel was not particular.

The Bohuns were one of the very few aristocratic families really dating from the Middle Ages, and their pennon had actually seen Palestine. But it is a great mistake to suppose that such houses stand high in chivalric tradition. Few except the poor preserve traditions. Aristocrats live not in traditions but in fashions. The Bohuns had been Mohocks under Queen Anne and Mashers under Queen Victoria. But like more than one of the really ancient houses, they had rotted in the last two centuries into mere drunkards and dandy degenerates, till there had even come a whisper of insanity. Certainly there was something hardly human about the colonel's wolfish pursuit of pleasure, and his chronic resolution not to go home till morning had a touch of the hideous clarity of insomnia. He was a tall, fine animal, elderly, but with hair still startlingly yellow. He would have looked merely blond and leonine, but his blue eyes were sunk so deep in his face that they looked black. They were a little too close together. He had very long yellow moustaches; on each side of them a fold or furrow from nostril to jaw, so that a sneer seemed cut into his face. Over his evening clothes he wore a curious pale yellow coat that looked more like a very light dressing-gown than an overcoat, and on the back of his head was stuck an extraordinary broad-brimmed hat of a bright green colour, evidently some oriental curiosity caught up at random. He was proud of appearing in such incongruous attires – proud of the fact that he always made them look congruous.

His brother the curate had also the yellow hair and the elegance, but he was buttoned up to the chin in black, and his face was clean-shaven, cultivated, and a little nervous. He seemed to live for nothing but his religion; but there were some who said (notably the blacksmith, who was a Presbyterian) that it was a love of Gothic architecture rather than of God, and that his haunting of the church like a ghost was another and purer turn of the almost morbid thirst for beauty which sent his brother raging after women and wine. This charge was doubtful, while the man's practical piety was indubitable. Indeed, the charge was mostly an ignorant misunderstanding of the love of solitude and secret prayer, and was founded on his being often found kneeling, not before the altar, but in peculiar places, in the crypts or gallery, or even in the belfry. He was at the moment about to enter the church through the yard of the smithy, but stopped and frowned a little as he saw his brother's cavernous eyes staring in the same direction. On the hypothesis that the colonel was interested in the church he did not waste any speculations. There only remained the blacksmith's shop, and though the blacksmith was a Puritan and none of his people, Wilfred Bohun had heard some scandals about a beautiful and rather celebrated wife. He flung a suspicious look across the shed, and the colonel stood up laughing to speak to him.

'Good morning, Wilfred,' he said. 'Like a good landlord I am watching sleeplessly over my people. I am going to call on the blacksmith.'

Wilfred looked at the ground, and said: 'The blacksmith is out. He is over at Greenford.'

'I know,' answered the other with silent laughter; 'that is why I am calling on him.'

'Norman,' said the cleric, with his eye on a pebble in the road, 'are you afraid of thunderbolts?'

'What do you mean?' asked the colonel. 'Is your hobby meteorology?'

'I mean,' said Wilfred, without looking up, 'do you ever think that God might strike you in the street?'

'I beg your pardon,' said the colonel; 'I see your hobby is folk-lore.'

'I know your hobby is blasphemy,' retorted the religious man, stung in the one live place of his nature. 'But if you do not fear God, you have good reason to fear man.'

The elder raised his eyebrows politely. 'Fear man?' he said.

'Barnes the blacksmith is the biggest and strongest man for forty miles round,' said the clergyman sternly. 'I know you are no coward or weakling, but he could throw you over the wall.'

This struck home, being true, and the lowering line by mouth and nostril darkened and deepened. For a moment he stood with the heavy sneer on his face. But in an instant Colonel Bohun had recovered his own cruel good humour and laughed, showing two dog-like front teeth under his yellow moustache. 'In that case, my dear Wilfred,' he said quite carelessly, 'it was wise for the last of the Bohuns to come out partially in armour.'

And he took off the queer round hat covered with green, showing that it was lined within with steel. Wilfred recognized it indeed as a light Japanese or Chinese helmet torn down from a trophy that hung in the old family hall.

'It was the first hat to hand,' explained his brother airily; 'always the nearest hat – and the nearest woman.'

'The blacksmith is away at Greenford,' said Wilfred quietly; 'the time of his return is unsettled.'

And with that he turned and went into the church with bowed head, crossing himself like one who wishes to be quit of an unclean spirit. He was anxious to forget such grossness in the cool twilight of his tall Gothic cloisters; but on that morning it was fated that his still round of religious exercises should be everywhere arrested by small shocks. As he entered the church, hitherto always empty at that hour, a kneeling figure rose hastily to its feet and came towards the full daylight of the doorway. When the curate saw it he stood still with surprise. For the early worshipper was none other than the village idiot, a nephew of the blacksmith, one who neither would nor could care for the church or for anything else. He was always called 'Mad Joe,' and seemed to have no other name; he was a dark, strong, slouching lad, with a heavy white face, dark straight hair, and a mouth always open. As he passed the priest, his moon-calf countenance gave no hint of what he had been doing or thinking of. He had never been known to pray before. What sort of prayers was he saying now? Extraordinary prayers surely.

Wilfred Bohun stood rooted to the spot long enough to see the idiot go out into the sunshine, and even to see his dissolute brother hail him with a sort of avuncular jocularity. The last thing he saw was the colonel throwing pennies at the open mouth of Joe, with the serious appearance of trying to hit it.

This ugly sunlight picture of the stupidity and cruelty of the earth sent the ascetic finally to his prayers for purification and new thoughts. He went up to a pew in the gallery, which brought him under a coloured window which he loved and always quieted his spirit; a blue window with an angel carrying lilies. There he began to think less about the half-wit, with his livid face and mouth like a fish. He began to think less of his evil brother, pacing like a lean lion in his horrible hunger. He sank deeper and deeper into those cold and sweet colours of silver blossoms and sapphire sky.

In this place half an hour afterwards he was found by Gibbs, the village cobbler, who had been sent for him in some haste. He got to his feet with promptitude, for he knew that no small matter would have brought Gibbs into such a place at all. The cobbler was, as in many villages, an atheist, and his appearance in church was a shade more extraordinary than Mad Joe's. It was a morning of theological enigmas.

'What is it?' asked Wilfred Bohun rather stiffly, but putting out a trembling hand for his hat.

The atheist spoke in a tone that, coming from him, was quite startlingly respectful, and even, as it were, huskily sympathetic.

'You must excuse me, sir,' he said in a hoarse whisper, 'but we didn't think it right not to let you know at once. I'm afraid a rather dreadful thing has happened, sir. I'm afraid your brother – '

Wilfred clenched his frail hands. 'What devilry has he done now?' he cried in involuntary passion.

'Why, sir,' said the cobbler, coughing, 'I'm afraid he's done nothing, and won't do anything. I'm afraid he's done for. You had really better come down, sir.'

The curate followed the cobbler down a short winding stair, which brought them out at an entrance rather higher than the street. Bohun saw the tragedy in one glance, flat underneath him like a plan. In the yard of the smithy were standing five or six men mostly in black, one in an inspector's uniform. They included the doctor, the Presbyterian minister, and the priest from the Roman Catholic chapel, to which the blacksmith's wife belonged. The latter was speaking to her, indeed, very rapidly, in an undertone, as she, a magnificent woman with red-gold hair, was sobbing blindly on a bench. Between these two groups, and just clear of the main heap of hammers, lay a man in evening dress, spreadeagled and flat on his face. From the height above Wilfred could have sworn to every item of his costume and appearance, down to the Bohun rings upon his fingers; but the skull was only a hideous splash, like a star of blackness and blood.

Wilfred Bohun gave but one glance, and ran down the steps into the yard. The doctor, who was the family physician, saluted him, but he scarcely took any notice. He could only stammer out: 'My brother is dead. What does it mean? What is this horrible mystery?' There was an unhappy silence; and then the cobbler, the most outspoken man present, answered: 'Plenty of horror, sir,' he said, 'but not much mystery.'

'What do you mean?' asked Wilfred, with a white face.

'It's plain enough,' answered Gibbs. 'There is only one man for forty miles round that could have struck such a blow as that, and he's the man that had most reason to.'

'We must not prejudge anything,' put in the doctor, a tall, black-bearded man, rather nervously; 'but it is competent for me to corroborate what Mr Gibbs says about the nature of the blow, sir; it is an incredible blow. Mr Gibbs says that only one man in this district could have done it. I should have said myself that nobody could have done it.'

A shudder of superstition went through the slight figure of the curate. 'I can hardly understand,' he said.

'Mr Bohun,' said the doctor in a low voice, 'metaphors literally fail me. It is inadequate to say that the skull was smashed to bits like an egg-shell. Fragments of bone were driven into the body and the ground like bullets into a mud wall. It was the hand of a giant.'

He was silent a moment, looking grimly through his glasses; then he added: 'The thing has one advantage – that it clears most people of suspicion at one stroke. If you or I or any normally made man in the country were accused of this crime, we should be acquitted as an infant would be acquitted of stealing the Nelson Column.'

'That's what I say,' repeated the cobbler obstinately; 'there's only one man that could have done it, and he's the man that would have done it. Where's Simeon Barnes, the blacksmith?'

'He's over at Greenford,' faltered the curate.

'More likely over in France,' muttered the cobbler.

'No; he is in neither of those places,' said a small and colourless voice, which came from the little Roman priest who had joined the group. 'As a matter of fact, he is coming up the road at this moment.'

The little priest was not an interesting man to look at, having stubbly brown hair and a round and stolid face. But if he had been as splendid as Apollo no one would have looked at him at that moment. Everyone turned round and peered at the pathway which wound across the plain below, along which was indeed walking, at his own huge stride and with a hammer on his shoulder, Simeon the smith. He was a bony and gigantic man, with deep, dark, sinister eyes and a dark chin beard. He was walking and talking quietly with two other men; and though he was never specially cheerful, he seemed quite at his ease.

'My God!' cried the atheistic cobbler, 'and there's the hammer he did it with.'

'No,' said the inspector, a sensible-looking man with a sandy moustache, speaking for the first time. 'There's the hammer he did it with over there by the church wall. We have left it and the body exactly as they are.'

All glanced round, and the short priest went across and looked down in silence at the tool where it lay. It was one of the smallest and the lightest of the hammers, and would not have caught the eye among the rest; but on the iron edge of it were blood and yellow hair.

After a silence the short priest spoke without looking up, and there was a new note in his dull voice. 'Mr Gibbs was hardly right,' he said, 'in saying that there is no mystery. There is at least the mystery of why so big a man should attempt so big a blow with so little a hammer.'

'Oh, never mind that,' cried Gibbs, in a fever. 'What are we to do with Simeon Barnes?'

'Leave him alone,' said the priest quietly. 'He is coming here of himself. I know those two men with him. They are very good fellows from Greenford, and they have come over about the Presbyterian chapel.'

Even as he spoke the tall smith swung round the corner of the church, and strode into his own yard. Then he stood there quite still, and the hammer fell from his hand. The inspector, who had preserved impenetrable propriety, immediately went up to him.

'I won't ask you, Mr Barnes,' he said, 'whether you know anything about what has happened here. You are not bound to say. I hope you don't know, and that you will be able to prove it. But I must go through the form of arresting you in the King's name for the murder of Colonel Norman Bohun.'

'You are not bound to say anything,' said the cobbler in officious excitement. 'They've got to prove everything. They haven't proved yet that it is Colonel Bohun, with the head all smashed up like that.'

'That won't wash,' said the doctor aside to the priest. 'That's out of the detective stories. I was the colonel's medical man, and I knew his body better than he did. He had very fine hands, but quite peculiar ones. The second and third fingers were the same in length. Oh, that's the colonel right enough.'

As he glanced at the brained corpse upon the ground the iron eyes of the motionless blacksmith followed them and rested there also.

'Is Colonel Bohun dead?' said the smith quite calmly. 'Then he's damned.'

'Don't say anything! Oh, don't say anything,' cried the atheist cobbler, dancing about in an ecstasy of admiration of the English legal system. For no man is such a legalist as the good Secularist.

The blacksmith turned on him over his shoulder the august face of a fanatic.

'It's well for you infidels to dodge like foxes because the world's law favours you,' he said; 'but God guards His own in His pocket, as you shall see this day.'

Then he pointed to the colonel and said: 'When did this dog die in his sins?'

'Moderate your language,' said the doctor.

'Moderate the Bible's language, and I'll moderate mine. When did he die?'

'I saw him alive at six o'clock this morning,' stammered Wilfred Bohun.

'God is good,' said the smith. 'Mr Inspector, I have not the slightest objection to being arrested. It is you who may object to arresting me. I don't mind leaving the court without a stain on my character. You do mind, perhaps, leaving the court with a bad set-back in your career.'

The solid inspector for the first time looked at the blacksmith with a lively eye; as did everybody else, except the short, strange priest, who was still looking down at the little hammer that had dealt the dreadful blow.

'There are two men standing outside this shop,' went on the blacksmith with ponderous lucidity, 'good tradesmen in Greenford whom you all know, who will swear that they saw me from before midnight till daybreak and long after in the committee-room of our Revival Mission, which sits all night, we save souls so fast. In Greenford itself twenty people could swear to me for all that time. If I were a heathen, Mr Inspector, I would let you walk on to your downfall. But as a Christian man I feel bound to give you your chance, and ask you whether you will hear my alibi now or in court.'

The inspector seemed for the first time disturbed, and said, 'Of course I should be glad to clear you altogether now.'

The smith walked out of his yard with the same long and easy stride, and returned to his two friends from Greenford, who were indeed friends of nearly everyone present. Each of them said a few words which no one ever thought of disbelieving. When they had spoken, the innocence of Simeon stood up as solid as the great church above them.

One of those silences struck the group which are more strange and insufferable than any speech. Madly, in order to make conversation, the curate said to the Catholic priest:

'You seem very much interested in that hammer, Father Brown.'

'Yes, I am,' said Father Brown; 'why is it such a small hammer?'

The doctor swung round on him.

'By George, that's true,' he cried; 'who would use a little hammer with ten larger hammers lying about?'

Then he lowered his voice in the curate's ear and said: 'Only the kind of person that can't lift a large hammer. It is not a question of force or courage between the sexes. It's a question of lifting power in the shoulders. A bold woman could commit ten murders with a light hammer and never turn a hair. She could not kill a beetle with a heavy one.'

Wilfred Bohun was staring at him with a sort of hypnotized horror, while Father Brown listened with his head a little on one side, really interested and attentive. The doctor went on with more hissing emphasis:

'Why do these idiots always assume that the only person who hates the wife's lover is the wife's husband? Nine times out of ten the person who most hates the wife's lover is the wife. Who knows what insolence or treachery he had shown her – look there.'

He made a momentary gesture towards the red-haired woman on the bench. She had lifted her head at last and the tears were drying on her splendid face. But the eyes were fixed on the corpse with an electric glare that had in it something of idiocy.

The Rev. Wilfred Bohun made a limp gesture as if waving away all desire to know; but Father Brown, dusting off his sleeve some ashes blown from the furnace, spoke in his indifferent way.

'You are like so many doctors,' he said; 'your mental science is really suggestive. It is your physical science that is utterly impossible. I agree that the woman wants to kill the co-respondent much more than the petitioner does. And I agree that a woman will always pick up a small hammer instead of a big one. But the difficulty is one of physical impossibility. No woman ever born could have smashed a man's skull out flat like that.' Then he added reflectively, after a pause: 'These people haven't grasped the whole of it. The man was actually wearing an iron helmet, and the blow scattered it like broken glass. Look at that woman. Look at her arms.'

Silence held them all up again, and then the doctor said rather sulkily: 'Well, I may be wrong; there are objections to everything. But I stick to the main point. No man but an idiot would pick up that little hammer if he could use a big hammer.'

With that the lean and quivering hands of Wilfred Bohun went up to his head and seemed to clutch his scanty yellow hair. After an instant they dropped, and he cried: 'That was the word I wanted; you have said the word.'

Then he continued, mastering his discomposure: 'The words you said were, "No man but an idiot would pick up the small hammer."'

'Yes,' said the doctor. 'Well?'

'Well,' said the curate, 'no man but an idiot did.' The rest stared at him with eyes arrested and riveted, and he went on in a febrile and feminine agitation.

'I am a priest,' he cried unsteadily, 'and a priest should be no shedder of blood. I – I mean that he should bring no one to the gallows. And I thank God that I see the criminal clearly now – because he is a criminal who cannot be brought to the gallows.'

'You will not denounce him?' inquired the doctor.

'He would not be hanged if I did denounce him,' answered Wilfred with a wild but curiously happy smile. 'When I went into the church this morning I found a madman praying there – that poor Joe, who has been wrong all his life. God knows what he prayed; but with such strange folk it is not incredible to suppose that their prayers are all upside down. Very likely a lunatic would pray before killing a man. When I last saw poor Joe he was with my brother. My brother was mocking him.'

'By Jove!' cried the doctor, 'this is talking at last. But how do you explain – '

The Rev. Wilfred was almost trembling with the excitement of his own glimpse of the truth. 'Don't you see; don't you see,' he cried feverishly; 'that is the only theory that covers both the queer things, that answers both the riddles. The two riddles are the little hammer and the big blow. The smith might have struck the big blow, but would not have chosen the little hammer. His wife would have chosen the little hammer, but she could not have struck the big blow. But the madman might have done both. As for the little hammer – why, he was mad and might have picked up anything. And for the big blow, have you never heard, doctor, that a maniac in his paroxysm may have the strength of ten men?'

The doctor drew a deep breath and then said, 'By golly, I believe you've got it.'

Father Brown had fixed his eyes on the speaker so long and steadily as to prove that his large grey, ox-like eyes were not quite so insignificant as the rest of his face. When silence had fallen he said with marked respect: 'Mr Bohun, yours is the only theory yet propounded which holds water every way and is essentially unassailable. I think, therefore, that you deserve to be told, on my positive knowledge, that it is not the true one.' And with that the old little man walked away and stared again at the hammer.

'That fellow seems to know more than he ought to,' whispered the doctor peevishly to Wilfred. 'Those popish priests are deucedly sly.'

'No, no,' said Bohun, with a sort of wild fatigue. 'It was the lunatic. It was the lunatic.'

The group of the two clerics and the doctor had fallen away from the more official group containing the inspector and the man he had arrested. Now, however, that their own party had broken up, they heard voices from the others. The priest looked up quietly and then looked down again as he heard the blacksmith say in a loud voice:

'I hope I've convinced you, Mr Inspector. I'm a strong man, as you say, but I couldn't have flung my hammer bang here from Greenford. My hammer hasn't any wings that it should come flying half a mile over hedges and fields.'

The inspector laughed amicably and said: 'No, I think you can be considered out of it, though it's one of the rummiest coincidences I ever saw. I can only ask you to give us all the assistance you can in finding a man as big and strong as yourself. By George! you might be useful, if only to hold him! I suppose you yourself have no guess at the man?'

'I may have a guess,' said the pale smith, 'but it is not at a man.'

Then, seeing the scared eyes turn towards his wife on the bench, he put his huge hand on her shoulder and said: 'Nor a woman either.'

'What do you mean?' asked the inspector jocularly. 'You don't think cows use hammers, do you?'

'I think no thing of flesh held that hammer,' said the blacksmith in a stifled voice; 'mortally speaking, I think the man died alone.'

Wilfred made a sudden forward movement and peered at him with burning eyes.

'Do you mean to say, Barnes,' came the sharp voice of the cobbler, 'that the hammer jumped up of itself and knocked the man down?'

'Oh, you gentlemen may stare and snigger,' cried Simeon; 'you clergymen who tell us on Sunday in what a stillness the Lord smote Sennacherib. I believe that One who walks invisible in every house defended the honour of mine, and laid the defiler dead before the door of it. I believe the force in that blow was just the force there is in earthquakes, and no force less.'

Wilfred said, with a voice utterly undescribable: 'I told Norman myself to beware of the thunderbolt.'

'That agent is outside my jurisdiction,' said the inspector with a slight smile.

'You are not outside His,' answered the smith; 'see you to it,' and, turning his broad back, he went into the house.

The shaken Wilfred was led away by Father Brown, who had an easy and friendly way with him. 'Let us get out of this horrid place, Mr Bohun,' he said. 'May I look inside your church? I hear it's one of the oldest in England. We take some interest, you know,' he added with a comical grimace, 'in old English churches.'

Wilfred Bohun did not smile, for humour was never his strong point. But he nodded rather eagerly, being only too ready to explain the Gothic splendours to someone more likely to be sympathetic than the Presbyterian blacksmith or the atheist cobbler.

'By all means,' he said; 'let us go in at this side.' And he led the way into the high side entrance at the top of the flight of steps. Father Brown was mounting the first step to follow him when he felt a hand on his shoulder, and turned to behold the dark, thin figure of the doctor, his face darker yet with suspicion.

'Sir,' said the physician harshly, 'you appear to know some secrets in this black business. May I ask if you are going to keep them to yourself?'

'Why, doctor,' answered the priest, smiling quite pleasantly, 'there is one very good reason why a man of my trade should keep things to himself when he is not sure of them, and that is that it is so constantly his duty to keep them to himself when he is sure of them. But if you think I have been discourteously reticent with you or anyone, I will go to the extreme limit of my custom. I will give you two very large hints.'

'Well, sir?' said the doctor gloomily.

'First,' said Father Brown quietly, 'the thing is quite in your own province. It is a matter of physical science. The blacksmith is mistaken, not perhaps in saying that the blow was divine, but certainly in saying that it came by a miracle. It was no miracle, doctor, except in so far as a man is himself a miracle, with his strange and wicked and yet half-heroic heart. The force that smashed that skull was a force well known to scientists – one of the most frequently debated of the laws of nature.'

The doctor, who was looking at him with frowning intentness, only said: 'And the other hint?'

'The other hint is this,' said the priest. 'Do you remember the blacksmith, though he believes in miracles, talking scornfully of the impossible fairy tale that his hammer had wings and flew half a mile across country?'

'Yes,' said the doctor, 'I remember that.'

'Well,' added Father Brown, with a broad smile, 'that fairy tale was the nearest thing to the real truth that has been said today.' And with that he turned his back and stumped up the steps after the curate.

The Rev. Wilfred, who had been waiting for him, pale and impatient, as if this little delay were the last straw for his nerves, led him immediately to his favourite corner of the church, that part of the gallery closest to the carved roof and lit by the wonderful window with the angel. The little Latin priest explored and admired everything exhaustively, talking cheerfully but in a low voice all the time. When in the course of his investigation he found the side exit and the winding stair down which Wilfred had rushed to find his brother dead, Father Brown ran not down but up, with the agility of a monkey, and his clear voice came from an outer platform above.

'Come up here, Mr Bohun,' he called. 'The air will do you good.'

Bohun followed him, and came out on a kind of stone gallery or balcony outside the building, from which one could see the illimitable plain in which their small hill stood, wooded away to the purple horizon and dotted with villages and farms. Clear and square, but quite small beneath them, was the blacksmith's yard, where the inspector still stood taking notes and the corpse still lay like a smashed fly.

'Might be the map of the world, mightn't it?' said Father Brown.

'Yes,' said Bohun very gravely, and nodded his head.

Immediately beneath and about them the lines of the Gothic building plunged outwards into the void with a sickening swiftness akin to suicide. There is that element of Titan energy in the architecture of the Middle Ages that, from whatever aspect it be seen, it always seems to be rushing away, like the strong back of some maddened horse. This church was hewn out of ancient and silent stone, bearded with old fungoids and stained with the nests of birds. And yet, when they saw it from below, it sprang like a fountain at the stars; and when they saw it, as now, from above, it poured like a cataract into a voiceless pit. For these two men on the tower were left alone with the most terrible aspect of the Gothic; the monstrous foreshortening and disproportion, the dizzy perspectives, the glimpses of great things small and small things great; a topsy-turvydom of stone in the mid-air. Details of stone, enormous by their proximity, were relieved against a pattern of fields and farms, pygmy in their distance. A carved bird or beast at a corner seemed like some vast walking or flying dragon wasting the pastures and villages below. The whole atmosphere was dizzy and dangerous, as if men were upheld in air amid the gyrating wings of colossal genii; and the whole of that old church, as tall and rich as a cathedral, seemed to sit upon the sunlit country like a cloud-burst.

'I think there is something rather dangerous about standing on these high places even to pray,' said Father Brown. 'Heights were made to be looked at, not to be looked from.'

'Do you mean that one may fall over,' asked Wilfred.

'I mean that one's soul may fall if one's body doesn't,' said the other priest.

'I scarcely understand you,' remarked Bohun indistinctly.

'Look at that blacksmith, for instance,' went on Father Brown calmly; 'a good man, but not a Christian – hard, imperious, unforgiving. Well, his Scotch religion was made up by men who prayed on hills and high crags, and learnt to look down on the world more than to look up at heaven. Humility is the mother of giants. One sees great things from the valley; only small things from the peak.'

'But he – he didn't do it,' said Bohun tremulously.

'No,' said the other in an odd voice; 'we know he didn't do it.'

After a moment he resumed, looking tranquilly out over the plain with his pale grey eyes. 'I knew a man,' he said, 'who began by worshipping with others before the altar, but who grew fond of high and lonely places to pray from, corners or niches in the belfry or the spire. And once in one of those dizzy places, where the whole world seemed to turn under him like a wheel, his brain turned also, and he fancied he was God. So that though he was a good man, he committed a great crime.'

Wilfred's face was turned away, but his bony hands turned blue and white as they tightened on the parapet of stone.

'He thought it was given to *him* to judge the world and strike down the sinner. He would never have had such a thought if he had been kneeling with other men upon a floor. But he saw all men walking about like insects. He saw one especially strutting just below him, insolent and evident by a bright green hat – a poisonous insect.'

Rooks cawed round the corners of the belfry; but there was no other sound till Father Brown went on.

'This also tempted him, that he had in his hand one of the most awful engines of nature; I mean gravitation, that mad and quickening rush by which all earth's creatures fly back to her heart when released. See, the inspector is strutting just below us in the smithy. If I were to toss a pebble over this parapet it would be something like a bullet by the time it struck him. If I were to drop a hammer – even a small hammer – '

Wilfred Bohun threw one leg over the parapet, and Father Brown had him in a minute by the collar.

'Not by that door,' he said gently; 'that door leads to hell.'

Bohun staggered back against the wall, and stared at him with frightful eyes.

'How do you know all this?' he cried. 'Are you a devil?'

'I am a man,' answered Father Brown gravely; 'and therefore have all devils in my heart. Listen to me,' he said after a short pause. 'I know what you did – at least, I can guess the great part of it. When you left your brother you were racked with no unrighteous rage to the extent even that you snatched up a small hammer, half inclined to kill him with his foulness on his mouth. Recoiling, you thrust it under your buttoned coat instead, and rushed into the church. You pray wildly in many places, under the angel window, upon the platform above, and on a higher platform still, from which you could see the colonel's Eastern hat like the back of a green beetle crawling about. Then something snapped in your soul, and you let God's thunderbolt fall.'

Wilfred put a weak hand to his head, and asked in a low voice: 'How did you know that his hat looked like a green beetle?'

'Oh, that,' said the other with the shadow of a smile, 'that was common sense. But hear me further. I say I know all this; but no one else shall know it. The next step is for you; I shall take no more steps; I will seal this with the seal of confession. If you ask me why, there are many reasons, and only one that concerns you. I leave things to you because you have not yet gone very far wrong, as assassins go. You did not help to fix the crime on the smith when it was easy; or on his wife, when that was easy. You tried to fix it on the imbecile because you knew that he could not suffer. That was one of the gleams that it is my business to find in assassins. And now come down into the village, and go your own way as free as the wind; for I have said my last word.'

They went down the winding stairs in utter silence, and came out into the sunlight by the smithy. Wilfred Bohun carefully unlatched the wooden gate of the yard, and going up to the inspector, said: 'I wish to give myself up; I have killed my brother.'

THE AWFUL REASON OF THE VICAR'S VISIT

G. K. Chesterton

THE revolt of Matter against Man (which I believe to exist) has not been reduced to a singular condition. It is the small things rather than the large things which make war against us and, I may add, beat us. The bones of the last mammoth have long ago decayed, a mighty wreck; the tempests no longer devour our navies, nor the mountains with hearts of fire heap hell over our cities. But we are engaged in a bitter and eternal war with small things; chiefly with microbes and with collar studs. The stud with which I was engaged (on fierce and equal terms) as I made the above reflections, was one which I was trying to introduce into my shirt collar when a loud knock came at the door.

My first thought was as to whether Basil Grant had called to fetch me. He and I were to turn up at the same dinner-party (for which I was in the act of dressing), and it might be that he had taken it into his head to come my way, though we had arranged to go separately. It was a small and confidential affair at the table of a good but unconventional political lady, an old friend of his. She had asked us both to meet a third guest, a Captain Fraser, who had made something of a name and was an authority on chimpanzees. As Basil was an old friend of the hostess and I had never seen her, I felt that it was quite possible that he (with his usual social sagacity) might have decided to take me along in order to break the ice. The theory, like all my theories, was complete; but as a fact it was not Basil.

I was handed a visiting card inscribed: 'Rev. Ellis Shorter,' and

underneath was written in pencil, but in a hand in which even hurry
could not conceal a depressing and gentlemanly excellence, 'Asking
the favour of a few moments' conversation on a most urgent matter.'

I had already subdued the stud, thereby proclaiming that the
image of God has supremacy over all matters (a valuable truth), and
throwing on my dress-coat and waistcoat, hurried into the drawing-
room. He rose at my entrance, flapping like a seal; I can use no
other description. He flapped a plaid shawl over his right arm; he
flapped a pair of pathetic black gloves; he flapped his clothes; I may
say, without exaggeration, that he flapped his eyelids, as he rose.
He was a bald-browed, white-haired, white-whiskered old clergyman, of a flappy and floppy type. He said:

'I am so sorry. I am so very sorry. I am so extremely sorry. I
come – I can only say – I can only say in my defence, that I come
– upon an important matter. Pray forgive me.'

I told him I forgave perfectly and waited.

'What I have to say,' he said, brokenly, 'is so dreadful – it is so
dreadful – I have lived a quiet life.'

I was burning to get away, for it was already doubtful if I should
be in time for dinner. But there was something about the old man's
honest air of bitterness that seemed to open to me the possibilities
of life larger and more tragic than my own.

I said gently: 'Pray go on.'

Nevertheless the old gentleman, being a gentleman as well as old,
noticed my secret impatience and seemed still more unmanned.

'I'm so sorry,' he said weakly; 'I wouldn't have come – but for –
your friend Major Brown recommended me to come here.'

'Major Brown!' I said, with some interest.

'Yes,' said the Reverend Mr Shorter, feverishly flapping his plaid
shawl about. 'He told me you helped him in a great difficulty – and
my difficulty! Oh, my dear sir, it's a matter of life and death.'

I rose abruptly, in an acute perplexity. 'Will it take long, Mr
Shorter?' I asked. 'I have to go out to dinner almost at once.'

He rose also, trembling from head to foot, and yet somehow,
with all his moral palsy, he rose to the dignity of his age and his
office.

'I have no right, Mr Swinburne – I have no right at all,' he said.
'If you have to go out to dinner, you have of course – a perfect

right – of course a perfect right. But when you come back – a man will be dead.'

And he sat down, quaking like a jelly.

The triviality of the dinner had been in those two minutes dwarfed and drowned in my mind. I did not want to go and see a political widow, and a captain who collected apes; I wanted to hear what had brought this dear, doddering old vicar into relation with immediate perils.

'Will you have a cigar?' I said.

'No thank you,' he said, with indescribable embarrassment, as if not smoking cigars was a social disgrace.

'A glass of wine?' I said.

'No, thank you, no, thank you; not just now,' he repeated with that hysterical eagerness with which people who do not drink at all often try to convey that on any other night of the week they would sit up all night drinking rum-punch. 'Not just now, thank you.'

'Nothing else I can get for you?' I said, feeling genuinely sorry for the well-mannered old donkey. 'A cup of tea?'

I saw a struggle in his eye and I conquered. When the cup of tea came he drank it like a dipsomaniac gulping brandy. Then he fell back and said:

'I have had such a time, Mr Swinburne. I am not used to these excitements. As Vicar of Chuntsey, in Essex' – he threw this in with an indescribable airiness of vanity – 'I have never known such things happen.'

'What things happen?' I asked.

He straightened himself with sudden dignity.

'As Vicar of Chuntsey, in Essex,' he said, 'I have never been forcibly dressed up as an old woman and made to take part in a crime in the character of an old woman. Never once. My experience may be small. It may be insufficient. But it has never occurred to me before.'

'I have never heard of it,' I said, 'as among the duties of a clergyman. But I am not well up in church matters. Excuse me if perhaps I failed to follow you correctly. Dressed up – as what?'

'As an old woman,' said the vicar solemnly, 'as an old woman.'

I thought in my heart that it required no great transformation to make an old woman of him, but the thing was evidently more tragic than comic, and I said respectfully:

'May I ask how it occurred?'

'I will begin at the beginning,' said Mr Shorter, 'and I will tell my story with the utmost possible precision. At seventeen minutes past eleven this morning I left the vicarage to keep certain appointments and pay certain visits in the village. My first visit was to Mr Jervis, the treasurer of our League of Christian Amusements, with whom I concluded some business touching the claim made by Parkes the gardener in the matter of the rolling of our tennis lawn. I then visited Mrs Arnett, a very earnest churchwoman, but permanently bedridden. She is the author of several small works of devotion, and a book of verse, entitled (unless my memory misleads me) *Eglantine.*'

He uttered all this not only with deliberation, but with something that can only be called, by a contradictory phrase, eager deliberation. He had, I think, a vague memory in his head of the detectives in the detective stories, who always sternly require that nothing should be kept back.

'I then proceeded,' he went on, with the same maddening conscientiousness of manner, 'to Mr Carr (not Mr James Carr, of course; Mr Robert Carr) who is temporarily assisting our organist, and having consulted with him (on the subject of a choir boy who is accused, I cannot as yet say whether justly or not, of cutting holes in the organ pipes), I finally dropped in upon a Dorcas meeting at the house of Miss Brett. The Dorcas meetings are usually held at the vicarage, but my wife being unwell, Miss Brett, a newcomer in our village, but very active in church work, had very kindly consented to hold them. The Dorcas society is entirely under my wife's management as a rule, and except for Miss Brett, who, as I say, is very active, I scarcely know any members of it. I had, however, promised to drop in on them, and I did so.

'When I arrived there were only four other maiden ladies with Miss Brett, but they were sewing very busily. It is very difficult, of course, for any person, however strongly impressed with the necessity in these matters of full and exact exposition of the facts, to remember and repeat the actual details of a conversation, particularly a conversation which (though inspired with a most worthy and admirable zeal for good work) was one which did not greatly impress the hearer's mind at the time and was, in fact – er – mostly about socks. I can, however, remember distinctly that one of the spinster ladies (she was a thin person with a woollen shawl, who appeared to feel the cold, and I am almost sure she was introduced to me as Miss James) remarked that the weather was very change-able. Miss Brett then offered me a cup of tea, which I accepted, I cannot recall in what words. Miss Brett is a short and stout lady with white hair. The only other figure in the group that caught my attention was a Miss Mowbray, a small and neat lady of aristocratic manners, silver hair, and a high voice and colour. She was the most emphatic member of the party; and her views on the subject of pinafores, though expressed with a natural deference to myself, were in themselves strong and advanced. Besides her (although all five ladies were dressed simply in black) it could not be denied that the others looked in some way what you men of the world would call dowdy.

'After about ten minutes' conversation I rose to go, and as I did so I heard something which – I cannot describe it – something which seemed to – but I really cannot describe it.'

'What did you hear?' I asked, with some impatience.

'I heard,' said the vicar solemnly, 'I heard Miss Mowbray (the lady with the silver hair) say to Miss James (the lady with the woollen shawl), the following extraordinary words. I committed them to memory on the spot, and as soon as circumstances set me free to do so, I noted them down on a piece of paper. I believe I have it here.' He fumbled in his breast-pocket, bringing out mild things, note-books, circulars and programmes of village concerts. 'I heard Miss Mowbray say to Miss James, the following words: "Now's your time, Bill." '

He gazed at me for a few moments after making this announce-ment, gravely and unflinchingly, as if conscious that here he was unshaken about his facts. Then he resumed, turning his bald head more towards the fire.

'This appeared to me remarkable. I could not by any means understand it. It seemed to me first of all peculiar that one maiden lady should address another maiden lady as "Bill." My experience, as I have said, may be incomplete; maiden ladies may have among

themselves and in exclusively spinster circles wilder customs than I
am aware of. But it seemed to me odd, and I could almost have
sworn (if you will not misunderstand the phrase) I should have been
strongly impelled to maintain at the time that the words, "Now's
your time, Bill," were by no means pronounced with that upper-
class intonation which, as I have already said, had up to now charac-
terized Miss Mowbray's conversation. In fact, the words, "Now's
your time, Bill," would have been, I fancy, unsuitable if pronounced
with that upper-class intonation.

'I was surprised,' I repeat, then, at the remark. But I was still
more surprised when looking round me in bewilderment, my hat
and umbrella in hand, I saw the lean lady with the woollen shawl
leaning upright against the door out of which I was just about to
make my exit. She was still knitting, and I supposed that this erect
posture against the door was only an eccentricity of spinsterhood
and an oblivion of my intended departure.

'I said genially "I am so sorry to disturb you, Miss James, but I
really must be going. I have – er – " I stopped here, for the words
she had uttered in reply, though singularly brief and in tone
extremely businesslike, were such as to render that arrest of my
remarks, I think, natural and excusable. I have these words also
noted down. I have not the least idea of their meaning; so I have
only been able to render them phonetically. But she said,' and Mr
Shorter peered shortsightedly at his papers, 'she said: "Chuck it, fat
'ed," and she added something that sounded like, "It's a kop," or
(possibly) "a kopt." And then the last cord, either of my sanity or
the sanity of the universe snapped suddenly. My esteemed friend
and helper, Miss Brett, standing by the mantelpiece, said: "Put 'is
old 'ead in a bag, Sam, and tie 'im up before you start jawin'. You'll
be kopt yourselves some o' these days with this way of doin' things,
har lar theater."

'My head went round and round. Was it really true, as I had
suddenly fancied a moment before, that unmarried ladies had some
dreadful riotous society of their own from which all others were
excluded? I remembered dimly in my classical days (I was a scholar
in a small way once, but now, alas! rusty), I remembered the mysteries of the Bona Dea and their strange female freemasonry. I remembered the witches' Sabbaths. I was just in my absurd light-head-

edness, trying to remember a line of verse about Diana's nymphs, when Miss Mowbray threw her arm round me from behind. The moment it held me I knew it was not a woman's arm.

'Miss Brett – or what I had called Miss Brett – was standing in front of me with a big revolver in her hand and broad grin on her face. Miss James was still leaning against the door, but had fallen into an attitude so totally new, so totally unfeminine, that it gave one a shock. She was kicking her heels, with her hands in her pockets and her cap on one side. She was a man. I mean he was a wo – no, that is I saw that instead of being a woman she – he, I mean – that is, it was a man.'

Mr Shorter became indescribably flurried and flapping in endeavouring to arrange these genders and his plaid shawl at the same time. He resumed with a higher fever of nervousness:

'As for Miss Mowbray, she – he, held me in a ring of iron. He had her arm – that is she had his arm – round her neck – my neck I mean – and I could not cry out. Miss Brett – that is Mr Brett, at least Mr something was who not Miss Brett – had the revolver pointed at me. The other two ladies – or er – gentlemen, were rummaging in some bag in the background. It was all clear at last: they were criminals dressed up as women, to kidnap me! To kidnap the Vicar of Chuntsey, in Essex. But why? Was it to be Nonconformists?

'The brute leaning against the door called out carelessly, "'Urry up, 'Arry. Show the old bloke what the game is and let's get off."

' "Curse 'is eyes," said Miss Brett – I mean the man with the revolver – "why should we show 'im the game?"

' "If you take my advice you bloomin' well will," said the man at the door, whom they called Bill. "A man wot knows wot 'e's doing' is worth ten wot don't, even if 'e's a potty old parson."

' "Bill's right enough," said the coarse voice of the man who held me (it had been Miss Mowbray's). "Bring out the picture, 'Arry."

'The man with the revolver walked across the room to where the other two women – I mean men – were turning over baggage, and asked them for something which they gave him. He came back with it across the room and held it out in front of me. And compared to the surprise of that display, all the previous surprises of this awful day shrank suddenly.

'It was a portrait of myself. That such a picture should be in the hands of these scoundrels might in any case have caused a mild surprise; but no more. It was no mild surprise that I felt. The likeness was an extremely good one, worked up with all the accessories of the conventional photographic studio. I was leaning my head on my hand and was relieved against a painted landscape of woodland. It was obvious that it was no snapshot; it was clear that I had sat for this photograph. And the truth was that I had never sat for such a photograph. It was a photograph that I had never had taken.

'I stared at it again and again. It seemed to me to be touched up a good deal; it was glazed as well as framed, and the glass blurred some of the details. But there unmistakably was my face, my eyes, my nose and mouth, my head and hand, posed for a professional photographer. And I had never posed so for any photographer.

' "Be'old the bloomin' miracle," said the man with the revolver, with ill-timed facetiousness. "Parson, prepare to meet your God." And with this he slid the glass out of the frame. As the glass moved, I saw that part of the picture was painted on it in Chinese white, notably a pair of white whiskers and a clerical collar. And underneath was a portrait of an old lady in a quiet black dress, leaning her head on her hand against the woodland landscape. The old lady was as like me as one pin is like another. It had required only the whiskers and the collar to make it me in every hair.

' "Entertainin' ain't it?" said the man described as 'Arry, as he shot the glass back again. "Remarkable resemblance, parson. Gratifyin' to the lady. Gratifyin' to you. And hi may hadd, particlery gratifyin' to us, as bein' the probable source of a very tolerable haul. You know Colonel Hawker, the man whose come to live in these parts, don't you?"

'I nodded.

' "Well," said the man 'Arry, pointing to the picture, "that's 'is mother. 'Oo ran to catch 'im when 'e fell? She did," and he flung his fingers in a general gesture towards the photograph of the old lady who was exactly like me.

' "Tell the old gent wot 'e's got to do and be done with it," broke out Bill from the door. "Look 'ere, Reverend Shorter, we ain't goin' to do you no 'arm. We'll give you a sov. for your trouble if you like. And as for the old woman's clothes – why, you'll look lovely in 'em."

' "You ain't much of an 'and at a description, Bill," said the man behind me. "Mr Shorter, it's like this. We've got to see this man Hawker to-night. Maybe he'll kiss us all and 'ave up the champagne when 'e sees us. Maybe on the other 'and – 'e won't. Maybe 'e'll be dead when we goes away. Maybe not. But we've got to see 'im. Now as you know, 'e shuts 'isself up and never opens the door to a soul; only you don't know why and we does. The only one as can ever get at 'im is 'is mother. Well, it's a confounded funny coincidence," he said, accenting the penultimate, "it's a very unusual piece of good luck, but you're 'is mother."

' "When first I saw 'er picture," said the man Bill, shaking his head in a ruminant manner "when I first saw it I said – old Shorter. Those were my exact words – old Shorter."

' "What do you mean, you wild creatures?" I gasped. "What am I to do?"

' "That's easy said, your 'oliness," said the man with the revolver good-humouredly; "you've got to put on those clothes," and he pointed to a poke-bonnet and a heap of female clothes in the corner of the room.

'I will not dwell, Mr Swinburne, upon the details of what followed. I had no choice. I could not fight five men, to say nothing of a loaded pistol. In five minutes, sir, the Vicar of Chuntsey was dressed as an old woman – as somebody else's mother, if you please, and was dragged out of the house to take part in a crime.

'It was already late in the afternoon, and the nights of winter were closing in fast. On a dark road, in a blowing wind, we set out towards the lonely house of Colonel Hawker, perhaps the queerest cortege that ever straggled up that or any other road. To every human eye, in every external, we were six very respectable old ladies of small means, in black dresses and refined but antiquated bonnets; and we were really five criminals and a clergyman.

'I will cut a long story short. My brain was whirling like a windmill as I walked, trying to think of some manner of escape. To cry out, so long as we were far from houses, would be suicidal, for it would be easy for the ruffians to knife me or to gag me and fling me in a ditch. On the other hand, to attempt to stop strangers and explain the situation was impossible, because of the frantic folly of the situation itself. Long before I had persuaded the chance postman or carrier of so absurd a story, my companions would certainly have got off themselves, and in all probability would have carried me off, as a friend of theirs who had the misfortune to be mad or drunk. The last thought, however, was an inspiration; though a very terrible one. Had it come to this, that the Vicar of Chuntsey must pretend to be mad or drunk? It had come to this.

'I walked along with the rest up the deserted road, imitating and keeping pace, as far as I could, with their rapid and yet lady-like step, until at length I saw a lamppost and a policeman standing under it. I had made up my mind. Until we reached them, we were all equally demure and silent and swift. When we reached them I suddenly flung myself against the railings and roared out: "Hooray! Hooray! Hooray! Rule Britannia! Get your 'air cut. Houp-la! Boo!" It was a condition of no little novelty for a man in my position.

'The constable instantly flashed his lantern on me, or the draggled, drunken old woman that was my travesty. "Now, then, mum," he began gruffly.

' "Come along quiet, or I'll eat your heart," cried Sam in my ear hoarsely. "Stop, or I'll flay you." It was frightful to hear the words and see the neatly-shawled old spinster who whispered them.

'I yelled and yelled – I was in for it now. I screamed comic refrains that vulgar young men had sung, to my regret, at our village concerts; I rolled to and fro like a ninepin about to fall.

' "If you can't get your friend on quiet, ladies," said the policeman, "I shall have to take 'er up. Drunk and disorderly she is right enough."

'I redoubled my efforts. I had not been brought up to this sort of thing; but I believe I eclipsed myself. Words that I did not know I had ever heard of seemed to come pouring out of my open mouth.

' "When we get you past," whispered Bill, "you'll howl louder; you'll howl louder when we're burning your feet off."

'I screamed in my terror those awful songs of joy. In all the nightmares that men have ever dreamed, there has never been anything so blighting and horrible as the faces of those five men, looking out of their poke-bonnets; the figures of district visitors with the faces of devils. I cannot think there is anything so heart-breaking in hell.

'For a sickening instant I thought that the bustle of my companions and the perfect respectability of all our dresses would overcome the policeman and induce him to let us pass. He wavered, so far as one can describe anything so solid as a policeman as wavering. I lurched suddenly forward and ran my head into his chest, calling out (if I remember correctly) "Oh, crikey, blimey, Bill." It was at that moment that I remembered most clearly that I was the Vicar of Chuntsey, in Essex.

'My desperate coup saved me. The policeman had me hard by the back of the neck.

"You come along with me," he began, but Bill cut in with his perfect imitation of a lady's finnicking voice.

' "Oh, pray, constable, don't make a disturbance with our poor friend. We will get her quietly home. She does drink too much, but she is quite a lady – only eccentric."

' "She butted me in the stomach," said the policeman, briefly.

' "Eccentricities of genius," said Sam earnestly.

' "Pray let me take her home," reiterated Bill, in the resumed character of Miss James, "she wants looking after."

' "She does," said the policeman, "but I'll look after her."

' "That's no good," cried Bill, feverishly. "She wants her friends. She wants a particular medicine we've got."

' "Yes," assented Miss Mowbray, with excitement, "no other medicine any good, constable. Complaint quite unique."

' "I'm all righ'. Cutchy, cutchy, coo!" remarked, to his eternal shame, the Vicar of Chuntsey.

' "Look here, ladies," said the constable sternly, "I don't like the eccentricity of your friend, and I don't like 'er songs, or 'er 'ead in my stomach. And now I come to think of it, I don't like the looks of you. I've seen many as quiet-dressed as you as was wrong 'uns. Who are you?"

' "We've not our cards with us," said Miss Mowbray, with indescribable dignity. "Nor do we see why we should be insulted by any Jack-in-the-office who chooses to be rude to ladies, when he is paid to protect them. If you choose to take advantage of the weakness of our unfortunate friend, no doubt you are legally entitled to take her. But if you fancy you have any legal right to bully us, you will find yourself in the wrong box."

'The truth and dignity of this staggered the policeman for a moment. Under cover of their advantage my five persecutors turned for an instant on me faces like faces of the damned and then swished off into the darkness. When the constable first turned his lantern and his suspicions on to them, I had seen the telegraphic look flash from face to face saying that only retreat was possible now.

'By this time I was sinking slowly to the pavement, in a state of acute reflection. So long as the ruffians were with me, I dared not quit the rôle of drunkard. For if I had begun to talk reasonably and explain the real case, the officer would merely have thought that I was slightly recovered and would have put me in charge of my friends. Now, however, if I liked I might safely undeceive him.

'But I confess I did not like. The chances of life are many, and it may doubtless sometimes lie in the narrow path of duty for a clergyman of the Church of England to pretend to be a drunken old woman; but such necessities are, I imagine, sufficiently rare to appear to many improbable. Suppose the story got about that I had pretended to be drunk. Suppose people did not all think it was pretence!

'I lurched up, the policeman half-lifting me. I went along weakly and quietly for about a hundred yards. The officer evidently thought that I was too sleepy and feeble to effect an escape, and so held me lightly and easily enough. Past one turning, two turnings, three turnings, four turnings, he trailed me with him, a limp and slow and reluctant figure. At the fourth turning, I suddenly broke from his hand and tore down the street like a maddened stag. He was unprepared, he was heavy, and it was dark. I ran and ran and ran, and in five minutes' running, found I was gaining. In half an hour I was out in the fields under the holy and blessed stars, where I tore off my accursed shawl and bonnet and buried them in clean earth.'

The old gentleman had finished his story and leant back in his chair. Both the matter and the manner of his narration had, as time went on, impressed me favourably. He was an old duffer and pedant, but behind these things he was a country-bred man and gentleman, and had showed courage and a sporting instinct in the hour of desperation. He had told his story with many quaint formalities of diction, but also with a very convincing realism.

'And now – ' I began.

'And now,' said Shorter, leaning forward again with something like servile energy, 'and now, Mr Swinburne, what about that unhappy man Hawker. I cannot tell what those men meant, or how far what they said was real. But surely there is danger. I cannot go to the police, for reasons that you perceive. Among other things, they wouldn't believe me. What is to be done?'

I took out my watch. It was already half-past twelve.

'My friend Basil Grant,' I said, 'is the best man we can go to. He and I were to have gone to the same dinner to-night; but he will just have come back by now. Have you any objection to taking a cab?'

'Not at all,' he replied, rising politely, and gathering up his absurd plaid shawl.

A rattle in a hansom brought us underneath the sombre pile of workmen's flats in Lambeth which Grant inhabited; a climb up a wearisome wooden staircase brought us to his garret. When I entered that wooden and scrappy interior, the white gleam of Basil's shirt-front and the lustre of his fur coat flung on the wooden settle, struck me as a contrast. He was drinking a glass of wine before retiring. I was right; he had come back from the dinner-party.

He listened to the repetition of the story of the Rev. Ellis Shorter with the genuine simplicity and respect which he never failed to exhibit in dealing with any human being. When it was over he said simply:

'Do you know a man named Captain Fraser?'

I was so startled at this totally irrelevant reference to the worthy collector of chimpanzees with whom I ought to have dined that evening, that I glanced sharply at Grant. The result was that I did not look at Mr Shorter. I only heard him answer, in his most nervous tone, 'No.'

Basil, however, seemed to find something very curious about his answer or his demeanour generally, for he kept his big blue eyes fixed on the old clergyman, and though the eyes were quite quiet they stood out more and more from his head.

'You are quite sure, Mr Shorter,' he repeated, 'that you don't know Captain Fraser?'

'Quite,' answered the vicar, and I was certainly puzzled to find him returning so much to the timidity, not to say the demoralization of his tone when he first entered my presence.

Basil sprang smartly to his feet.

'Then our course is clear,' he said. 'You have not even begun your investigation, my dear Mr Shorter; the first thing for us to do is to go together to see Captain Fraser.'

'When?' asked the clergyman, stammering.

'Now,' said Basil, putting one arm in his fur coat.

The old clergyman rose to his feet, quaking all over.

'I really do not think that it is necessary,' he said.

Basil took his arm out of the fur coat, threw it over the chair again, and put his hands in his pockets.

'Oh,' he said, with emphasis. 'Oh – you don't think it necessary; then,' and he added the words with great clearness and deliberation, 'then, Mr Ellis Shorter, I can only say that I would like to see you without your whiskers.'

And at these words I also rose to my feet, for the great tragedy of my life had come. Splendid and exciting as life was in continual contact with an intellect like Basil's, I had always the feeling that that splendour and excitement were on the borderland of sanity. He lived perpetually near the vision of the reason of things which makes men lose their reason. And I felt of his insanity as men feel of the death of friends with heart disease. It might come anywhere, in a field, in a hansom cab, looking at a sunset, smoking a cigarette. It had come now. At the very moment of delivering a judgment for the salvation of a fellow creature, Basil Grant had gone mad.

'Your whiskers,' he cried, advancing with blazing eyes. 'Give me your whiskers. And your bald head.'

The old vicar naturally retreated a step or two. I stepped between.

'Sit down, Basil,' I implored, 'you're a little excited. Finish your wine.'

'Whiskers,' he answered sternly, 'whiskers.'

And with that he made a dash at the old gentleman, who made a dash for the door, but was intercepted. And then, before I knew where I was, the quiet room was turned into something between a pantomime and a pandemonium by those two. Chairs were flung over with a crash, tables were vaulted with a noise like thunder, screens were smashed, crockery shattered in smithereens, and still Basil Grant bounded and bellowed after the Rev. Ellis Shorter.

And now I began to perceive something else, which added the last half-witted touch to my mystification. The Rev. Ellis Shorter, of Chuntsey, in Essex, was by no means behaving as I had previously noticed him to behave, or, as considering his age and station I should have expected him to behave. His power of dodging, leaping, and fighting would have been amazing in a lad of seventeen, and in this doddering old vicar looked like a sort of farcical fairy-tale. Moreover, he did not seem to be so much astonished as I had thought. There was even a look of something like enjoyment in his eyes; so there was in the eye of Basil. In fact, the unintelligible truth must be told. They were both laughing.

At length Shorter was cornered.

'Come, come, Mr Grant,' he panted, 'you can't do anything to me. It's quite legal. And it doesn't do any one the least harm. It's only a social fiction. A result of our complex society, Mr Grant.'

'I don't blame you, my man,' said Basil coolly. 'But I want your whiskers. And your bald head. Do they belong to Captain Fraser?'

'No, no,' said Mr Shorter, laughing, 'we provide them ourselves. They don't belong to Captain Fraser.'

'What the deuce does all this mean?' I almost screamed. 'Are you all in an infernal nightmare? Why should Mr Shorter's bald head belong to Captain Fraser? How could it? What the deuce has Captain Fraser to do with the affair? What is the matter with him? You dined with him. Basil.'

'No,' said Grant, 'I didn't.'

'Didn't you go to Mrs Thornton's dinner-party?' I asked, staring. 'Why not?'

'Well,' said Basil, with a slow and singular smile, 'the fact is I was detained by a visitor. I have him, as a point of fact, in my bedroom.'

'In your bedroom?' I repeated; but my imagination had reached that point when he might have said in his coal scuttle or his waistcoat pocket.

Grant stepped to the door of an inner room, flung it open, and walked in. Then he came out again with the last of the bodily wonders of that wild night. He introduced into the sitting-room, in an apologetic manner, and by the nape of the neck, a limp clergyman with a bald head, white whiskers and a plaid shawl.

'Sit down, gentlemen,' cried Grant, striking his hands heartily. 'Sit down all of you and have a glass of wine. As you say, there is no harm in it, and if Captain Fraser had simply dropped me a hint I could have saved him from dropping a good sum of money. Not that you would have liked that, eh?'

The two duplicate clergymen, who were sipping their Burgundy with two duplicate grins, laughed heartily at this, and one of them carelessly pulled off his whiskers and laid them on the table.

'Basil,' I said, 'if you are my friend, save me. What is all this?'

He laughed again.

'Only another addition, Cherub, to your collection of Queer Trades. These two gentlemen (whose health I have now the pleasure of drinking) are Professional Detainers.'

'And what on earth's that?' I asked.

'It's really very simple, Mr Swinburne,' began he who had once been the Rev. Ellis Shorter, of Chuntsey, in Essex; and it gave me a shock indescribable to hear out of that pompous and familiar form come no longer its own pompous and familiar voice, but the brisk sharp tones of a young city man. 'It is really nothing very important. We are paid by our clients to detain in conversation, on some harmless pretext, people whom they want out of the way for a few hours. And Captain Fraser – ' and with that he hesitated and smiled.

Basil smiled also. He intervened.

'The fact is that Captain Fraser, who is one of my best friends, wanted us both out of the way very much. He is sailing to-night for East Africa, and the lady with whom we were all to have dined is – er – what is I believed described as "the romance of his life." He wanted that two hours with her, and employed these two reverend gentlemen to detain us at our houses so as to let him have the field to himself.'

'And of course,' said the late Mr Shorter, apologetically to me, 'as I had to keep a gentleman at home from keeping an appointment with a lady, I had to come with something rather hot and strong – rather urgent. It wouldn't have done to have been tame.'

'Oh,' I said, 'I acquit you of tameness.'

'Thank you, sir,' said the man, respectfully, 'always very grateful for any recommendation, sir.'

The other man idly pushed back his artificial bald head, revealing close red hair, and spoke dreamily, perhaps under the influence of Basil's admirable Burgundy.

'It's wonderful how common it's getting, gentlemen. Our office is busy from morning till night. I've no doubt you've often knocked up against us before. You just take notice. When an old bachelor goes on boring you with hunting stories, when you're burning to be introduced to somebody, he's from our bureau. When a lady calls on parish work and stops hours, just when you wanted to go to the Robinsons', she's from our bureau. The Robinson hand, sir, may be darkly seen.'

'There is one thing I don't understand,' I said. 'Why you are both vicars.'

A shade crossed the brow of the temporary incumbent of Chuntsey, in Essex.

'That may have been a mistake, sir,' he said. 'But it was not our fault. It was all the munificence of Captain Fraser. He requested that the highest price and talent on our tariff should be employed to detain you gentlemen. Now the highest payment in our office goes to those who impersonate vicars, as being the most respectable and more of a strain. We are paid five guineas a visit. We have had the good fortune to satisfy the firm with our work; and we are now permanently vicars. Before that we had two years as colonels, the next in our scale. Colonels are four guineas.'

THE GENUINE TABARD

E. C. Bentley

IT was quite by chance, at a dinner-party given by the American Naval Attaché, that Philip Trent met the Langleys, who were visiting Europe for the first time. During the cocktail-time, before dinner was served, he had gravitated towards George D. Langley, because he was the finest-looking man in the room – tall, strongly-built, carrying his years lightly, pink of face, with vigorous, massive features and thick grey hair.

They had talked about the Tower of London, the Cheshire Cheese, and the Zoo, all of which the Langleys had visited that day. Langley, so the Attaché had told Trent, was a distant relative of his own; he had made a large fortune manufacturing engineers' drawing-office equipment, was a prominent citizen of Cordova, Ohio, the headquarters of his business, and had married a Schuyler. Trent, though not sure what a Schuyler was, gathered that it was an excellent thing to marry, and this impression was confirmed when he found himself placed next to Mrs Langley at dinner.

Mrs Langley always went on the assumption that her own affairs were the most interesting subject of conversation; and as she was a vivacious and humorous talker and a very handsome and good-hearted woman, she usually turned out to be right. She informed Trent that she was crazy about old churches, of which she had seen and photographed she did not know how many in France, Germany, and England. Trent, who loved thirteenth-century stained glass, mentioned Chartres, which Mrs Langley said, truly enough, was too perfect for words. He asked if she had been to Fairford in Gloucestershire. She had; and that was, she declared with emphasis, the greatest day of all their time in Europe; not because of the church, though that was certainly lovely, but because of the treasure they had found that afternoon.

Trent asked to be told about this; and Mrs Langley said that it was quite a story. Mr Gifford had driven them down to Fairford in his car. Did Trent know Mr Gifford – W. N. Gifford, who lived at the Suffolk Hotel? He was visiting Paris just now. Trent ought to meet him, because Mr Gifford knew everything there was to know about stained glass, and church ornaments, and brasses, and antiques in general. They had met him when he was sketching some traceries in Westminster Abbey, and they had become great friends. He had driven them about to quite a few places within reach of London. He knew all about Fairford, of course, and they had a lovely time there.

On the way back to London, after passing through Abingdon, Mr Gifford had said it was time for a cup of coffee, as he always did around five o'clock; he made his own coffee, which was excellent, and carried it in a thermos. They slowed down, looking for a good place to stop, and Mrs Langley's eye was caught by a strange name on a signpost at a turning off the road – something Episcopi. She knew that meant bishops, which was interesting; so she asked Mr Gifford to halt the car while she made out the weather-beaten lettering. The sign said 'Silcote Episcopi ½ mile.'

Had Trent heard of the place? Neither had Mr Gifford. But that lovely name, Mrs Langley said, was enough for her. There must be a church, and an old one; and anyway she would love to have Silcote Episcopi in her collection. As it was so near, she asked Mr Gifford if they could go there so she could take a few snaps while the light was good, and perhaps have coffee there.

They found the church, with the parsonage near by, and a village in sight some way beyond. The church stood back of the church-yard, and as they were going along the footpath they noticed a grave with tall railings round it; not a standing-up stone but a flat one, raised on a little foundation. They noticed it because, though it was an old stone, it had not been just left to fall into decay, but had been kept clean of moss and dirt, so you could make out the inscription, and the grass around it was trim and tidy. They read

Sir Rowland Verey's epitaph; and Mrs Langley – so she assured
Trent – screamed with joy.

There was a man trimming the churchyard boundary hedge with
shears, who looked at them, she thought, suspiciously when she
screamed. She thought he was probably the sexton; so she assumed
a winning manner, and asked him if there was any objection to her
taking a photograph of the inscription on the stone. The man said
that he didn't know as there was; but maybe she ought to ask vicar,
because it was his grave, in a manner of speaking. It was vicar's
great-grandfather's grave, that was; and he always had it kep' in
good order. He would be in the church now, very like, if they had
a mind to see him.

Mr Gifford said that in any case they would have a look at the
church, which he thought might be worth the trouble. He observed
that it was not very old – about mid-seventeenth century, he would
say – a poor little kid church, Mrs Langley commented with gay
sarcasm. In a place so named, Mr Gifford said, there had probably
been a church for centuries farther back; but it might have been
burnt down, or fallen into ruin, and replaced by this building. So
they went into the church; and at once Mr Gifford had been
delighted with it. He pointed out how the pulpit, the screen, the
pews, the glass, the organ-case in the west gallery, were all of the
same period. Mrs Langley was busy with her camera when a pleas-
ant-faced man of middle age, in clerical attire, emerged from the
vestry with a large book under his arm.

Mr Gifford introduced himself and his friends as a party of chance
visitors who had been struck by the beauty of the church and had
ventured to explore its interior. Could the vicar tell them anything
about the armorial glass in the nave windows? The vicar could and
did; but Mrs Langley was not just then interested in any family
history but the vicar's own, and soon she broached the subject of
his great-grandfather's gravestone.

The vicar, smiling, said that he bore Sir Rowland's name, and
had felt it a duty to look after the grave properly, as this was the
only Verey to be buried in that place. He added that the living was
in the gift of the head of the family, and that he was the third Verey
to be vicar of Silcote Episcopi in the course of two hundred years.
He said that Mrs Langley was most welcome to take a photograph

of the stone, but he doubted if it could be done successfully with a hand-camera from over the railings – and of course, said Mrs Langley, he was perfectly right. Then the vicar asked if she would like to have a copy of the epitaph, which he could write for her if they would all come over to his house, and his wife would give them some tea; and at this, as Trent could imagine, they were just tickled to death.

'But what was it, Mrs Langley, that delighted you so much about the epitaph?' Trent asked. 'It seems to have been about a Sir Rowland Verey – that's all I have been told so far.'

'I was going to show it to you,' Mrs Langley said, opening her hand-bag. 'Maybe you will not think it so precious as we do. I have had a lot of copies made, to send to friends at home.' She unfolded a small typed sheet, on which Trent read what follows:

Within this Vault are interred
the Remains of
Lt.-Gen. Sir Rowland Edmund Verey,
Garter Principal King of Arms,
Gentleman Usher of the Black Rod
and
Clerk of the Hanaper,
who departed this Life
on the 2nd May 1795
in the 73rd Year of his Age
calmly relying
on the Merits of the Redeemer
for the Salvation of
his Soul.
Also of Lavinia Prudence,
Wife of the Above,
who entered into Rest
on the 12th March 1799
in the 68th Year of her Age.
She was a Woman of fine Sense
genteel Behaviour,
prudent Oeconomy
and

great Integrity.
'This is the Gate of the Lord:
The Righteous shall enter into it.'

'You have certainly got a fine specimen of that style,' Trent
observed. 'Nowadays we don't run to much more, as a rule, than
"in loving memory," followed by the essential facts. As for the
titles, I don't wonder at your admiring them; they are like the sound
of trumpets. There is also a faint jingle of money, I think. In Sir
Rowland's time, Black Rod's was probably a job worth having; and
though I don't know what a Hanaper is, I do remember that its
Clerkship was one of the fat sinecures that made it well worth while
being a courtier.'

Mrs Langley put away her treasure, patting the bag with affection.
'Mr Gifford said the Clerk had to collect some sort of legal fees for
the Crown, and that he would draw maybe seven or eight thousand
pounds a year for it, paying another man two or three hundred for
doing the actual work. Well, we found the vicarage just perfect –
an old house with everything beautifully mellow and personal about
it. There was a long oar hanging on the wall in the hall, and when
I asked about it the vicar said he had rowed for All Souls College
when he was at Oxford. His wife was charming, too. And now
listen! While she was giving us tea, and her husband was making a
copy of the epitaph for me, he was talking about his ancestor, and
he said the first duty that Sir Rowland had to perform after his
appointment as King of Arms was to proclaim the Peace of Versailles
from the steps of the Palace of St James's. Imagine that, Mr Trent!'

Trent looked at her uncertainly. 'So they had a Peace of Versailles
all that time ago.'

'Yes, they did,' Mrs Langley said, a little tartly. 'And quite an
important Peace, at that. We remember it in America, if you don't.
It was the first treaty to be signed by the United States, and in that
treaty the British Government took a licking, called off the war,
and recognized our independence. Now when the vicar said that
about his ancestor having proclaimed peace with the United States,
I saw George Langley prick up his ears; and I knew why.

'You see, George is a collector of Revolution pieces, and he has
some pretty nice things, if I do say it. He began asking questions;

and the first thing anybody knew, the vicaress had brought down the old King of Arms' tabard and was showing it off. You know what a tabard is, Mr Trent, of course. Such a lovely garment! I fell for it on the spot, and as for George, his eyes stuck out like a crab's. That wonderful shade of red satin, and the Royal Arms embroidered in those stunning colours, red and gold and blue and silver, as you don't often see them.

'Presently George got talking to Mr Gifford in a corner, and I could see Mr Gifford screwing up his mouth and shaking his head; but George only stuck out his chin, and soon after, when the vicaress was showing off the garden, he got the vicar by himself and talked turkey.

'Mr Verey didn't like it at all, George told me; but George can be a very smooth worker when he likes, and at last the vicar had to allow that he was tempted, what with having his sons to start in the world, and the income tax being higher than a cat's back, and the death duties and all. And finally he said yes. I won't tell you or anybody what George offered him, Mr Trent, because George swore me to secrecy; but, as he says, it was no good acting like a piker in this kind of a deal, and he could sense that the vicar wouldn't stand for any bargaining back and forth. And anyway, it was worth every cent of it to George, to have something that no other curio-hunter possessed. He said he would come for the tabard next day and bring the money in notes, and the vicar said very well, then we must all three come to lunch, and he would have a paper ready giving the history of the tabard over his signature. So that was what we did; and the tabard is in our suite at the Greville, locked in a wardrobe, and George has it out and gloats over it first thing in the morning and last thing at night.'

Trent said with sincerity that no story of real life had ever interested him more. 'I wonder,' he said, 'if your husband would let me have a look at his prize. I'm not much of an antiquary, but I am interested in heraldry, and the only tabards I have ever seen were quite modern ones.'

'Why, of course,' Mrs Langley said. 'You make a date with him after dinner. He will be delighted. He has no idea of hiding it under a bushel, believe me!'

The following afternoon, in the Langley's sitting room at the Greville, the tabard was displayed on a coat-hanger before the thought-
ful gaze of Trent, while its new owner looked on with a pride not
untouched with anxiety.

'Well, Mr Trent,' he said. 'How do you like it? You don't doubt
this is a genuine tabard, I suppose?'

Trent rubbed his chin. 'Oh yes, it's a tabard. I have seen a few
before, and I have painted one, with a man inside it, when Richmond
Herald wanted his portrait done in the complete get-up. Everything
about it is right. Such things are hard to come by. Until recent
times, I believe, a herald's tabard remained his property, and stayed
in the family, and if they got hard up they might perhaps sell it
privately, as this was sold to you. It's different now – so Richmond
Herald told me. When a herald dies, his tabard goes back to the
College of Arms, where he got it from.'

Langley drew a breath of relief. 'I'm glad to hear you say my
tabard is genuine. When you asked me if you could see it, I got the
impression you thought there might be something phoney about
it.'

Mrs Langley, her keen eyes on Trent's face, shook her head. 'He
thinks so still, George, I believe. Isn't that so Mr Trent?'

'Yes, I am sorry to say it is. You see, this was sold to you as a
particular tabard, with an interesting history of its own; and when
Mrs Langley described it to me, I felt pretty sure that you had been
swindled. You see, she had noticed nothing odd about the Royal
Arms. I wanted to see it just to make sure. It certainly did not
belong to Garter King of Arms in the year 1783.'

A very ugly look wiped all the benevolence from Langley's face,
and it grew several shades more pink. 'If what you say is true, Mr
Trent, and if that old fraud was playing me for a sucker, I will get
him jailed if it's my last act. But it certainly is hard to believe – a
preacher – and belonging to one of your best families – settled in
that lovely, peaceful old place, with his flock to look after and
everything. Are you really sure of what you say?'

'What I know is that the Royal Arms on this tabard are all wrong.'

An exclamation came from the lady. 'Why, Mr Trent, how you
talk! We have seen the Royal Arms quite a few times, and they are

just the same as this – and you have told us it is a genuine tabard, anyway. I don't get this at all.'

'I must apologize,' Trent said unhappily, 'for the Royal Arms. You see, they have a past. In the fourteenth century Edward III laid claim to the Kingdom of France, and it took a hundred years of war to convince his descendants that that claim wasn't practical politics. All the same, they went on including the lilies of France in the Royal Arms, and they never dropped them until the beginning of the nineteenth century.'

'Mercy!' Mrs Langley's voice was faint.

'Besides that, the first four Georges and the fourth William were Kings of Hanover; so until Queen Victoria came along, and could not inherit Hanover because she was a female, the Arms of the House of Brunswick were jammed in along with our own. In fact, the tabard of the Garter King of Arms in the year when he proclaimed the peace with the United States of America was a horrible mess of the leopards of England, the lion of Scotland, the harp of Ireland, the lilies of France, together with a few more lions, and a white horse, and some hearts, as worn in Hanover. It was a fairly tight fit for one shield, but they managed it somehow – and you can see that the Arms on this tabard of yours are not nearly such a bad dream as that. It is a Victorian tabard – a nice, gentlemanly coat, such as no well-dressed herald should be without.'

Langley thumped the table. 'Well, I intend to be without it anyway, if I can get my money back.'

'We can but try,' Trent said. 'It may be possible. But the reason why I asked to be allowed to see this thing, Mr Langley, was that I thought I might be able to save you some unpleasantness. You see, if you went home with your treasure, and showed it to people, and talked about its history, and it was mentioned in the newspapers, and then somebody got inquiring into its authenticity, and found out what I have been telling you, and made it public – well, it wouldn't be very nice for you.'

Langley flushed again, and a significant glance passed between him and his wife.

'You're damn right, it wouldn't,' he said. 'And I know the name of the buzzard who would do that to me, too, as soon as I had gone the limit in making a monkey of myself. Why, I would lose the money twenty times over, and then a bundle, rather than have that happen to me. I am grateful to you, Mr Trent – I am indeed. I'll say frankly that at home we aim to be looked up to socially, and we judged that we would certainly figure if we brought this dog-goned thing back and had it talked about. Gosh! When I think – but never mind that now. The thing is to go right back to that old crook and make him squeal. I'll have my money out of him, if I have to use a can-opener.'

Trent shook his head. 'I don't feel very sanguine about that, Mr Langley. But how would you like to run down to his place to-morrow with me and a friend of mine, who takes an interest in affairs of this kind, and who would be able to help you if any one can?'

Langley said, with emphasis, that that suited him.

The car which called for Langley next morning did not look as if it belonged, but did belong, to Scotland Yard; and the same could be said of its dapper chauffeur. Inside was Trent, with a black-haired, round-faced man whom he introduced as Superintendent Owen. It was at his request that Langley, during the journey, told with as much detail as he could recall the story of his acquisition of the tabard, which he had hopefully brought with him in a suitcase.

A few miles short of Abingdon the chauffeur was told to go slow. 'You tell me it was not very far this side of Abingdon, Mr Langley, that you turned off the main road,' the superintendent said. 'If you will keep a look-out now, you might be able to point out the spot.'

Langley stared at him. 'Why, doesn't your man have a map?'

'Yes; but there isn't any place called Silcote Episcopi on his map.'

'Nor,' Trent added, 'on any other map. No, I am not suggesting that you dreamed it all; but the fact is so.'

Langley, remarking shortly that this beat him, glared out of the window eagerly; and soon he gave the word to stop. 'I am pretty sure this is the turning,' he said. 'I recognize it by these two hay-stacks in the meadow, and the pond with osiers over it. But there certainly was a signpost there, and now there isn't one. If I was not dreaming then, I guess I must be now.' And as the car ran swiftly down the side-road he went on, 'Yes; that certainly is the church on ahead – and the covered gate, and the graveyard – and there is the vicarage, with the yew trees and the garden and everything.

Well, gentlemen, right now is when he gets what is coming to him, I don't care what the name of the darn place is.'

'The name of the darn place on the map,' Trent said, 'is Oak-hanger.'

The three men got out and passed through the lychgate.

'Where is the gravestone?' Trent asked.

Langley pointed. 'Right there.' They went across to the railed-in grave, and the American put a hand to his head. 'I must be nuts!' he groaned. 'I *know* this is the grave – but it says that here is laid to rest the body of James Roderick Stevens, of this parish.'

'Who seems to have died about thirty years after Sir Rowland Verey,' Trent remarked, studying the inscription; while the superintendent gently smote his thigh in an ecstasy of silent admiration. 'And now let us see if the vicar can throw any light on the subject.'

They went on to the parsonage; and a dark-haired, bright-faced girl, opening the door at Mr Owen's ring, smiled recognizingly at Langley. 'Well, you're genuine, anyway!' he exclaimed. 'Ellen is what they call you, isn't it? And you remember me, I see. Now I feel better. We would like to see the vicar. Is he at home?'

'The canon came home two days ago, sir,' the girl said, with a perceptible stress on the term of rank. 'He is down in the village now; but he may be back any minute. Would you like to wait for him?'

'We surely would,' Langley declared positively; and they were shown into the large room where the tabard had changed hands.

'So he has been away from home?' Trent asked. 'And he is a canon, you say?'

'Canon Maberley, sir; yes, sir, he was in Italy for a month. The lady and gentleman who were here till last week had taken the house furnished while he was away. Me and cook stayed on to do for them.'

'And did that gentleman – Mr Verey – do the canon's duty during his absence?' Trent inquired with a ghost of a smile.

'No, sir; the canon had an arrangement with Mr Giles, the vicar of Cotmore, about that. The canon never knew that Mr Verey was a clergyman. He never saw him. You see, it was Mrs Verey who came to see over the place and settled everything; and it seems she never mentioned it. When we told the canon, after they had gone, he was quite took aback. "I can't make it out at all," he says. "Why should he conceal it?" he says. "Well, sir," I says, "they were very nice people, anyhow, and the friends they had to see them here was very nice, and their chauffeur was a perfectly respectable man," I says.'

Trent nodded. 'Ah! They had friends to see them.'

The girl was thoroughly enjoying this gossip. 'Oh yes, sir. The gentleman as brought you down, sir' – she turned to Langley – 'he brought down several others before that. They was Americans too, I think.'

'You mean they didn't have an English accent, I suppose,' Langley suggested dryly.

'Yes, sir; and they had such nice manners, like yourself,' the girl said, quite unconscious of Langley's confusion, and of the grins covertly exchanged between Trent and the superintendent, who now took up the running.

'This respectable chauffeur of theirs – was he a small, thin man with a long nose, partly bald, always smoking cigarettes?'

'Oh yes, sir; just like that. You must know him.'

'I do,' Superintendent Owen said grimly.

'So do I!' Langley exclaimed. 'He was the man we spoke to in the churchyard.'

'Did Mr and Mrs Verey have any – er – ornaments of their own with them?' the superintendent asked.

Ellen's eyes rounded with enthusiasm. 'Oh yes, sir – some lovely things they had. But they was only put out when they had friends coming. Other times they was kept somewhere in Mr Verey's bedroom, I think. Cook and me thought perhaps they was afraid of burglars.'

The superintendent pressed a hand over his stubby moustache. 'Yes, I expect that was it,' he said gravely. 'But what kind of lovely things do you mean? Silver – china – that sort of thing?'

'No, sir; nothing ordinary, as you might say. One day they had out a beautiful goblet, like, all gold, with little figures and patterns worked on it in colours, and precious stones, blue and green and white, stuck all round it – regular dazzled me to look at, it did.'

'The Debenham Chalice!' exclaimed the superintendent.

'Is it a well-known thing, then, sir?' the girl asked.

'No, not at all,' Mr Owen said. 'It is an heirloom – a private family possession. Only we happen to have heard of it.'

'Fancy taking such things about with them,' Ellen remarked. 'Then there was a big book they had out once, lying open on that table in the window. It was all done in funny gold letters on yellow paper, with lovely little pictures all round the edges, gold and silver and all colours.'

'The Murrane Psalter!' said Mr Owen. 'Come, we're getting on.'

'And,' the girl pursued, addressing herself to Langley, 'there was that beautiful red coat with the arms on it, like you see on a half-crown. You remember they got it out for you to look at, sir; and when I brought in the tea it was hanging up in front of the tallboy.'

Langley grimaced. 'I believe I do remember it,' he said, 'now you remind me.'

'There is the canon coming up the path now,' Ellen said, with a glance through the window. 'I will tell him you gentlemen are here.'

She hurried from the room, and soon there entered a tall, stooping old man with a gentle face and the indescribable air of a scholar.

The superintendent went to meet him.

'I am a police officer, Canon Maberley,' he said. 'I and my friends have called to see you in pursuit of an official inquiry in connection with the people to whom your house was let last month. I do not think I shall have to trouble you much, though, because your parlour-maid has given us already most of the information we are likely to get, I suspect.'

'Ah! That girl,' the canon said vaguely. 'She has been talking to you, has she? She will go on talking for ever, if you let her. Please sit down, gentlemen. About the Vereys – ah yes! But surely there was nothing wrong about the Vereys? Mrs Verey was quite a nice, well-bred person, and they left the place in perfectly good order. They paid me in advance, too, because they live in New Zealand, as she explained, and know nobody in London. They were on a visit to England, and they wanted a temporary home in the heart of the country, because that is the real England, as she said. That was so sensible of them, I thought – instead of flying to the grime and turmoil of London, as most of our friends from overseas do. In a way, I was quite touched by it, and I was glad to let them have the vicarage.'

The superintendent shook his head. 'People as clever as they are make things very difficult for us, sir. And the lady never mentioned that her husband was a clergyman, I understand.'

'No, and that puzzled me when I heard of it,' the canon said. 'But it didn't matter, and no doubt there was a reason.'

'The reason was, I think,' Mr Owen said, 'that if she had mentioned it, you might have been too much interested, and asked questions which would have been all right for a genuine parson's wife, but which she couldn't answer without putting her foot in it. Her husband could do a vicar well enough to pass with laymen, especially if they were not English laymen. I am sorry to say, canon, that your tenants were imposters. Their name was certainly not Verey, to begin with. I don't know who they are – I wish I did – they are new to us and they have invented a new method. But I can tell you what they are. They are thieves and swindlers.'

The canon fell back in his chair. 'Thieves and swindlers!' he gasped.

'And very talented performers too,' Trent assured him. 'Why, they have had in this house of yours part of the loot of several country-house burglaries which took place last year, and which puzzled the police because it seemed impossible that some of the things taken could ever be turned into cash. One of them was a herald's tabard, which Superintendent Owen tells me had been worn by the father of Sir Andrew Ritchie. He was Maltravers Herald in his day. It was taken when Sir Andrew's place in Lincolnshire was broken into, and a lot of very valuable jewellery was stolen. It was dangerous to try to sell the tabard in the open market, and it was worth little, anyhow, apart from any associations it might have. What they did was to fake up a story about the tabard which might appeal to an American purchaser, and, having found a victim, to induce him to buy it. I believe he parted with quite a large sum.'

'The poor simp!' growled Langley.

Canon Maberley held up a shaking hand. 'I fear I do not understand,' he said. 'What had their taking my house to do with all this?'

'It was a vital part of the plan. We know exactly how they went to work about the tabard; and no doubt the other things were got rid of in very much the same way. There were four of them in the gang. Besides your tenants, there was an agreeable and cultured person – I should think a man with real knowledge of antiquities and objects of art – whose job was to make the acquaintance of wealthy people visiting London, gain their confidence, take them about to places of interest, exchange hospitality with them, and finally get them down to this vicarage. In this case it was made to appear as if the proposal to look over your church came from the visitors themselves. They could not suspect anything. They were attracted by the romantic name of the place on a signpost up there at the corner of the main road.'

The canon shook his head helplessly. 'But there is no signpost at that corner.'

'No, but there was one at the time when they were due to be passing that corner in the confederate's car. It was a false signpost, you see, with a false name on it – so that if anything went wrong, the place where the swindle was worked would be difficult to trace. Then, when they entered the churchyard their attention was attracted by a certain gravestone with an inscription that interested them. I won't waste your time by giving the whole story – the point is that the gravestone, or rather the top layer which had been fitted on to it, was false too. The sham inscription on it was meant to lead up to the swindle, and so it did.'

The canon drew himself up in his chair. 'It was an abominable act of sacrilege!' he exclaimed. 'The man calling himself Verey – '

'I don't think,' Trent said, 'it was the man calling himself Verey who actually did the abominable act. We believe it was the fourth member of the gang, who masqueraded as the Verey's chauffeur – a very interesting character. Superintendent Owen can tell you about him.'

Mr Owen twisted his moustache thoughtfully. 'Yes; he is the only one of them that we can place. Alfred Coveney, his name is; a man of some education and any amount of talent. He used to be a stage-carpenter and property-maker – a regular artist, he was. Give him a tub of papier-mâché, and there was nothing he couldn't model and colour to look exactly like the real thing. That was how the false top to the gravestone was made, I've no doubt. It may have been made to fit on like a lid, to be slipped on and off as required. The inscription was a bit above Alf, though – I expect it was Gifford who drafted that for him, and he copied the lettering from other old stones in the churchyard. Of course the fake signpost was Alf's work too – stuck up when required, and taken down when the show was over.

'Well, Alf got into bad company. They found how clever he was with his hands, and he became an expert burglar. He has served two terms of imprisonment. He is one of a few who have always been under suspicion for the job at Sir Andrew Ritchie's place, and the other two when the chalice was lifted from Eynsham Park and the Psalter from Lord Swanbourne's house. With what they collected in this house and the jewellery that was taken in all three burglaries, they must have done very well indeed for themselves; and by this time they are going to be hard to catch.'

Canon Maberley, who had now recovered himself somewhat, looked at the others with the beginnings of a smile. 'It is a new experience for me,' he said, 'to be made use of by a gang of criminals. But it is highly interesting. I suppose that when these confiding strangers had been got down here, my tenant appeared in the character of the parson, and invited them into the house, where you tell me they were induced to make a purchase of stolen property. I do not see, I must confess, how anything could have been better designed to prevent any possibility of suspicion arising. The vicar of a parish, at home in his own vicarage! Who could imagine anything being wrong? I only hope, for the credit of my cloth, that the deception was well carried out.'

'As far as I know,' Trent said, 'he made only one mistake. It was a small one; but the moment I heard of it I knew that he must have been a fraud. You see, he was asked about the oar you have hanging up in the hall. I didn't go to Oxford myself, but I believe when a man is given his oar it means that he rowed in an eight that did something unusually good.'

A light came into the canon's spectacled eyes. 'In the year I got my colours the Wadham boat went up five places on the river. It was the happiest week of my life.'

'Yet you had other triumphs,' Trent suggested. 'For instance, didn't you get a Fellowship at All Souls, after leaving Wadham?'

'Yes, and that did please me, naturally,' the canon said. 'But that is a different sort of happiness, my dear sir, and, believe me, nothing like so keen. And by the way, how did you know about that?'

'I thought it might be so, because of the little mistake your tenant made. When he was asked about the oar, he said he had rowed for All Souls.'

Canon Maberley burst out laughing, while Langley and the superintendent stared at him blankly.

'I think I see what happened,' he said. 'The rascal must have been browsing about in my library, in search of ideas for the part he was to play. I was a resident Fellow for five years, and a number of my books have a bookplate with my name and the name and arms of All Souls. His mistake was natural.' And again the old gentleman laughed delightedly.

Langley exploded. 'I like a joke myself,' he said, 'but I'll be skinned alive if I can see the point of this one.'

'Why, the point is,' Trent told him, 'that nobody ever rowed for All Souls. There never were more than four undergraduates there at one time, all the other members being Fellows.'

THE BUNCH OF GRAPES

H. C. Bailey

MR FORTUNE stood over the remains of a bunch of large black grapes and contemplated them in a gentle melancholy. He was in his laboratory.

Slowly and sighing he turned to an apparatus of glass tube and bottles and poured some fluid into one. Bubbles of gas began to pass from that bottle to the other. His assistant, watching, showed with respect a lack of interest.

The fluid into which the gas came was suffused with a faint tawny colour: a cloud formed in it, orange red.

A faint sound escaped from the assistant. 'Yes. Yes. I know you're disappointed.' Mr Fortune murmured. 'That's the only consolin' factor present. But irrelevant to the problem.'

'Sorry, sir.' The assistant studied the orange cloud, which did not become more substantial. 'Only a small amount here.'

'My dear chap! Oh, my dear chap!' Mr Fortune murmured. 'Did you happen to think that will simplify things?'

'I don't see my way at all,' the assistant grumbled.

'It's something to know that,' said Mr Fortune cheerfully. 'I knew I didn't some time ago. We'll try the other test, please.' He went back to the grapes and looked at each one with minute care. He smelt them.

The activities of the assistant were stopped a moment by a spasm of surprise.

The grapes were reduced to fluid, another apparatus of bottle and tube was prepared, and gas generated in the grape fluid passed into a clear solution. In that came darkness and black mist.

Mr Fortune sighed again. 'Which bein' thus, we have to work

out the quantity. What is life that one should seek it?' For he does not love calculations.

They worked on and at the end his assistant looked at him with puzzled curiosity. 'Call it three grains. Say the rest of the bunch had the same proportion, about six in all. Small dose, isn't it?'

'Yes. Yes. Economical for a poisoner. They're generally generous. But less than a grain has killed. I wonder.' He contemplated the assistant with gentle sorrow. 'Anything else occur to you, Jenks?'

'Well, it's a very happy-go-lucky affair,' Jenks complained.

'I wouldn't say that. No. You're so professional. You don't allow for the limited resources of the amateur. Signs of careful work by an ingenious amateur. And that's very tiresome, Jenks. The country is so cold.' He moaned and went to the window and looked at a sullen October sky and wandered out.

This was his first investigation of the case which his sister considers his best. But she is a woman of sentiment – though she would not forgive the description.

She is the sister who married a bishop: a fact of which his friends consider Mr Fortune apt to boast. He professes himself afraid of the Bishop, but there are those who believe the Bishop more afraid of him. It is a wholesome condition for brothers-in-law, promoting family affection.

At this point in the case Mr Fortune told his sister by telephone that the world was a vale of tears and he would like to come and weep with her at Laxbury.

'My dear child!' said the telephone. 'How sweet of you! Come along. Bill will love it. I was really just going to ask you. We haven't seen you in ages. Bill was saying so.'

'Bless him!' said Mr Fortune, and rang off. She is a little too fond of bringing the Bishop into her conversation.

But the Bishop of Laxbury, a large impressive bishop, was most delighted to see Reginald and took pains about it. Reggie purred: he likes people to be nice to him: and the gaiety of his sister (she was in spirits) alleviated the zeal of the episcopal welcome. Yet he was nervous, he felt unworthy.

They gave him an admirable dinner in the episcopal palatial style. Mrs Brandon left the table, and struggling against exhaustion he was alone with the Bishop and the port.

'I hope you like that,' said the Bishop earnestly.

'Oh, yes. Rather.' Reggie roused himself to drink. 'Wonderful.'

'It's the '78,' the Bishop explained with decent pride. 'There is not much left.'

'My dear chap!' Reggie sipped again. For port he has no reverence – that is one of his dearest heresies – but he appreciated the honour. 'Wonderful.' His heavy eyes opened a little wider. He was wondering why the pride of the episcopal cellar was offered to a casual brother-in-law.

But the Bishop talked fervently of vintages and then with indignation of the decay of faith from which arose the cult of tawny port.

Reggie was not required to take part in the conversation. He came back to life on the necessity of declining any more of the '78. Its level was low. 'Well, then, let us smoke a cigar in the library.' The Bishop rose and in a mild, dazed alarm Reggie was shepherded away. It was without precedent that they should not go to Pamela. Behold the awful reason for '78 port. And what in wonder could Bill the Bishop be confidential about? A ghastly question.

The Bishop stood in front of the fire and cleared his throat. 'I was so pleased you could spare us a day or two, Reginald. I have been anxious to consult you. In point of fact I had resolved to go to town. You won't think me selfish if I put the matter before you now?'

'My dear fellow!' Reggie beamed.

'You're very kind. It is causing me a great deal of anxiety,' and the Bishop looked it.

Reggie moved in his chair. 'Something personal, Bill?'

'Dear me, no, not at all. Except as touching my office.' But the Bishop was still uncomfortable. 'I don't know whether I am justified in forcing an evil affair upon another man's mind. But you are of great experience in such things.'

'Yes. My job's sin,' said Reggie with some acidity. 'What sin's this?'

'I have received an anonymous letter,' the Bishop announced.

'Oh, my aunt!' Reggie moaned. 'Is that unusual?'

'It has occurred before. But hitherto only upon church affairs. This is of quite a different nature. This – let me show it you,

Reginald.' The Bishop strode to a dispatch box and came back holding, as if it were filthy, an envelope.

Reggie received it without gratitude. 'Thanks. Cheap stationery. Postmark, Laxbury. Addressed in laboured hand, Bishop of Laxbury, The Palace. Letter apparently in same writing. "Bishop of Laxbury – Sir, This is to say you ought to know what's going on in Morton parish." ' He looked up at the Bishop. 'Morton?' he asked.

'A large parish, two miles out of the town. It has a very interesting Norman church.'

'Is that so?' Reggie murmured. 'And did you know what's goin' on in Morton parish?'

'My dear Reginald, I know the parish well. But this – pray read on.'

' "Mr Waring is as good as a saint and he won't see anything though 'tis open scandal for all how his wife is with Mr Ivor Gould. If someone don't stop them soon there'll be a wicked end to it. She is that set on Mr Gould, she cares for nothing else now, not her husband nor her dear boy. Nor the shame of it. – A Friend!" '

Reggie sat back 'Yes. Amiable composition. Common type. With points of interest. Any reason to believe it?'

'I don't know how to answer you, Reginald.'

'Oh! Like that. Who is the saintly Waring?'

'The Vicar. A dear good fellow, a fine spirit, the most unworldly of men.'

'Letter accurate so far. And the other members of the triangle?'

'I can only tell you, Reginald, I am not surprised.'

'Oh, my hat!' Reggie moaned.

'You see what a distressing situation I am in. Here is danger of a terrible scandal. Should I warn poor Waring? Or would it be better to approach his wife? She might be very difficult – '

'Yes. She might,' Reggie murmured.

'But I must endeavour to do what is right.'

'Yes. Very painful state of mind. Yes. Led to a lot of trouble.'

'Pray give me your advice.'

'Have you asked Pamela?' said Reggie.

'My dear Reginald!' The Bishop was horrified. 'I could not discuss such an affair with Pamela.'

'Sorry. My error. Well, as you don't know anything, you'd better not do anything.'

The Bishop was startled. 'But really, Reginald, can I honestly say I don't know anything?'

'It's all you can honestly say.'

'I should be most happy to repose in your judgment, my dear fellow. But – '

'You can repose all right.' Reggie was tired of him.

'But I am not sure you realize the grave issues – '

'Only a life or two. That's all, Bill.' Reggie looked at him with dislike.

'Quite so. Quite.' The Bishop cleared his throat importantly.

'Well, I meant to stay a bit.' Reggie got out of his chair. 'I'll look into it. Good-night.'

He was in his bedroom, he was out of his coat and in a dressing gown, he had composed himself in a chair before the fire to meditation upon the parish of Morton when the door opened and Pamela came in.

'Well, well!' Reggie smiled upon her. 'Bless you, my child. You look about fourteen. And very nice, too.'

She was in a kimono, her hair down. She kissed the top of his head and sat cross-legged on the rug at his feet and looked up at him like an earnest child. 'Bill told you all about it?'

'Not to notice. No.' Reggie's face became blank. 'What do you happen to mean?'

'This wretched anonymous letter.'

'Which is that?'

'Oh, don't you be discreet,' she cried. 'The letter about the Vicar at Morton and Mrs Waring.'

'Think of that!' Reggie sighed. 'Are you a good little girl? No. The ruling of Bill is that we couldn't possibly discuss such an affair with Pamela.'

'Bless him!' She laughed a little. 'I was so glad you could come, Reggie.'

'Yes, I noticed that. Now I know why. Very gratifyin'. So he did show you the letter?'

'Well, not exactly showed me,' said Pamela. 'I – I just gathered, Reggie.'

Reggie shook his head. 'Now and then – only now and then – I am a little sorry for Bill.'

'Poor dear.' Pamela looked charming. 'He's been so dreadfully troubled.'

'Yes, that was indicated,' Reggie murmured. 'But Pamela isn't?'

'It's a horrid letter.' Pamela's little nose wrinkled disgust. 'Oh, it's vile. I was afraid Bill would do something hopeless. You won't let him, will you?'

'Oh! That was your idea. You don't believe it?'

'My dear!' She looked up at him, a sad child. 'One doesn't, does one – that sort of thing? And I'm sure the letter's not true. There isn't any open scandal. I should know. Morton's quite near. But it's so difficult. Mr Waring is a sort of learned saint and she's different. And she has been a great deal about with this Mr Gould. Oh, I'm horrid. I should never have thought anything of it except for this letter. But it is true.'

'Yes. Ingenious letter. Yes. And you don't care for Mrs Waring, Pam?'

'Why, I don't know. She's just not interesting. Quite an ordinary woman. Rather fine to look at in a big, hearty way, and she has a dear little boy. She's very much alive. Everybody likes her well enough.'

'And the Mr Gould?'

'Oh, he's a rich hunting man. I don't care for him. A hard, pushful creature. But he's quite well liked, too.'

'Somebody don't like somebody,' Reggie murmured. 'Any idea who would write the letter, Pam?'

'My dear child, it might be hundreds of people. I thought it was a woman. It's just like servants' talk. Morton's quite close to Laxbury, and you know what a cathedral town is for gossip. How can one tell? There are hosts would know enough to make it up.'

'Yes. Takin' it for false. Anyone who would know if it was true?'

Pamela was frightened. 'That would have to be just chance, wouldn't it?' she cried.

'Does anybody much live out at Morton – except these people?'

Pamela meditated. 'I don't know. It's an ordinary county parish. The only other big house is the Lyntons'. But he's a futile little man and she's the gentlest creature. She's been ill, too, just lately.'

'Oh! Serious?'

'I don't know. Something internal.'

'Well, well,' Reggie sighed. 'What is life that one should seek it? Is there anything to look at in the parish of Morton?'

'How do you mean?' She was startled.

'Anything to attract the intelligent stranger?'

'There's the church, of course. It's Norman and all that. It has a priest's chamber and a funny little staircase up to it – wooden but all squiggly, spiral; it's very wonderful. I've forgotten what they call it.'

'They call it a newel stair,' said Reggie severely. 'In wood it is unusual. I will go and look at the wooden newel stair. Go to bed, Pam.' He stood up, lifting her to her feet.

'You are a dear, Reggie.' She kissed him. 'It's so comfortable with you. I feel people are safe. You're nice.'

'I rather like you,' said Reggie.

But when she had gone, 'Oh, my aunt!' he groaned. 'Safe! What a mess! What a mess!'

As an example of scientific method, Reggie considers that the value of the case is its demonstration of the importance of the open mind. At this stage his mind was very open. The possibilities seemed to him practically infinite. That was what kept him awake for an hour – an event very rare.

It was not Morton Church he went to in the morning but the county police station.

The Chief Constable received him with anxious solemnity. 'Very good of you to come down. This is Dr Antony, Mrs Lynton's doctor.'

Reggie shook hands. 'Any further illness?'

'She's made a fair recovery. She's about again. I'm afraid you have something serious to tell us, Mr Fortune?'

'Yes. It's going to be a tiresome case.'

'You found arsenic?'

'Oh, no. No. Not a trace. I didn't think I should. Your account of the symptoms was very good and clear.'

'Dear me.' Dr Antony was disconcerted. 'I thought there was strong suspicion of arsenic.'

'Effects do simulate each other,' Reggie consoled him. 'But the pulse, you know, the breathing.'

'What did you find, then, Mr Fortune?'

'Oh, antimony. Antimony. We found about three grains in the grapes. Assumin' the amount employed was equally distributed in the whole bunch, it was six grains or more. Our conclusion is, some grains of antimony were consumed by Mrs Lynton. Rather indefinite, but adequate.'

'Antimony!' said the Chief Constable. 'That's out of the way, isn't it?'

'Yes. Not one of the popular poisons. Rather old-fashioned. Victorian. But it works all right.'

'Two or three grains,' the doctor reflected. 'I never saw a case, myself, but surely that's a small dose, Mr Fortune?'

'Quite enough for the symptoms. And the hypothetical six could easily be fatal. Still the amount is small. That's one of the interesting points.'

'What does it mean, Mr Fortune?' said the Chief Constable eagerly.

'I haven't the slightest idea. Hopeful ignorance of the poisoner – poisoner's fear of being too obvious – many other meanings possible. Attractive field for speculation.'

'It was diabolically clever, putting the stuff in grapes,' said the Chief Constable.

'You think so?' Reggie murmured.

'That's never been done before, has it?'

'I don't recall grapes. The raisin is suspect. Yes the use of the grapes also has interest.' He gazed with dreamy eyes at Dr Antony, who became uncomfortable.

'Clever work to get it into them,' the Chief Constable persisted.

'Quite neat, yes. There's no actual difficulty for a light hand. It was generally inserted at the juncture with the stem. One or two punctures also. On ordinary inspection the grapes looked all right. Did you notice anything, Doctor?'

'I did think the bunch looked a little knocked about,' said Dr Antony with some hesitation.

'Yes. Was that after your attention had been drawn to it?'

'Oh, certainly. Of course. I didn't see the grapes till after Mrs Lynton said she believed it was they made her ill. Naturally I didn't.'

'Quite,' Reggie murmured, watching him.

'Do you know what was used, Mr Fortune?' the doctor asked eagerly.

'Oh, tartrate of antimony. Tartar emetic. I rather suspected wine of antimony. I thought I could smell sherry. But there was only a faint trace of alcohol.'

'You're going beyond me,' the Chief Constable complained. 'What is wine of antimony?'

'Common drug once, wasn't it, Doctor?' Reggie smiled.

'Really, I don't know,' the doctor snapped. 'I never use it.'

'Of course not. No. Quite obsolete. Victorian.' Reggie turned to the Chief Constable. 'It's tartar emetic dissolved in sherry: a cure-all of the Dark Ages.'

'I see. I've heard of tartar emetic. That's common enough. Vet's use it, don't they?'

'Oh, yes. Yes. Quite easy to get. Well, all this bein' thus, let's have the history of Mrs Lynton.'

'Poor lady, she hasn't any,' the Chief Constable laughed.

'She has enough to suggest poison to somebody,' said Reggie.

'That's true, of course. But I mean there's absolutely nothing about her to give a motive.'

'Queer things, motives,' Reggie murmured. 'Well, Doctor, what's her history?'

'You mean her medical history, Mr Fortune?' The doctor was nervous.

'All you know about her,' said Reggie sharply.

'Well, really – I'm not a personal friend, you know. She's only a patient. She's a woman of about forty; she's lived twenty years at Morton, much respected. I think we can say she's happily married.' He looked at the Chief Constable.

'Certainly you can. Sweet woman – and Lynton's an excellent fellow. Very quiet and retiring, but one of the best. Perfect marriage, I should say. No children, of course.'

'There you have them, Mr Fortune,' the doctor went on. 'It's always been a very pleasant household. Mrs Lynton hasn't had good health recently.'

'Any previous suspicion?'

'Not the least. She has been rather run down and depressed. Nothing more than you see in many women. This came on me like a bolt from the blue. Absolutely. A bolt from the blue. I had an urgent call from Morton House. Mr Lynton's account was that she had been staying in for some days on account of a cold, but when they thought it had passed off she was suddenly taken with what seemed to be severe indigestion. She was very sick and had a lot of stomach pain. I found her, as I wrote, in a very disturbing condition: pulse small and very irregular, great irregularity of respiration, temperature below normal, a good deal of sweat, state of collapse. She said, and her husband confirmed it, the sickness came on just after eating these grapes. Before that, she had been quite comfortable. The food she'd been having previously was Byng's Invalid Diet and a little fish; on account of the cold. It was clear to my mind she must be suffering from some form of poisoning. I own I suspected arsenic.'

'Oh, yes. Did you tell them so?'

'I didn't feel justified. I said I thought something she had eaten had upset her. They quite agreed. They said that it must have been the grapes. They were both very anxious and bewildered. I told them I had better examine what she'd been eating and took the grapes and what was left of the Diet and fish she had – '

'Very thorough. Yes. I appreciated that. Both quite innocent. It was only the grapes. As suggested. And then?'

'Then I treated her for arsenic poisoning, demulcents and so forth, and she's made quite a good recovery, as I told you.'

'Very satisfactory. Yes.' Reggie looked at him with half-shut eyes. 'And are they satisfied, Doctor?'

'Well, naturally, they have shown some curiosity.' Dr Antony was embarrassed. 'Mr Lynton has asked me more than once if I found anything wrong with the grapes. I told him I was having them examined. Mrs Lynton has several times asked me if I think she is likely to have another attack.'

'And do you?' Reggie drawled.

'Dear me, Mr Fortune, how can I possibly say?' The doctor shifted in his chair.

'But we've got to say,' Reggie murmured. 'And leavin' things as they are, I should say she is.'

'Good God!' the doctor cried.

'Why the surprise?' Reggie stared.

'Why, Mr Fortune, I have been assuming it was arsenic, you see,' the doctor hesitated. 'I thought one of these arsenical washes used on the grape vine – '

'Yes. Very ingenious. Yes. Only it wasn't. Whose vine were you thinking of?'

'I was not,' the doctor exploded in vague anger.

'Oh, don't be cross. What's the origin of the grapes?'

'I gathered they were brought by Mrs Waring. The Vicar's wife, you know. She called with her little boy.'

'Did she really?' Reggie sat up. His mouth stayed a little open, his eyes were puckered as though he had a glimpse of something that startled him. He sighed and his round face became plaintive again. 'The Vicar's wife,' he murmured. 'Oh, yes. Do vicars grow grapes much?'

'Wouldn't be her own growing,' said the Chief Constable. 'The Warings haven't any glass. These were Black Colmar.'

'Yes, I noticed that. Yes. And very fine, too. Where would she get them?'

'Really, I don't know.' The doctor fidgeted in his chair. 'I – I should think it most likely she had them from Ivor Gould. He does send grapes and so forth to the vicarage. For the sick, you know. He's very generous.'

'Oh, is he? I see. Mr Ivor Gould sends grapes to Mrs Waring for the sick. Mrs Waring brings them to her friend, Mrs Lynton, who has a cold. And they contain antimony in a probably lethal dose. Yes.' Reggie turned to the Chief Constable. 'There's your case, Major. Easy, isn't it?'

'As nasty a one as I want,' the Chief Constable growled.

'Baffling, absolutely baffling,' Dr Antony stood up. 'It's – it's incredible.'

'Only it happened,' Reggie said.

'Well, it's quite beyond me, Mr Fortune. I can only leave it in your hands. Of course, I'm at your service; but you've had everything I know about it.' He fussed out of the room.

'Rather shy, isn't he?' Reggie murmured.

'Perhaps he is,' the Chief Constable nodded. 'But it's not a pleasant situation for him. All these people are his patients. He's been as frank as we could expect.'

'You think so? Well, you know him.'

'After all, he brought me the case and asked for investigation. If he wanted to hush it up, no need to let me know there was anything fishy.'

'I wonder,' Reggie murmured. 'I should say he hadn't much choice. The Lyntons had suspicions of something queer. He let that out. They're still worryin' him about it. Very desirable to protect himself.'

The Chief Constable was shocked. 'I say, that's a nasty suggestion, Mr Fortune.'

'Oh, no. No. The suggestion is, Dr Antony has been quite correct. But not anxious to assist.'

'I really don't know what more he could have told us.'

'Nor do I. I should like to. What he did tell us was only what we should get from the Lyntons as soon as we asked. And he don't mean to tell us anything else.'

'He was in a fluster,' the Chief Constable admitted.

'Yes. I think so. Nervous reticence by Dr Antony. All these people are his patients. He's been in and out of Mrs Lynton's house for umpteen years. But he protests she's not a personal friend. And he don't want to talk about how she came to be poisoned in grapes provided by the other patients. Yet that little point should interest him.'

'I suppose he feels bound to the others, too.'

'Yes. As you were sayin'. That was strongly indicated. I wonder where he went to in such a hurry.'

'Good God! You don't mean he's involved?'

'I didn't say that. No. But he ran away just as we were coming to the point. Havin' dodged it some time.'

'But I don't follow you,' the Chief Constable complained.

'The motive. Why was Mrs Lynton poisoned? Why was the poison put in grapes which came from Mr Gould by way of Mrs Waring?'

'I don't mind owning, I can't imagine why anybody should poison

Mrs Lynton,' the Chief Constable declared. 'She's the most harmless woman alive.'

'And Mrs Waring and our Mr Gould – are they harmless?'

'Absolutely different types, of course. I've nothing against 'em.'

'Anything in the association?' Reggie murmured.

'I see what you mean.' The Chief Constable pulled his moustache. 'An intrigue between 'em – Mrs Lynton came to know of it – and they wanted to stop her mouth.'

'Yes. Ever heard of that before?' Reggie watched him.

'I have heard a joke or two about them, now you ask me. Smoking-room talk. My God, it's possible.'

'Rather indicated when our doctor ran away,' Reggie murmured. 'I wonder.'

'That makes a devilish case of it, doesn't it?' The Chief Constable meditated.

'Yes. Poisonin' seldom is induced by the nobler emotions.'

The Chief Constable meditated more profoundly and at length. 'We can't leave it like this,' he announced.

'I wasn't going to,' Reggie moaned.

'If this is the motive and these two arranged it, we've got to expect there'll be further attempts.'

'Yes. Something more will happen,' Reggie murmured. 'I don't know what, though.'

'Well, what are we going to do? Better put these two on the carpet and have it out with them, I suppose.'

'As at present advised – yes. Pendin' the effects of our doctor's efforts. Don't be in a hurry.'

'What do you mean?'

'My dear chap! Oh, my dear chap! Dr Antony went to warn 'em.'

'Good God, if he's done that!' the Chief Constable exploded.

'Yes? What then?'

'Why, it looks deuced ugly for him.'

'I wonder,' Reggie murmured. 'I meant him to, you know. Instructive to watch the reaction. See you again in the morning.'

He went out and bought a guidebook to the county and read it over a lunch in the wrong hotel. It had much to say of Morton Church: of the saddle-back tower and the strange beasts at the south door, of the priest's chamber over the chancel, of the small newel stair of oak carved with angels by which it was reached, and the black-letter books in the chamber. Reggie saw no difficulty in being the curious visitor to the church of Morton.

His car brought him to the village and his head came slowly out of his coat collar, for the air was crisp, which pains him. The village was comely but without human life. The church tower could be seen some way beyond. Church and vicarage stood together as though the church were in the vicarage garden or the vicarage in the churchyard.

Reggie surveyed one and the other dreamily. The vicarage also seemed to enjoy a lifeless peace. But from somewhere behind it a child's voice sang joyfully:

> '*Wiv a fearful, fwightful, fwantic fwown*
> *I bared my big wight arm,*
> *I seized him by his little pigtail*
> *As on his knees fell he,*
> *An' my sabre twue cut clearly fwough*
> *His sersical wertebwæ.*'

'Well, well!' Reggie sighed, and gazed at the grim Norman mass of the church. That song in that guileless voice made a queer harmony with the grotesque horror of the beasts cut in the stone above the door. Slowly he moved to the door and opened it: stood a moment: called to his chauffeur and ran in.

On the floor of the chancel lay a man's body. A woman was kneeling beside it. Reggie came to her. 'I am a doctor, madam. Let me see him.'

'A doctor?' She stared at him. She was flushed and panting. 'I think he's dead. He fell – he must have fallen down the stairs – he was in that room up there.' She pointed to the newel stair.

Reggie glanced over his shoulder. 'Oh, yes. I see.' He bent over the body. Sam, the chauffeur, arrived, and as he came doors banged. Reggie looked around again. 'What was that?' he said sharply.

'Sorry, sir, I left the door in my 'urry. It's the wind.'

Reggie worked upon the still body. . . .

'Is he dead, Doctor?' the woman said eagerly.

'No. No.' Reggie looked at her. 'I can't promise you anything, madam.'

She clasped her hands. She gave a cry of fear.

'We must have him in hospital at once.'

'Oh, no! The vicarage is just close by. He's my husband, you know.'

'It's a case for a hospital. You can't treat it in your house,' Reggie said sharply, and she looked away from him, breathing fast. 'Have you a telephone?' She nodded. 'Sam, run across and telephone Laxbury hospital for an ambulance. Mr Fortune is bringing a bad accident case.' Sam departed. 'Were you here when it happened, madam?'

'No, I wasn't. I – I'd been in the church putting flowers on the altar. My husband was in the priest's chamber up there. I heard a noise and came back and found him. He must have fallen down the stairs.'

'I see. Well, the ambulance will be here in a few minutes. You'd better get some things for him.'

'I shall go with him, of course.' She started up.

'If you please,' Reggie said gravely. She was gone. He stood up and peered round the church and after a moment moved to the newel stair. It was a short and narrow spiral. He frowned at it, looked up to the door of the chamber above, and slowly, examining each stair, climbed, and entered the chamber, a dark place with a black old table and chair and chest. The chest, which had books in it, stood open. On the table a book lay open, too. 'Well, well,' Reggie murmured, and wandered about the room. He came back to the door and knelt on the threshold and looked along the edges of that and the newel stair, then ran down and pored over the chancel floor. 'Oh, my hat!' he moaned. He turned away and was walking down the nave when Sam put his head in.

'Ambulance just coming along the road, sir.'

'Good. Tell Mrs Waring.'

Sam vanished and Reggie walked on. Opposite the south door by which they had entered was another. He tried it and it opened. He stepped out upon a path which led by a stile in the churchyard wall to fields, and no creature but sheep could be seen in them. He sighed and turned back.

On the other side of the churchyard the ambulance drew up. The

Vicar's unconscious body was being placed in it when his wife came breathless.

'You may be more comfortable in my car, madam,' said Reggie.

'You are going to the hospital?'

'Oh, yes. Yes, I shall be wanted.'

She looked at him fiercely, defiant or desperate. 'I'll go with him in the ambulance,' she said, and turned to get in.

'Very well. By the way, did you happen to see anyone else about the church?'

She stopped with her foot on the step. She did not look round. 'I didn't,' she said in a moment. 'There was no one.'

'Thank you.' Reggie shut the door on her and waved the ambulance on. He contemplated his chauffeur gloomily, 'Did you, Sam?'

'What, sir, see anyone? Not me. Not a sign.'

'Oh, yes. Both doors banged,' Reggie murmured. 'Well, well. Let's get on. As quick as you like.'

While Sam turned the car he saw the face of a small boy appear and vanish at the corner of the vicarage hedge, the face of a boy doing what he should not, a troubled, reckless face.

The car shot away, but in a hundred yards was checked by the coming of another down the narrow lane, and each crawled to a point where they could pass. Reggie obstructed the passing by a head out of window. 'Dr Antony, I think. Fancy meeting you!'

'Mr Fortune!' Dr Antony stopped his car. His face showed no kind of pleasure at the meeting. 'I didn't know you were here.'

'No. No. I gathered that.'

'Have you been to the vicarage?'

'Oh, no. Only to the church.'

'I'm told the Vicar has had an accident?'

'Yes. That is so. Who told you?'

'I just heard of it – I heard of it in the village. Is it serious?'

'Considerably smashed, yes. I've sent him to Laxbury hospital.'

'How terrible for Mrs Waring!'

'Yes. Yes. Not very nice for him.'

'Dear me, no, poor fellow. But what has happened?'

'Oh, weren't you told that? A fall. Good-bye.'

Some hours afterwards Reggie wandered into the Chief Constable's office and sank wearily into its one easy chair. 'Well, well!'

he moaned. 'Todgers's can do it when it chooses. And you do, you really do. I wanted a reaction to the discovery of the poison and I've got it. Could there be weak tea and bread and butter? Quite a plain tea. The mind is much confused.'

'Of course, of course.' The Chief Constable ordered it. 'How is he?'

'As well as a man can be with concussion and a dislocated shoulder and two ribs and a leg broken. Nothing else happened to him.'

The Chief Constable considered that it was enough.

'Yes, Yes. If not as much as intended,' Reggie murmured. And a policeman came with the tea and interrupted the Chief Constable's exclamation.

'Good God! Do you mean – do you mean he was assaulted?'

'Speakin' legally, no,' Reggie mumbled through bread and butter. 'Speakin' morally, yes.'

'Has he spoken?'

'Yes, I thought so. The house surgeon didn't. I thought he said he fell.'

'Well then – '

'Oh, yes, he probably believes it. And anyway, it's true. All the injuries were caused by a fall from the priest's chamber to the chancel. Do you know his church? Say twenty feet plus.' Reggie looked plaintively at the Chief Constable. 'The stair didn't break his fall. So he did fairly well.'

'Is he going to recover?'

'A good chance, yes.'

'Thank God.'

'I wonder. Yes, I suppose we ought to. It won't solve his problem, poor beggar. That's our little job, Major. And very confusin' to the simple mind.'

'He's not been murdered, anyway,' the Chief Constable said.

'Not yet, no. Nor was Mrs Lynton.'

'You put the two cases together?'

'Oh, yes. Yes. And it makes a complex mess.'

'But look here, Mr Fortune, as soon as Waring's better he can tell us all about it.'

'My only aunt!' Reggie was shrill. 'He don't know. That's the one certain factor. He don't know enough.'

'I don't follow,' the Chief Constable complained. 'You make it so involved.'

'Me! Oh, my hat! Not me. It's a nightmare of involutions. I'm strugglin' to keep touch with myself. Take this little bit. Waring is found smashed on his chancel floor with wife in attendance. Her statement – she heard a crash and ran in and found him; he had been up in the priest's chamber; she saw no one about the church. Quite plausible. But for the observed facts. When we left the door open, another door banged. When I went to the priest's chamber, I found he had left the book chest open and a book open on the table. I found also that the newel stair had recently been moved some way from the chamber door and moved back again: which would require two people or one hefty man. The inference is that while Waring was reading the stair was moved, that Waring had some sudden reason for coming away from his books and as the stair wasn't there fell smash, after which the stair was put back and someone went off, leaving the second door open.'

'My God! That means it was attempted murder and his wife was in it.'

'Yes. That is the obvious hypothesis. Yes. She was certainly lying. She knew there was someone else there. She was hit hard when I suggested it. Strong, determined woman. But I don't think she moved the stair by herself. I don't think she could. Say someone else moved the stair, then someone gave Waring a sudden call – and you account for the facts.'

'I see what you mean,' the Chief Constable nodded. 'Ivor Gould moved the stair and she called him down. What a devilish trick!'

'Well, our Mr Gould is strongly indicated. There's some further evidence. We had reason to believe Dr Antony was anxious about Mr Gould. Takin' it he went off and warned Gould there was trouble about the grapes, as intended, immediate activity of our Mr Gould is the reaction.'

'Guesswork though, isn't it?'

'Not wholly, no. Before I got away from Morton, Dr Antony drove up. He'd heard the Vicar had had an accident. Heard very quick, didn't he? He said he'd been told in the village. I don't think the village knew.'

'Antony in it, too!' the Chief Constable growled. 'It is a foul case.'

'Very uncomfortable, yes. We're just blunderin' about among 'em and they don't know what they're at. Feel almost wholly inadequate, don't you? Everybody else is all wrong and you're the only one sane. A state of feelin' very bad for the mind.'

'What on earth are we to do, Mr Fortune?'

'Well, you were goin' to have a talk with our Mr Gould in the morning. I should. Mrs Waring can wait.' Reggie stood up with difficulty. 'Other possible factors. You might have a man sniff round Morton in case anyone saw anyone. I want a map – a large map.' He yawned. 'Oh, Peter! I want my dinner,' he moaned, and wandered out.

In those benign moments when he likes to talk about himself he will claim as his chief intellectual virtues that he keeps an open mind and that he is naturally careful, and these from time to time make up for his besetting weakness, a lack of imagination. The virtues and the defect he points out were well displayed in this case. A useful imagination would have shown him the dominant force in it at an early stage – when Pamela sat on his bedroom rug – whereas he had to work painfully from one thing to another with no guidance but the sensation of being caught in a muddle of emotions.

That sensation brought him pensive and dreamy and a little late to dinner. Pamela gave him one quick glance and began to chatter; the Bishop talked earnestly of trifles. Reggie's attention was not required. When Pamela was gone, the Bishop's small-talk was cut off as by a tap. 'This is a terrible thing which has happened to poor Waring, Reginald. I heard just before I dressed. They tell me you know all about it.'

'Oh, my hat!' Reggie moaned. 'I went out to Morton to look round things. I found him smashed. I picked him up and I've been tryin' to put him together again. Speakin' physically, I think I've done it. That's all I know.'

'I understand he fell from the priest's chamber to the chancel.'

'Yes. So do I.'

'A dreadful accident.' The Bishop in a majestic way exhibited curiosity. Reggie did not respond. 'I cannot but think it a strange thing it should have happened just now.'

'You'd better not think,' said Reggie.

The Bishop recovered from shock. 'My dear Reginald, I value your discretion – '

The return of Pamela interrupted him. 'Bill, Mr Lynton has rung up. He says they've just heard of Mr Waring's accident – '

'Oh. You know, do you?' Reggie murmured.

'Yes, of course, dear. He's been to the vicarage to inquire and heard Mrs Waring was in Laxbury. He wanted to know if we knew where.'

The Bishop shook his head, declining to know anything of such a woman. 'I really couldn't say, my dear.'

'You see, Mr Lynton found the little boy alone and rather sorrowful and wanted to take him to their house if Mrs Waring didn't mind.'

'I really couldn't advise,' said the Bishop primly.

Reggie had made a little sound. Pamela turned to him, but he was looking at neither of them. His lips were parted in a small smile, his eyes bright and eager as though he had seen something which he wanted. 'What do you think, Reggie?' Pamela said.

'The little boy. Oh, yes. Very nice of Mr Lynton. The little boy has been overlooked, hasn't he?'

'Do you think the Lyntons might have him, dear?' said Pamela.

'Eh?' Reggie gazed at her as if she had just occurred. 'Oh, you know 'em. I don't.'

'They'll be sweet to him, of course. Mrs Lynton's a dear with children.'

'Well, well.' Reggie smiled at her. 'If she satisfies you, she won't hurt him. Make it so.' But when Pamela had gone, the smile vanished and his round face was set in plaintive perplexity. He gazed with the fascination of fear at the Bishop offering port. 'Oh, no. No. I want to go to bed.'

The Bishop was surprised but indulgent. He always likes his guests to go to bed. 'I'm afraid you have had a trying day, Reginald.'

Reggie moaned and made haste away. But before he got into bed he spent some time over a map of the parish of Morton, six inches to the mile.

Still pathetic and puzzled, like a child in a strange and terrible world, he presented himself next morning to the Chief Constable.

'Here we are again. Same like the clown says. He also says how are you tomorrow. And very sensible of him. That is the main question.'

The Chief Constable was too earnest to listen. 'It's opening out, Mr Fortune. I sent two men out to Morton last night as you said and they've got something. Gould was seen there – came across the fields from his house – went off another way in a deuce of a hurry: seemed to be going to Laxton – that's where Antony lives. So you may say we have Gould. You were right.'

'Oh, yes. Yes.' Reggie sighed. 'Quite clear. Very gratifyin'. Neither walk bringin' him naturally by the stile in the north wall of the churchyard and the north door.'

'I really couldn't say. I – '

'I can. Always wise to get up your facts. But generally disheartenin'.'

'Very likely he dodged round to hide.'

'It could be. Yes. Your fellows heard of no one else?'

'Mrs Waring was about, of course. Not actually seen with Gould.'

'And her little boy?' Reggie murmured.

'Why, the child wouldn't be noticed. Good God, you don't think he was in it?'

'My dear chap!' Reggie sighed. 'How old is he? Seven or eight. Of course, he wouldn't be noticed.' He sat up. 'Who is that, Major?'

It was someone whistling a song from the *Mikado*: 'The criminal cried as he dropped him down – ' the song which Mrs Waring's little boy had sung in the vicarage garden.

The Chief Constable frowned disciplinary wrath at whistling in his office. 'May be that fellow Gould. I wrote him to come at ten. We'll have him in, eh?'

Mr Gould was brought, a loose-build, big man, with a florid face which looked ample resources of will and a manner of assured insolence. ''Morning, Major. What's doing?'

'Sit down,' the Chief Constable grunted. 'This is Mr Fortune of the Criminal Investigation Department.'

'How d'ye do?' Gould nodded. 'By the way, how's old Waring, Major?'

'Haven't you seen his wife to-day?' the Chief Constable snapped. 'We'll take one thing at a time, please. A month ago Mrs Lynton fell ill after eating some grapes brought to her by Mrs Waring which Mrs Waring received from you. Those grapes have been analyzed and found to contain poison. I want to know if you care to give any explanation.'

'No. I don't care to. Because I can't. If there was any poison in the grapes which came from my place, take it from me, I didn't put it there.' Gould laughed. 'Rum idea, what? Poison inside grapes! Is somebody telling the tale?'

'I found poison there,' said Reggie. 'The woman might have died. Any idea who poisoned her, Mr Gould?'

'Search me. What was the poison?'

'Does that matter to you?' Reggie murmured.

Gould's eyes flickered. 'No. I thought you wanted to talk it over.'

'I want information. About a crime. You're not bein' helpful.'

'What the devil do you expect me to say? The grapes passed through plenty of hands after they left my place.'

'Oh! You put it on Mrs Waring?'

'You be damned. I never said so.'

'No. You didn't say it,' Reggie murmured.

'I didn't mean it, either. There's servants, God knows who. The old girl may have poisoned herself.'

'You think so? Why?'

'Don't try and trick me. There's nothing doing.'

'The tricks aren't this side of the table, Gould,' the Chief Constable said sharply. 'You're doing yourself no good.'

'Well, well, let's get on,' Reggie sighed. 'Mr Gould, is this the first time you've heard the grapes were poisoned?'

Gould took time to consider that. Then he asked, 'What do you mean?'

'Don't you remember talking to Dr Antony yesterday?'

But Gould was ready for that. He went on fluent and loud. 'Oh, you've got at him, have you? You might just as well go straight. You won't catch me. I've nothing to hide. Antony told me there was some tomfool suspicion of the grapes. That showed me I had to get things clear with Mrs Waring. So I went over. I saw her and her husband going into the church. That didn't suit me. I waited about till she came out. She said she couldn't talk to me, her husband was up in the room over the chancel and might be down any moment. I said I'd have a look, buzzed into the church, and moved the stair so he couldn't get down and told her he was all right. Then I had it out with her – '

'Arranged what you were to say, you mean,' the Chief Constable growled.

'Arrange nothing. Ask her. She got the wind up. While we were talking, there was a crash in the church and we went in and found old Waring on the floor. Silly ass hadn't noticed the stair was gone and taken a toss.'

'That's what you wanted, eh?' the Chief Constable said. 'You fixed it so he should break his neck.'

'Go to hell! He didn't. And if he wasn't a ruddy ass he wouldn't have been hurt at all. I put the stair back and went off and told Antony he was wanted for an accident to the Vicar. There you are, Major.' Gould grinned. 'That's the lot.'

'Is it?' The Chief Constable scowled at him. 'I warn you, you'll probably hear more of it.'

'That be damned! You can't touch me.'

'You think not?' Reggie murmured. 'I wonder.'

Gould's pale eyes turned on him a moment. 'Going to try?'

'Good-bye, Mr Gould,' said Reggie. 'You're finished.' The Chief Constable pointed to the door and with a laugh and a swagger Gould went out.

'There's a dirty dog,' said the Chief Constable.

'Oh, yes. Absolutely. I should say he was tellin' the truth, you know.'

'I daresay he was. That's the devil of it.'

Reggie smiled. 'Yes. I feel that. Yes.'

'He wants hanging.'

'Kicking,' Reggie corrected. 'Good and hard.'

The Chief Constable was in a measure comforted. 'I'll attend to that, believe me,' he said with relish. 'Things can be made very nasty for him socially. I'll pass the good word along.'

'Very gratifyin'! Yes, I should say he won't wait for it. He's funkin' like sin, you know. Quite a yellow man.' Reggie stood up.

'Skunk!' said the Chief Constable. 'But look here, Mr Fortune, we're not out of the wood. He's put the poison on Mrs Waring. The next thing is, we'll have to get her story.'

'Not now,' Reggie said. 'I left her sitting with her husband.'

'Shaken up, is she? Well, she's got herself in a nice mess – and all for that swine, Gould.'

'Rather shattered, yes.'

'Well, when you've seen her again – '

'Oh, yes. I'll see her again.' Reggie drifted out. But he did not go to see Mrs Waring. He ate a slow and pensive lunch and directed his car to Morton House.

He found it among shrubberies, a plain Victorian place in grey brick. He found Mr Lynton also prim, a little bearded man with gold spectacles, shy but anxious to be civil and unable to conceal curiosity.

'Mr Fortune? Am I right, sir, you are the surgeon who was so kind to poor Waring? All his friends will be very grateful to you. I am so sorry my wife can't see you at the moment. She is lying down. I have to insist on her lying down for two hours every afternoon. Perhaps you have heard, she has been seriously ill?'

Reggie was so sorry. He mustn't disturb Mrs Lynton. Quite unnecessary. He'd come over to see the Warings' little boy. Lynton said it was very kind – hoped Mrs Waring wasn't worrying – Michael was perfectly well and happy – a dear child – they were so glad to have him.

'How nice of you,' Reggie murmured. 'Where is he?'

'He's in my den, you know. I call it my den. A sort of workshop I have in the grounds. Michael loves to play with my tools. There's nothing to hurt him and he's a very good, careful boy. But I'll send for him.'

'Don't bother. I'll go out.'

'Oh, really, if you don't mind – but hadn't I better – just as you like, of course – '

Reggie made plain that he was going.

'It's rather untidy, I'm afraid.' Lynton tripped along at his side. It was a wooden hut in one of the shrubberies, with a carpenter's bench and racks of little tools and many incomplete masterpieces of fretwork. On the floor sat a small boy gloating over a box of fireworks.

'Michael, here's a gentleman to see you. It's Mr Fortune, the doctor who's looking after your father,' said Lynton. 'Isn't that kind of him, Michael?'

'Thanks very much,' said Reggie sharply. 'Now, may I have a talk with him?'

'Oh, certainly.' Lynton backed away. 'By all means, Mr Fortune. Well, I'll just leave you. You'll stay to tea, won't you? My wife will so want to see you.' He fled.

The small boy was on his feet staring at Reggie with solemn eyes. 'You're ve man who came in ve big car,' he stated.

'You're the boy who sang the song,' Reggie said in equal solemnity; and he whistled, "With a fearful, frightful, frantic frown – " 'Where did you learn that?'

'Mr Gould,' the small boy muttered.

'Like him?'

The boy shook his head. 'Mum doesn't like me to sing it.'

'Well, well. Don't bother about Mr Gould.'

'I didn't mean to sing it ven. I didn't know. I'm never going to sing it any more. Is Dad going to be all wight, please?'

'We're making him all right again.'

'Oo.' The boy's eyes confessed tears. 'Does it hurt him much?'

'Like being ill, you know.'

'I do hate Mr Gould. Mum always did hate him.'

'Oh, yes. Why was that?'

'He was always vere,' said the small boy vehemently. 'We didn't want him.'

'Don't worry. No more Mr Gould. Is it all right here?'

'Mrs Lynton's vewy nice,' the boy said with care. 'Awfully nice. I like being home best.'

'Want to go home now?'

'I want to see my wabbits.' The boy looked wistful.

'Right. Run off now. I'll talk to Mrs Lynton.'

'Could I weally go?'

'Just nip off through the shrubbery, so they don't see. I'll make it all right. You come back to tea.'

Reggie watched him vanish in the bushes, turned back and bent for some time over the box of fireworks. Then he walked slowly back to the house.

At the door he was met by Mrs Lynton, a frail woman, flushed and breathless, with anxious eyes. 'Mr Fortune! But how very good of you,' she panted. 'George should have told me at once. I did so want to see you. Have you heard anything of poor Mrs Waring?'

'She's with her husband.'

'Oh, really, is she? We couldn't hear where she was. I'm so glad. I suppose one shouldn't say that, but it's so difficult. Do come in. Have you had your talk with Michael?'

'Oh, yes. In the hut. Nice place for him. So kind of you to get him fireworks.'

'Poor child, for Guy Fawkes' Day, you know. I wanted – Oh, my God!'

A blaze of flames broke from the hut: it was filled with a glare and dense smoke enveloped it. She ran forward crying, 'Michael! Michael!'

Reggie followed at leisure.

She did not stop or falter, she rushed into the fire. Then Reggie ran after her.

He caught her as she reeled, groping through fume and flame, and swung her out to clear air again. 'Don't – ' she gasped. 'Let me go – Michael – find him.'

'Michael's not there. Michael's all right. He's just run off to the vicarage. It's only your fireworks blown up.'

Then she fainted.

Her husband arrived saying wild words.

Reggie picked her up. 'Don't worry. She's rather burnt her hands. That's all.'

'Oh, thank God, thank God!' the little man gurgled.

'Yes. I think so,' Reggie said gravely, and moved away with her.

'She's so fond of Michael, you know,' the little man explained.

'She's proved that. Yes.' Reggie carried her to her room and she began to come to herself. 'Well, now. I'd better dress these burns. Have you got a medicine chest?'

'Certainly, yes, a medicine cupboard. You're very kind.'

Reggie was taken to it. He found many shelves, an array of grandmother's remedies. 'Well, well,' he mumbled. 'Some good old drugs here.'

'Yes, indeed. My family used to give all the parish medicine, I believe.'

Reggie was moving some of the bottles. 'Takin' a chance, what? Still a useful method.' He surveyed the little man with a benign smile. 'However – among the genuine antiques here's some modern croton oil. Now, if you just let me see to Mrs Lynton, I think I can make her comfortable.'

He was left alone with her; he dressed hands and arms and sat down by the bedside.

'It was rather fine, goin' into the fire for that boy,' he said gently.

'It didn't do any good. I wasn't wanted.'

'Oh, yes, it did. Quite a lot. Showed the sort of woman you are. Worth finding out, Mrs Lynton. I don't believe you knew yourself.'

'I've always loved Michael,' she cried.

'I can believe that.'

'I haven't one of my own, you see.'

'I know. That was the trouble, wasn't it? You'll love him better after this.'

'What do you mean?'

'Rather hard lovin' what isn't yours sometimes. I'm goin' to tell you what nobody knows but me and you. It hurt you Mrs Waring should have Michael and you no child at all. You wanted to hurt her. You believed she was in love with Ivor Gould. It came into your head, if you could make it look like he and she had tried to poison you, she'd be ruined. You had a cupboard full of old wives' medicines. There was wine of antimony, wasn't there – not very much perhaps, but enough to make you ill? When Mrs Waring sent you a bunch of Gould's grapes you put that stuff into them and you were ill. But the doctor didn't get the right suspicions. So you sent the Bishop an anonymous letter about Gould and Mrs Waring. And still nothing happened. Then yesterday you went to Morton to watch. Perhaps you'd been before. You came to the church by the north door. You saw Gould and Mrs Waring talking; you knew the vicar was in the priest's chamber; you called to him so he should come and see them and he fell right down and was nearly killed.'

'I didn't mean that. I didn't mean that,' she sobbed.

'No. I don't think you really meant anything you've done. It was not loving Michael the right way. That's why I'm not going to say anything to anyone but you. This is the end of it. You begin again.'

She lay sobbing. 'Oh, I'm wicked. I'm a wicked woman.'

'No. You're a better woman than you thought you were. That's what's hurting you now. It's going to be all right.'

'How can you say that – you? How can you trust me?'

'Because I know a little,' said Reggie. 'Goodbye.'

An hour or two later he appeared before the Chief Constable dreamy and benign. 'Well, Major, the Vicar's doin' nicely, thank you, and Mrs Vicar's dozin' by the bedside.'

'Is she? When are we going to ask her about the poison?'

'We aren't. Because she don't know anything.'

'Are you satisfied of that?'

'Oh, yes. Absolutely. I satisfied her, too.' Reggie smiled. 'She believes it was Gould. She's had a tryin' time. Not a nice man, our Mr Gould. Beast o' prey.'

'I know he is. But you don't believe he doctored the grapes. Who did?'

'Speakin' from experience' – Reggie eyed him solemnly – 'I should say you'll never know. And they all lived happy ever after. Eliminatin' Gould. But a very interestin' case. Glad you gave it me.'

'Well – if you're content with it – '

'My dear chap! Oh, my dear chap! Very neat, I think.' Reggie made an affectionate farewell.

Pamela came into her drawing room to find him curled up eating muffins. 'My dear child!' She smiled upon him. 'How nice you look!'

'I am,' Reggie mumbled.

'As pleased with yourself as a cat. I know you've settled things when you're that way.' She rumpled his hair. 'Who was it, Reggie?'

'Exit our Mr Gould. Peace reigns in Morton.'

'But who was it?' Reggie did not answer. 'I always thought it was Mrs Lynton, you know.'

Reggie opened round eyes. 'Well, well,' he murmured. 'Then thank Heaven you didn't say so.'

MISS HINCH

H. S. Harrison

IN going from a given point on 126th Street to the subway station
at 125th, it is not usual to begin by circling the block of 127th
Street, especially in sleet, darkness, and deadly cold. When two
people pursue such a course at the same time, moving unobtrusively
on opposite sides of the street, in the nature of things the coincidence
is likely to attract the attention of one or the other of them.

In the bright light of the entrance to the tube they came almost
face to face, and the clergyman took a good look at her. Certainly
she was a decent-looking old body, if any woman was: white-
haired, wrinkled, spectacled, and stooped. A poor but thoroughly
respectable domestic servant of the better class she looked, in her
old black hat, wispy veil, and grey shawl; and her brief glance at
the reverend gentleman was precisely what it should have been from
her to him – open deference itself. Nevertheless, he, going more
slowly down the draughty steps, continued to study her from behind
with a singular intentness.

An express was just thundering in, which the clergyman, handi-
capped as he was by his clubfoot and stout cane, was barely in time
to catch. He entered the same car with the woman, and chanced to
take a seat directly across from her. It must have been then after
twelve o'clock, and the wildness of the weather was discouraging
to travel. The car was almost deserted. Even in this underground
retreat the bitter breath of the night blew and bit, and the old woman
shivered under her shawl. At last, her teeth chattering, she got up
in an apologetic sort of way, and moved toward the better protected
rear of the car, feeling the empty seats as she went, in a palpable
search for hot pipes. The clergyman's eyes followed her candidly,

and watched her sink down, presently, into a seat on his own side of the car. A young couple sat between them now; he could no longer see the woman, beyond occasional glimpses of her black knees and her ancient bonnet, skewered on with a long steel hatpin.

Nothing could have seemed more natural or more trivial than this change of seats on the part of a thin-blooded and half-frozen passenger. But it happened to be a time of mutual doubt and suspicion, of alert suspicions and hair-trigger watchfulness, when men looked askance into every strange face and the smallest incidents were likely to take on an hysterical importance. Through days of fruitless searching for a fugitive outlaw of extraordinary gifts, the nerve of the city had been slowly strained to the breaking-point. All jumped, now, when anybody cried 'Boo!' and the hue and cry went up falsely twenty times a day.

The clergyman pondered; mechanically he turned up his coat collar and fell to stamping his icy feet. He was an Episcopal clergyman, by his garb – rather short, very full-bodied, not to say fat, bearded and somewhat puffy-faced, with heavy cheeks cut by deep creases. Well lined against the cold though he was, however, he, too, began to suffer visibly, and presently was forced to retreat in his turn, seeking out a new place where the heating apparatus gave a better account of itself. He found one two seats beyond the old serving-woman, limped into it, and soon relapsed into his own thoughts.

The young couple, now half the car-length away, were thoroughly absorbed in each other's society. The fifth traveller, a withered old gentleman sitting next to the middle door across the aisle, napped fitfully upon his cane. The woman in the hat and shawl sat in a sad kind of silence; and the train hurled itself roaringly through the tube. After a time, she glanced timidly at the meditating clergyman, and her look fell swiftly from his face to the discarded 'ten-o'clock extra' lying by his side. She removed her dim gaze and let it travel casually about the car; but before long it returned again, pointedly, to the newspaper. Then, with some obvious hesitation, she bent forward and said:

'Excuse me, Father, but would you please let me look at your paper a minute, sir?'

The clergyman came out of his reverie instantly, and looked up with almost an eager smile.

'Certainly. Keep it if you like: I am quite through with it. But,' he said, in a pleasant deep voice, 'I am an Episcopal minister, not a priest.'

'Oh, sir – I beg your pardon! I thought – '

He dismissed the apology with a smile and a good-natured hand.

The woman opened the paper with decent cotton-gloved fingers. The garish head-lines told the story at a glance: 'Earth Opened and Swallowed Miss Hinch – Headquarters Virtually Abandons Case – Even Jessie Dark' – so the bold capitals ran on – 'Seems Stumped.' Below the spread was a luridly written but flimsy narrative, 'By Jessie Dark,' which at once confirmed the odd implication of the caption. 'Jessie Dark,' it appeared, was one of those most extraordinary of the products of yellow journalism, a woman 'crime expert,' now in action. More than this, she was a 'crime expert' to be taken seriously, it seemed – no mere office-desk sleuth, but an actual performer with, unexpectedly enough, a somewhat formidable list of notches on her gun. So much, at least, was to be gathered from her paper's display of 'Jessie Dark's Triumphs':

March 2, 1901. Caught Julia Victorian, *alias* Gregory, the brains of the 'Healey Ring' kidnappers.

October 7–29, 1903. Found Mrs Trotwood and secured the letter that convicted her of the murder of her lover, Ellis E. Swan.

December 17, 1903. Ran down Charles Bartsch in a Newark laundry and trapped a confession from him.

July 4, 1904. Caught Mary Calloran and recovered the Stratford jewels.

And so on – nine 'triumphs' in all; and nearly every one of them, as the least observant reader could hardly fail to notice, involved the capture of a woman.

Nevertheless, it could not be pretended that the 'snappy' paragraphs in this evening's extra seemed to foreshadow a new or tenth triumph for Jessie Dark at any early date; and the old serving-woman in the car presently laid down the sheet with an irrepressible sigh.

The clergyman glanced toward her kindly. The sigh was so audible that it seemed to be almost an invitation; besides, public interest in the great case was a freemasonry that made conversation between total strangers the rule wherever two or three were gathered together.

'You were reading about this strange mystery, perhaps?'

The woman, with a sharp intake of breath, answered: 'Yes, sir. Oh, sir, it seems as if I couldn't think of anything else.'

'Ah?' he said, without surprise. 'It certainly appears to be a remarkable affair.'

Remarkable indeed the affair seemed. In a tiny little room within ten steps of Broadway, at half past nine o'clock on a fine evening, Miss Hinch had killed John Catherwood with the light sword she used in her famous representation of the Father of his Country. Catherwood, it was known, had come to tell of his approaching marriage; and ten thousand amateur detectives, athirst for rewards, had required no further 'motive' of a creature so notorious for fierce jealousy. So far the tragedy was commonplace enough, and even vulgar. What had redeemed it to romance from this point on was the extraordinary faculty of the woman, which had made her celebrated while she was still in her teens. Coarse, violent, utterly unmoral she might be, but she happened also to be the most astonishing impersonator of her time. Her brilliant 'act' consisted of a series of character changes, many of them done in full view of the audience with the assistance only of a small table of properties half concealed under a net. Some of these transformations were so amazing as to be beyond belief, even after one had sat and watched them. Not her appearance only, but voice, speech, manner, carriage, all shifted incredibly to fit the new part; so that the woman appeared to have no permanent form or fashion of her own, but to be only so much plastic human material out of which her cunning could mould at will man, woman or child, great lady of the Louisan court or Tammany statesman with the modernest of East Side modernisms upon his lip.

With this strange skill, hitherto used only to enthral huge audiences and wring extortionate contracts from managers, the woman known as Miss Hinch – she appeared to be without a first name – was now fighting for her life somewhere against the police of the world. Without artifice, she was a tall, thin-chested young woman with strongly marked features and considerable beauty of a bold sort. What she would look like at the present moment nobody could venture a guess. Having stabbed John Catherwood in her dressing-room at the Amphitheatre, she had put on her hat and coat, dropped two wigs and her make-up kit into a hand-bag, and walked out into Broadway. Within ten minutes the dead body of Catherwood was found and the chase begun. At the stage door, as she passed out, Miss Hinch had met an acquaintance, a young comedian named Dargis, and exchanged a word of greeting with him. That had been ten days ago. After Dargis, no one had seen her. The earth, indeed, seemed to have opened and swallowed her. Yet her natural features were almost as well known as a President's, and the newspapers of a continent were daily reprinting them in a thousand variations.

'A very remarkable case,' repeated the clergyman, rather absently; and his neighbour, the old woman, respectfully agreed that it was. After that she hesitated a moment, and then added with sudden bitterness:

'Oh, they'll never catch her, sir – never! She's too smart for 'em all, Miss Hinch is.'

Attracted by her tone, the stout divine inquired if she was particularly interested in the case.

'Yes, sir – I got reason to be. Jack Catherwood's mother and me was at school together, and great friends all our life long. Oh, sir,' she went on, as if in answer to his look of faint surprise, 'Jack was a fine gentleman, with manners and looks and all beyond his people. But he never grew away from his old mother – no, sir, never! And I don't believe ever a Sunday passed that he didn't go up and set the afternoon away with her, talking and laughing just like he was a little boy again. Maybe he done things he hadn't ought, as high-spirited lads will, but oh, sir, he was a good boy in his heart – a good boy. And it does seem too hard for him to die like that – and that hussy free to go her way, ruinin' and killin' – '

'My good woman,' said the clergyman presently, 'compose yourself. No matter how diabolical this woman's skill is, her sin will assuredly find her out.'

The woman dutifully lowered her handkerchief and tried to compose herself, as bidden.

'But oh, she's that clever – diabolical, just as ye say, sir. Through poor Jack we of course heard much gossip about her, and they do say that her best tricks was not done on the stage at all. They say, sir, that, sittin' around a table with her friends, she could begin and twist her face so strange and terrible that they would beg her to stop, and jump up and run from the table – frightened out of their lives, sir, grown-up people, by the terrible faces she could make. And let her only step behind her screen for a minute – for she kept her secrets well, Miss Hinch did – and she'd come walking out to you, and you could go right up to her in the full light and take her hand, and still you couldn't make yourself believe that it was her.'

'Yes,' said the clergyman. 'I have heard that she is remarkably clever – though, as a stranger in this part of the world, I never saw her act. I must say, it is all very interesting and strange.'

He turned his head and stared through the rear door of the car at the dark flying walls. At the same moment the woman turned her head and stared full at the clergyman. When he turned back, her gaze had gone off toward the front of the car, and he picked up the paper thoughtfully.

'I'm a visitor in the city, from Denver, Colorado,' he said presently, 'and knew little or nothing about the case until an evening or two ago, when I attended a meeting of gentlemen here. The men's club of St Matthias' Church – perhaps you know the place? Upon my word, they talked of nothing else. I confess they got me quite interested in their gossip. So to-night I bought this paper to see what this extraordinary woman detective it employs had to say about it. We don't have such things in the West, you know. But I must say I was disappointed, after all the talk about her.'

'Yes, sir, indeed, and no wonder, for she's told Mrs Catherwood herself that she's never made such a failure as this so far. It seemed like she could always catch women, up to this. It seemed like she knew in her own mind just what a woman would do, where she'd try to hide and all, and so she could find them time and time when the men detectives didn't know where to look. But oh, sir, she's never had to hunt for such a woman as Miss Hinch before!'

'No? I suppose not,' said the clergyman. 'Her story here in the paper certainly seems to me very poor.'

'*Story*, sir! Bless my soul!' suddenly exploded the old gentleman across the aisle, to the surprise of both. 'You don't suppose the clever little woman is going to show her hand in those stories, with Miss Hinch in the city and reading every line of them! In the city, sir – such is my positive belief!'

The approach to his station, it seemed, had roused him from his nap just in time to overhear the episcopate criticism. Now he answered the looks of the old woman and the clergyman with an elderly cackle.

'Excuse my intrusion, I'm sure! But I can't sit silent and hear anybody run down Jessie Dark – Miss Matthewson in private life, as perhaps you don't know. No, sir! Why, there's a man at my boarding-place – astonishing young fellow named Hardy, Tom Hardy – who's known her for *years*! As to those stories, sir, I can assure you that she puts in there *exactly the opposite to what she really thinks*!'

'You don't tell me!' said the clergyman encouragingly.

'Yes, sir! Oh, she plays the game – yes, yes! She has her private ideas, her clues, her schemes. The woman doesn't live who is clever enough to hoodwink Jessie Dark. I look for developments any day – any day, sir!'

A new voice joined in. The young couple down the car, their attention caught by the old man's pervasive tones, had been frankly listening: and it was illustrative of the public mind at the moment that, as they now rose for their station, the young fellow felt perfectly free to offer his contribution:

'Tremendously dramatic situation, isn't it, gentlemen? Those two clever women pitted against each other in a life-and-death struggle, fighting it out silently in the underground somewhere – keen professional pride on one side and the fear of the electric chair on the other. Good heavens there's – '

'Oh, yes! Oh, yes!' exclaimed the old gentleman rather testily. 'But, my dear sir, it's not *professional pride* that makes Jessie Dark so resolute to win. It's *sex jealousy*, if you follow me – no offence, madam! Yes, sir! Women never have the slightest respect for each other's abilities – not the slightest. No mercy for each other, either! I tell you, Jessie Dark'd be ashamed to be beaten by another woman. Read her stories between the lines, sir – as I do. Invincible determination – no weakening – no mercy! You catch my point, sir?'

'It sounds reasonable,' answered the Colorado clergyman, with his courteous smile. 'All women, we are told, are natural rivals at heart – '

'Oh, I'm for Jessie Dark every time!' the young fellow broke in eagerly, 'especially since the police have practically laid down. But – '

'Why, she's told my young friend Hardy,' the old gentleman rode him down, 'that she'll find Hinch if it takes her lifetime! Knows a thing or two about actresses, she says. Says the world isn't big enough for the creature to hide from her. Well! What do you think of that?'

'Tell what we were just talking about, George,' said the young wife, looking at her husband with grossly admiring eyes.

'But, oh, sir,' began the old woman timidly, 'Jack Catherwood's been dead ten days now, and – and – '

'Woman got on my car at nine o'clock to-night,' interjected the subway guard, who, having flung open the doors for the station, was listening excitedly to the symposium; 'wore a brown veil and goggles. I'd 'a' bet every dollar I had – '

'Ten days, madam! And what is that, pray?' exploded the old gentleman, rising triumphantly. 'A lifetime, if necessary! Oh, never fear! Mrs Victorian was considered pretty clever, eh? Wasn't she? Remember what Jessie Dark did for her? Nan Parmalee, too – though the police did their best to steal her credit. She'll do just as much for Miss Hinch – you may take it from me!'

'But how's she going to make the capture, gentlemen?' cried the young fellow, getting his chance at last. 'That's the point my wife and I've been discussing. Assuming that she succeeds in spotting this woman-devil, what will she do? Now – '

'Do! Yell for the police!' burst from the old gentleman at the door.

'And have Miss Hinch shoot her – and then herself, too? Wouldn't she have to – '

'Grand Central!' cried the guard for the second time; and the young fellow broke off reluctantly to find his bride towing him strongly toward the door.

'Hope she nabs her soon, anyway,' he called back to the clergyman over his shoulder. 'The thing's getting on my nerves. One of these kindergarten reward-chasers followed my wife for five blocks the other day, just because she's got a pointed chin, and I don't know what might have happened if I hadn't come along and – '

Doors rolled shut behind him, and the train flung itself on its way. Within the car a lengthy silence ensued. The clergyman stared thoughtfully at the floor, and the old woman fell back upon her borrowed paper. She appeared to be re-reading the observations of Jessie Dark with considerable care. Presently she lowered the paper and began a quiet search for something under the folds of her shawl; and at length, her hands emerging empty, she broke the silence with a timid request:

'Oh, sir – have you a pencil you could lend me, please? I'd like to mark something in the piece to send to Mrs Catherwood. It's what she says here about the disguises, sir.'

The kindly divine felt in his pockets, and after some hunting produced a pencil – a white one with blue lead. She thanked him gratefully.

'How is Mrs Catherwood bearing all this strain and anxiety?' he asked suddenly. 'Have you seen her to-day?'

'Oh, yes, sir. I've been spending the evening with her since nine o'clock, and am just back from there now. Oh, she's very much broke up, sir.'

She looked at him hesitatingly. He stared straight in front of him, saying nothing, though conceivably he knew, in common with the rest of the reading world, that Jack Catherwood's mother lived, not on 126th Street, but on East Houston Street. Possibly he might have wondered if his silence had not been an error of judgment. Perhaps that misstatement had not been a slip, but something cleverer?

The woman went on with a certain eagerness: 'Oh, sir, I only hope and pray those gentlemen may be right, but it does look to Mrs Catherwood, and me too, that if Jessie Dark was going to catch her at all, she'd have done it before now. Look at those big, bold blue eyes she had, sir, with lashes an inch long, they say, and that terrible long chin of hers. They do say she can change the colour of her eyes, not for ever of course, but put a few of her drops into them and make them look entirely different for a time. But that chin, ye'd say – '

She broke off; for the clergyman, without preliminaries of any sort, had picked up his heavy stick and suddenly risen.

'Here we are at Fourteenth Street,' he said, nodding pleasantly. 'I must change here. Good night. Success to Jessie Dark, I say!'

He was watching the woman's faded face and he saw just that look of respectful surprise break into it that he had expected.

'Fourteenth Street! I'd no notion at all we'd come so far. It's where I get out too, sir, the express is not stopping at my station.'

'Ah?' said the clergyman, with the utmost dryness.

He led the way, limping and leaning on his stick. They emerged upon the chill and cheerless platform, not exactly together, yet still with some reference to their acquaintanceship on the car. But the clergyman, after stumping along a few steps, all at once realized that he was walking alone, and turned. The woman had halted. Over the intervening space their eyes met.

'Come,' said the man gently. 'Come, let us walk about a little to keep warm.'

'Oh, sir – it's too kind of you, sir,' said the woman, coming forward.

From other cars two or three blue-nosed people had got off to make the change; one or two more came straggling in from the street; but, scattered over the bleak concrete expanse, they detracted little from the isolation that seemed to surround the woman and the clergyman. Step for step, the odd pair made their way to the extreme northern end of the platform.

'By the way,' said the clergyman, halting abruptly, 'may I see that paper again for a moment?'

'Oh, yes, sir – of course,' said the woman, producing it from beneath her shawl. 'I thought you had finished with it, and I – '

He said that he wanted only to glance at it for a moment; but he fell to looking through it page by page, with considerable care. The woman looked at him several times. Finally she said hesitatingly:

'I thought, sir, I'd ask the ticket-chopper could he say how long before the next train. I'm very late as it is, sir, and I still must stop to get something to eat before I go to bed.'

'An excellent idea,' said the clergyman.

He explained that he, too, was already an hour behind time, and was spending the night with cousins in Newark, to boot. Side by side, they retraced their steps down the platform, questioned the chopper with scant results, and then, as by some tacit consent, started slowly back again. However, before they had gone very far, the woman all at once stopped short and, with a white face, leaned against the wall.

'Oh, sir, I'm afraid I'll just have to stop and get a bite somewhere before I go on. You'll think me foolish, sir, but I missed my supper entirely to-night, and there is quite a faint feeling coming over me.'

The clergyman looked at her with apparent concern. 'Do you know, my friend, you seem to anticipate all my own wants? Your mentioning something to eat just now reminded me that I myself was all but famishing.' He glanced at his watch, appearing to deliberate. 'Yes – it will not take long. Come, we will find a modest eating-place together.'

'Oh, sir,' she stammered, 'but – you wouldn't want to eat with a poor old woman like me, sir.'

'And why not? Are we not all equal in the sight of God?'

They ascended the stairs together, like any prosperous parson and his poor parishioner, and coming out into Fourteenth Street, started west. On the first block they came to a restaurant, a brilliantly lighted, tiled and polished place of the quick-lunch variety. But the woman timidly preferred not to stop here, saying that the glare of such places was very bad for her old eyes. The divine accepted the objection as valid, without argument. Two blocks farther on they found on a corner a quieter resort, an unpretentious little haven which yet boasted a 'Ladies' Entrance' down the side street.

They entered by the front door, and sat down at a table, facing each other. The woman read the menu through, and finally, after some embarrassed uncertainty, ordered poached eggs on toast. The clergyman ordered the same. The simple meal was soon despatched. Just as they were finishing it, the woman said apologetically:

'If you'll excuse me, sir – could I see the bill of fare a minute? I think I'd best take a little pot of tea to warm me up, if they do not charge too high.'

'I haven't the bill of fare,' said the clergyman.

They looked diligently for the cardboard strip, but it was nowhere to be seen. The waiter drew near.

'Yes, sir! I left it there on the table when I took the order.'

'I'm sure I can't imagine what's become of it,' repeated the clergy-man, rather insistently.

He looked hard at the woman, and found that she was looking hard at him. Both pairs of eyes fell instantly.

The waiter brought another bill of fare; the woman ordered tea; the waiter came back with it. The clergyman paid for both orders with a bill that looked hard-earned.

The tea proved to be very hot: it could not be drunk down at a gulp. The clergyman, watching the woman intently as she sipped, seemed to grow more and more restless. His fingers drummed the tablecloth: he could hardly sit still. All at once he said: 'What is that calling in the street? It sounds like newsboys.'

The woman put her old head on one side and listened. 'Yes, sir. There seems to be an extra out.'

'Upon my word,' he said, after a pause. 'I believe I'll go get one. Good gracious! Crime is a very interesting thing, to be sure!'

He rose slowly, took down his shovel-hat from the hanger near him, and, grasping his heavy stick, limped to the door. Leaving it open behind him, much to the annoyance of the proprietor in the cashier's cage, he stood a moment in the little vestibule, looking up and down the street. Then he took a few slow steps eastward, beckoning with his hand as he went, and so passed out of sight of the woman at the table.

The eating-place was on the corner, and outside the clergyman paused for half a breath. North, east, south, and west he looked, and nowhere he found what his flying glance sought. He turned the corner into the darker cross-street, and began to walk, at first slowly, continually looking about him. Presently his pace quickened, quick-ened so that he no longer even stayed to use his stout cane. In another moment he was all but running, his club-foot pounding the icy pavement heavily as he went. A newsboy thrust an extra under his very nose, and he did not even see it.

Far down the street, nearly two blocks away, a tall figure in a blue coat stood and stamped in the freezing sleet; and the hurrying divine sped straight toward him. But he did not get very near. For, as he passed the side entrance at the extreme rear of the restaurant, a departing guest dashed out so recklessly as to run full into him, stopping him dead.

Without looking at her, he knew who it was. In fact, he did not look at her at all, but turned his head hurriedly east and west, sweeping the dark street with a swift eye. But the old woman, having drawn back with a sharp exclamation as they collided, rushed breathlessly into apologies:

'Oh, sir – excuse me! A newsboy popped his head into the side door just after you went out, and I ran to him to get you the paper. But he got away too quick for me, sir, and so I – '

'Exactly,' said the clergyman in his quiet deep voice. 'That must have been the very boy I myself was after.'

On the other side, two men had just turned into the street, well muffled against the night, talking cheerfully as they trudged along. Now the clergyman looked full at the woman, and she saw that there was a smile on his face.

'As he seems to have eluded us both, suppose we return to the subway?'

'Yes, sir; it's full time I – '

'The sidewalk is so slippery,' he went on gently, 'perhaps you had better take my arm.'

Behind the pair in the dingy restaurant, the waiter came forward to shut the door, and lingered to discuss with the proprietor the sudden departure of his two patrons. However, the score had been paid with a liberal tip for service, so there was no especial complaint to make. After listening to some unfavourable comments on the ways of the clergy, the waiter returned to his table to set it in order.

On the floor in the carpeted aisle between tables lay a white piece of cardboard, which his familiar eye recognized as part of one of his own bills of fare, face downward. He stooped and picked it up. On the back of it was some scribbling, made with a blue lead-pencil.

The handwriting was very loose and irregular, as if the writer had had his eyes elsewhere while he wrote, and it was with some difficulty that the waiter deciphered his message:

Miss Hinch 14th St. subway Get police quick

The waiter carried this curious document to the proprietor, who read it over a number of times. He was a dull man, and had a dull man's suspiciousness of a practical joke. However, after a good deal of irresolute discussion, he put on his overcoat and went out for a policeman. He turned west, and half-way up the block met an elderly bluecoat sauntering east. The policeman looked at the scribbling, and dismissed it profanely as a wag's foolishness of the sort that was bothering the life out of him a dozen times a day. He walked along with the proprietor, and as they drew near to the latter's place of business, both became aware of footsteps thudding nearer up the cross-street from the south. As they looked up, two young policemen, accompanied by a man in a uniform like a street-car conductor's, swept around the corner and dashed straight into the restaurant.

The first policeman and the proprietor ran in after them, and found them staring about rather vacantly. One of the arms of the law demanded if any suspicious characters had been seen about the place, and the dull proprietor said no. The officers, looking rather flat, explained their errand. It seemed that a few moments before, the third man, who was a ticket-chopper at the subway station, had found a mysterious message lying on the floor by his box. Whence it had come, how long it had lain there, he had not the slightest idea. However, there it was. The policeman exhibited a crumpled white scrap torn from a newspaper, on which was scrawled in blue pencil:

Miss Hinch Miller's Restaurant Get police quick

The first policeman, who was both the oldest and the fattest of the three, produced the message on the bill of fare, so utterly at odds with this. The dull proprietor, now bethinking himself, mentioned the clergyman and the old woman who had taken poached eggs and tea together, called for a second bill of fare, and departed so unexpectedly by different doors. The ticket-chopper recalled that he had seen the same pair at his station: they had come up, he remembered, and questioned him about trains. The three policemen were momentarily puzzled by this testimony. But it was soon plain to them that if either the woman or the clergyman really had any information about Miss Hinch – a highly improbable supposition in itself – they would never have stopped with peppering the neighbourhood with silly little contradictory messages.

'They're a pair of old fools tryin' to have sport with the police, and I'd like to run them in for it,' growled the fattest of the officers; and this was the general verdict.

The little conference broke up. The dull proprietor returned to his cage, the waiter to his table; the subway man departed on the run for his chopping box; the three policemen passed out into the bitter night. They walked together, grumbling, and their feet, perhaps by some subconscious impulse, turned eastward toward the subway. And in the middle of the next block a man came running up to them.

'Officer, look what I found on the sidewalk a minute ago. Read that scribble!'

He held up a white slab which proved to be part of a bill of fare from Miller's Restaurant. On the back of it the three peering officers saw, almost illegibly scrawled in blue pencil:

Police! Miss Hinch 14th St. subw

The hand trailed off on the *w* as thought the writer had been suddenly interrupted. The fat policeman blasphemed and threatened arrests. But the second policeman, who was dark and wiry, raised his head from the bill of fare and said suddenly: 'Tim, I believe there's something in this.'

'There'd ought to be ten days on the Island in it for them,' growled fat Tim.

'Suppose, now,' said the other policeman, staring intently at nothing, 'the old woman was Miss Hinch herself, f'r instance, and the parson was shadowing her while pretendin' he never suspicioned her, and Miss Hinch not darin' to cut and run for it till she was sure she had a clean getaway. Well, now, Tim, what better could he do – '

'That's right!' exclaimed the third policeman. ''Specially when ye think that Hinch carries a gun, an'll use it, too! Why not have a look in at the subway station anyway, the three of us?'

The proposal carried the day. The three officers started for the subway, the citizen following. They walked at a good pace and without more talk; and both their speed and their silence had a subtle psychological reaction. As the minds of the four men turned inward upon the odd behaviour of the pair in Miller's Restaurant, the conviction that, after all, something important might be afoot grew and strengthened within each one of them. Unconsciously their pace quickened. It was the wiry policeman who first broke into an open run, but the three other men had been for twenty paces on the verge of it.

However, these consultations and vacillations had taken time. The stout clergyman and the poor old woman had five minutes' start on the officers of the law, and that, as it happened, was all that the occasion required. On Fourteenth Street, as they made their way arm in arm to the station, they were seen, and remembered, by a number of belated pedestrians. It was observed by more than one that the woman lagged as if she were tired, while the club-footed divine, supporting her on his arm, steadily kept her up to his own brisk gait.

So walking, the pair descended the subway steps, came out upon the bare platform again, and presently stood once more at the extreme uptown end of it, just where they had waited half an hour before. Nearby a careless porter had overturned a bucket of water, and a splotch of thin ice ran out and over the edge of the concrete. Two young men who were taking lively turns up and down distinctly heard the clergyman warn the woman to look out for this ice. Far away to the north was to be heard the faint roar of an approaching train.

The woman stood nearest the track, and the clergyman stood in front of her. In the vague light their looks met, and each was struck by the pallor of the other's face. In addition, the woman was breathing hard, and her hands and feet betrayed some nervousness. It was difficult now to ignore the too patent fact that for an hour they had been clinging desperately to each other, at all costs; but the clergyman made a creditable effort to do so. He talked ramblingly, in a voice sounding only a little unnatural, for the most part of the deplorable weather and his train to Newark, for which he was now so late. And all the time both of them were incessantly turning their heads toward the station entrances, as if expecting some arrival.

As he talked, the clergyman kept his hands unobtrusively busy. From the bottom edge of his black sack-coat he drew a pin, and stuck it deep into the ball of his middle finger. He took out his handkerchief to dust the hard sleet from his hat; and under his overcoat he pressed the handkerchief against his bleeding finger.

While making these small arrangements, he held the woman's eyes with his own, talking on; and, still holding them, he suddenly broke off his random talk and peered at her cheek with concern.

'My good woman, you've scratched your cheek somehow! Why, bless me, its bleeding quite badly.'

'Never mind – never mind,' said the woman, and swept her eyes hurriedly toward the entrance.

'But, good gracious, I must mind! The blood will fall on your shawl. If you will permit me – ah!'

Too quick for her, he leaned forward and, through the thin veil, swept her cheek hard with the handkerchief; removing it, he held it up so that she might see the blood for herself. But she did not glance at the handkerchief, and neither did he. His gaze was riveted upon her cheek, which looked smooth and clear where he had smudged the clever wrinkles away.

Down the steps and upon the platform pounded the feet of three flying policemen. But it was evident now that the express would thunder in just ahead of them. The clergyman, standing close in front of the woman, took a firmer grip on his heavy stick and a look of stern triumph came into his face.

'You're not so terribly clever, after all!'

The woman had sprung back from him with an irrepressible exclamation, and in that instant she was aware of the police.

However, her foot slipped upon the treacherous ice – or it may have tripped on the stout cane, when the clergyman suddenly shifted its position. And in the next breath the express train roared past.

By one of those curious chances which sometimes refute all experience, the body of the woman was not mangled or mutilated in the least. There was a deep blue bruise on the left temple, and apparently that was all; even the ancient hat remained on her head, skewered fast by the long pin. It was the clergyman who found the body huddled at the side of the dark track where the train had flung it – he who covered the still face and superintended the removal to the platform. Two eye-witnesses of the tragedy pointed out the ice on which the unfortunate woman had slipped, and described their horror as they saw her companion spring forward just too late to save her.

Not wishing to bring on a delirium of excitement among the

bystanders, two policemen drew the clergyman quietly aside and showed him the three mysterious messages. Much affected by the shocking end of his sleuthery as he was, he readily admitted having written them. He briefly recounted how the woman's strange movements on 126th Street had arrested his attention and how watching her closely on the car, he had finally detected that she wore a wig. Unfortunately, however, her suspicions had been aroused by his interest in her, and thereafter a long battle of wits had ensued between them – he trying to summon the police without her knowledge, she dogging him close to prevent that, and at the same time watching her chance to give him the slip. He rehearsed how, in the restaurant, when he had invented an excuse to leave her for an instant, she had made a bolt and narrowly missed getting away; and finally how, having brought her back to the subway and seeing the police at last near, he had decided to risk exposing her make-up, with this unexpectedly shocking result.

'And now,' he concluded in a shaken voice, 'I am naturally most anxious to know whether I am right – or have made some terrible mistake. Will you look at her, officer, and tell me if it is indeed – she?'

But the fat policeman shook his head over the well-known ability of Miss Hinch to look like everybody else in the world but herself.

'It'll take God Almighty to tell ye that, sir – saving your presence. I'll leave it f'r headquarters,' he continued, as if that were the same thing. 'But, if it is her, she's gone to her reward, sir.'

'God pity her!' said the clergyman.

'Amen! Give me your name, sir. They'll likely want you in the morning.'

The clergyman gave it: Rev. Theodore Shaler, of Denver; city address, a number on East 126th Street. Having thus discharged his duty in the affair, he started sadly to go away; but, passing by the silent figure stretched on a bench under the ticket-seller's overcoat, he bared his head and stopped for one last look at it.

The parson's gentleness and efficiency had already won favourable comments from the bystanders, and of the first quality he now gave a final proof. The dead woman's balled-up handkerchief, which somebody had recovered from the track and laid upon her breast, had slipped to the floor; and the clergyman, observing it, stooped silently to restore it again. This last small service chanced to bring his head close to the head of the dead woman; and, as he straightened up again, her projecting hatpin struck his cheek and ripped a straight line down it. This in itself would have been a trifle, since scratches soon heal. But it happened that the point of the hatpin caught under the lining of the clergyman's perfect beard and ripped it clean from him; so that, as he rose with a suddenly shrilled cry, he turned upon the astonished onlookers the bare, smooth chin of a woman, curiously long and pointed.

There were not many such chins in the world, and the urchins in the street would have recognized this one. Amid a sudden uproar which ill became the presence of the dead, the police closed in on Miss Hinch and handcuffed her with violence, fearing suicide, if not some new witchery; and at the station-house an unemotional matron divested the famous impersonator of the last and best of all her many disguises.

This much the police did. But it was everywhere understood that it was Jessie Dark who had really made the capture, and the papers next morning printed pictures of the unconquerable little woman and of the hatpin with which she had reached back from another world to bring her greatest adversary to justice.

MISS BURNSIDE'S DILEMMA

Cyril Hare

I T'S the fact that it's the vicar that makes the whole business so *difficult*. I simply don't know what to do about it. Those were his very words to me when I taxed him with it after matins last Sunday. 'Well, Miss Burnside,' he said, 'and what do you propose to do about it?' He smiled at me as he said it, I remember – just a friendly, amused sort of smile over his shoulder as he locked the vestry door, and then he took off his hat in that courteous way of his and walked back to the vicarage, leaving me standing there without an answer. That was nearly a week ago. And I don't know what the answer is. And he knows quite well that I don't know. I can see it in his eye whenever we meet. And in a small place like this it does make for a really impossible situation.

My first thought was to go to the police about it. In fact, if it had not been for the chance that my nephew John was staying with me at the time I think I should have done so. I call it chance, but looking back on it now I feel that it was rather the hand of Providence. Because if I had obeyed that first impulse I can see now what a terrible scandal there would have been. And much worse than a mere scandal, indeed! It so happened that on that Sunday evening John – he is studying for the Bar and is a very clever boy indeed – was talking to me about a big law case there had been recently in which a poor woman was made to pay enormous damages for – what did he call it? – Malicious Prosecution. That made me think a great deal of the danger of acting rashly in the matter, and in the end I told him all about it and asked his advice. After all, he is very nearly a lawyer, and as he is not one of the village it didn't seem to matter. John was tremendously interested – more interested than shocked, I'm afraid, but I suppose that is only natural – and he spent nearly the whole evening considering the matter when he ought to have been studying the Law of Real Property, which is his next examination, and in the end he told me that he could not find that any crime had been committed. Well, that may be the law, and of course I believe what my nephew tells me, but it does seem to me very wrong that the law should permit such things to be done – especially by a minister of the Church of England.

Of course, I could write to the bishop about it. Indeed, I have considered very seriously whether it is not my *duty* to write to the bishop. But it is a step that one shrinks from. In some ways it seems almost more serious than informing the police. I mean, it does seem almost equal to invoking the help of a Higher Power – I trust I am not being irreverent in putting it in that way. But I do not think the seriousness of it would deter me if I were only sure that the bishop would be able to do anything about it, and of that I cannot be sure. I asked John, but he could not help me. It appears that Church Law is not one of the subjects they examine him in, which seems a pity. However, he was very kind and helpful in explaining all kinds of points about the Law of Wills and so on, so that I do at least understand the whole of the dreadful story now quite clearly. Not that that is very much comfort to me, indeed! Rather the reverse. And situated as I am, there is literally *nobody* to whom I can turn for guidance. It is just the sort of problem that I could have set before the vicar himself until this terrible thing happened. But now – !

I want to be perfectly just to the vicar. In all the time that he has been in the village nobody, I am sure, has had a word to say against him, except indeed old Judd, and he, I fear, is irreclaimably ill disposed to every influence for good in the village. Of course, one might say that he – the vicar, I mean – has merely been a hypocrite all these years and that we have all been woefully deceived in him. But I prefer to think of him as a man suddenly exposed to a great Temptation and being carried away, as might happen to any of us. True, I cannot forget the way in which he brazened it out with me on Sunday, but neither can I believe that I have been utterly mistaken

in the man, after knowing him so well for nearly ten years. That is
the time that he has been in the village, and I remember quite well
how good an impression he made when Mrs Wheeler presented him
to the living. It was quite soon after Mrs Wheeler settled down
among us, and bought the Hall and with it the patronage. I do not
myself altogether approve of such a thing as a cure of souls being
in the gift of a private person and I am very glad that Parliament
has done something about it, though I can never understand quite
what, but it seemed impossible to quarrel with Mrs Wheeler's choice,
and the fact that he was her godson as well as her nephew made it
so peculiarly appropriate. Certainly, we all agreed that it was a
mercy that the old vicar had survived until after Sir John sold the
place, for Sir John's intellect was beginning to fail, and what with
that and his dangerously Low Church tendencies one shudders to
think what his choice might have been.

Altogether, there is no denying that the double change, at the
Hall and the vicarage, was all to the good of the neighbourhood.
Everybody liked Mrs Wheeler. Even Judd had hardly a word to say
against her. True, she lived very quietly, as was after all only proper
for a widow who was no longer young; but until last year, when
her health began to fail, she took her full part in all the village
activities, and whenever help was needed she was unfailingly generous. As indeed she could well afford to be – not that I consider
that that detracts in any way from her kindness of heart, but it was
common knowledge that Mr Wheeler, whoever he may have been,
had left her very well provided for. The all-important thing was
that she used her wealth for the good of others.

But if it is true to say that we respected the new vicar and admired
Mrs Wheeler – and I think it is – there is no doubt that we loved
Miss Dalrymple. She, I should explain, was Mrs Wheeler's companion. There is a lot of nonsense talked about the companions of
rich old ladies who have no daughters of their own to look after
them. They are always represented as poor abject creatures, perpetually bullied and down-trodden by their employers. Miss Dalrymple
was not at all like that. She was a very cheerful, active young woman
– not really young, of course, only in comparison with Mrs Wheeler
she seemed so – and there was nothing in the least abject about her.
Of course, she kept herself well in the background when Mrs Whee-

ler was present, but that is no more than one would expect. And there was no doubt that they were very fond of each other. They were indeed just like mother and daughter – or, rather, like what mother and daughter should be but so often, alas, are *not*.

The only person in the place who did not seem absolutely devoted to Miss Dalrymple, strangely enough, was the vicar himself. It was strange, because in many ways they had so much in common. At one time, indeed, I had hopes that the pair of them would make a match of it. It seemed so extremely suitable, and I know that I did my little best to bring it to pass. Certainly, I have always felt that a bachelor vicar, however excellent, is out of place in a parish like ours – though I know that Saint Paul thought otherwise. But it was not to be, and as the years went on it was impossible not to notice a certain coolness – I wouldn't go so far as to call it hostility – between him and Miss Dalrymple; although, of course, they always remained scrupulously polite and acted together quite harmoniously on committees and bazaars and at other parish functions.

That was how matters stood when Mrs Wheeler came to the village, and that was how they remained for a very long time. Nothing changes very much with the years in a quiet place like this, except that we all grow a little older, and I think it was quite a shock to most of us to realize last year how very much older and more infirm dear Mrs Wheeler had become. She went out less and less, and Miss Dalrymple, too, withdrew almost entirely from our little activities owing to the necessity of having to look after her. Mrs Wheeler had some objection to a nurse, so that all the burden fell upon poor Miss Dalrymple. It was really very hard upon her, though she never complained, and I must say that she was quite as good and careful as any professional nurse could be.

A month or two ago, however, it became sadly evident that Mrs Wheeler was seriously ill. Dr Perry – who was always, I think, just the least bit afraid of her – plucked up the courage to insist that she should have a night nurse permanently on duty and this gave Miss Dalrymple a little more freedom to come out and see her friends. One evening, shortly after the nurse had been installed, she came round to see me. I had expected her to be tired and anxious, but I was not prepared to find her quite so depressed and utterly unlike her usual cheerful self.

Naturally my first question was after Mrs Wheeler.

'She is very ill indeed,' she told me. 'Dr Perry thinks that it is most unlikely that she will recover.'

It is always difficult to know what to say on such occasions. I said, 'Oh dear!' which, I am afraid, was rather inadequate, but I tried to put as much sympathy into my voice as possible.

Miss Dalrymple said nothing for a moment or two but sat there looking very low and miserable. Finally she said, 'The trouble is, Miss Burnside, that she doesn't realize how ill she is.'

'Surely that is all to the good,' I said. 'After all, if she is going to die, it is better that she should not be troubled with any forebodings about it. It isn't as if she was a Roman Catholic,' I added, 'and in need of making a confession or anything of that kind. Not that a dear, good woman like Mrs Wheeler could having anything to confess, in any case.'

'It isn't that,' she answered, looking more miserable than ever. 'You see, Dr Perry says that she might die at any minute, and I happen to know that she has not made any will.'

I confess that I could not help feeling a little shocked – disgusted even – that Miss Dalrymple should be thinking of such things at such a time, and I thought then – as I have thought many times since! – how mistaken one can be, even about somebody one has known for a long time. Of course, I knew, like everybody in the village, that Miss Dalrymple had absolutely nothing of her own, and I knew also, because Mrs Wheeler had told me so, that her employer had intentions of making some provision for her after her death. I could quite understand Miss Dalrymple feeling disappointed at having to go out and look for another post at her age. But at the same time I could not but think that it was rather improper to be thinking of such matters, much more discussing them, while the person in question was still alive.

I must have shown something of my feelings in my expression, although I certainly did my best not to, for Miss Dalrymple immediately said, 'Please don't imagine that I'm thinking of myself, Miss Burnside.'

Naturally, I said, 'Of course not!' though I wondered very much of whom else she could possibly be thinking. But what she said next surprised me very much indeed.

'It would be a lamentable thing,' she went on, 'and, absolutely contrary to Mrs Wheeler's own wishes, if all that money of hers were to go to her son.'

Now this was the very first time that I, or anybody else so far as I was aware, had ever so much as heard that Mrs Wheeler had a son, and that only goes to show how very reticent she had always been about her own affairs, and how very loyal a companion Miss Dalrymple had been, never once to have mentioned the fact to any of her friends in the village.

'Her son, Miss Dalrymple?' I said. 'Whatever do you mean?' And then she told me all about him.

It appeared that Mrs Wheeler had a son who, as is, I am afraid, so often the case with the children of the most excellent, religious people, had turned out very badly indeed. It crossed my mind that perhaps young Charles Wheeler – that was his name, apparently – took after his father, but this was really very uncharitable of me, for, of course, I knew nothing whatever about the late Mr Wheeler except that he had made a great deal of money, and that, after all, was nothing against his character – rather the reverse. At all events, as the result of his misconduct (and although Miss Dalrymple, most properly, entered into no *details*, I gathered that it had been very grave indeed), the young man had for many years entirely cut himself off from his family. Miss Dalrymple did not so much as know where he was living, except that it was somewhere abroad, and the only communication that his mother had received from him recently was an application for money a little time before she was taken ill, which she had, of course, refused to consider in any way.

And now there was a possibility of Mrs Wheeler's money being diverted to this wicked person, to be turned by him to the most disreputable purposes! I could well understand Miss Dalrymple's agitation at such a thing, although I may as well admit that I did not *wholly* credit her assertion that she was not thinking at all of her own prospects, because, after all, we are all *human*. Speaking for myself, I felt particularly alarmed when I reflected that Mrs Wheeler's property included the right of presentation to our living and that this might well fall into the hands of an outright rascal.

I was sadly perplexed in my mind as to what advice I should give Miss Dalrymple on this difficult question, for though I am always prepared to listen to other people's troubles, and my friends have told me that I am a particularly good listener, giving advice is a responsibility which I do not care to undertake. At last it occurred to me to suggest that she should consult the vicar, who, from his position, was particularly suited to bring Mrs Wheeler to a sense of the danger which she was in, and who was himself really interested in the matter in another way. I mean, until this moment everybody regarded him as Mrs Wheeler's nearest relative, although presumably he was well aware of the existence of his ill-behaved cousin.

I could see that Miss Dalrymple did not altogether like the prospect of confiding in the vicar, but she agreed to think it over, and a little later she went home, feeling, I am sure, all the better for having had a good chat. There is, I think, nothing better than a good chat with the right sort of person to make you look on the bright side of things.

Next morning, as soon as I had breakfasted, I put on my hat and went round to the Hall to enquire. I had done this many times since Mrs Wheeler had been taken ill, of course, but on this occasion, though I am not, I trust, superstitious, I did feel a certain sense of foreboding as I did so. And sure enough, as I came round the bend in the drive, I saw that the blinds of the house had been drawn, and knew at once that our dear friend had passed away. I was about to turn round and go home again, when the front door opened and Miss Dalrymple came out. She saw me and came straight up towards me, so that, without feeling that I was in any *intruding*, I was able to get the very first information about what had happened from her instead of having to rely upon village gossip, which is always rather undignified, in my opinion, and has the added disadvantage that one does not know what to believe!

Dear Mrs Wheeler, she told me, had take a sudden turn for the worse at about two o'clock that morning. Dr Perry had been sent for immediately, of course, but he was out attending a maternity case, and in spite of all that Miss Dalrymple and the nurse could do, by the time that he arrived, which was not until nearly seven, all was over. The doctor had said that he could have done nothing had he been there in time, and I was glad to learn that the end had been altogether peaceful.

I dare say that I should not have been thinking of such things at

such a moment, but, remembering our conversation of the evening
before, I could not forbear saying, 'Then I suppose poor Mrs Wheeler was never able to make a will after all?'

Then Miss Dalrymple told me her great news! It seemed that
after the first seizure Mrs Wheeler had rallied and remained quite
conscious and sensible for several hours. And during that time,
knowing that her last hour had come, she had been able to make
her will. By that will, Miss Dalrymple told me, she had bequeathed
one thousand pounds to her nephew, the vicar, and the whole of
the rest of her fortune to Miss Dalrymple herself!

I could hardly believe my ears. It really seemed too good to be
true, and I congratulated her most warmly, but, I hope, with the
solemnity that the occasion required. Still I found it difficult to
credit that the story should have had so happy an ending.

'Forgive me for asking you,' I said, 'but are you quite sure that
this is really so? Have you seen the will yourself?'

'Indeed, I have,' she told me. 'We sent for the vicar, of course,
as soon as we saw how gravely ill she was. The moment she
recovered consciousness, she told him to write down what she
wished. I saw her sign the paper, and then the vicar and I put our
names underneath hers as witnesses.'

When I had got as far as this in telling the story to my nephew
John, he made a most peculiar noise, something between a snort
and a laugh. Of course, with his knowledge, he saw at once what
was wrong; but we are not all lawyers – thank goodness! – and
neither Miss Dalrymple nor I had the least idea at the time that the
will was anything but perfectly legal. Nor, I am sure, had poor Mrs
Wheeler, unless the knowledge was vouchsafed to her in Heaven,
in which case it must have made her very unhappy, if such a thing
is possible in Heaven. But it is the fact, cruel and unfair though it
may seem, that the law does not allow a will to be legal unless it is
witnessed by two persons, and that neither of those two persons is
allowed to have any benefit from the will which they have witnessed. So that, as John put it, the only two people in the world
who could not receive any of Mrs Wheeler's money under her will
were the vicar and Miss Dalrymple, the only two people whom she
desired to give anything to! I said then, and I think still, that it
is most unreasonable and a kind of trap for innocent people like

companions and country clergy who could not be expected to know anything about the law, because, after all, who could be better suited to witness an old lady's will than her nephew and the woman who had looked after her for so many years? I think they should have thought of such things when the law was made, but I suppose it is too late to alter it now.

Of course, neither Miss Dalrymple nor I knew anything of this at the time, but we were speedily undeceived. The day after the funeral she came to see me in great distress and told me that she had been to consult a lawyer as to what was to be done about Mrs Wheeler's estate, and he had told her that by witnessing the will she and the vicar had signed away all their inheritance. She told me also that the vicar had called upon her and expressed his sorrow that his ignorance had led to her losing the reward of her long years of service, not to mention his own thousand pounds, which he admitted was a serious matter for him, for the living was not a good one.

After that Miss Dalrymple left the village, and I understand she secured another post with a lady at Cheltenham, where she was not well paid, and where, I am afraid, she was anything but happy. Meanwhile we in the village awaited the dreadful moment when Mr Charles Wheeler would descend upon us to take possession of the property which had in this strange way become his after all. A week or more went by, and then we heard the great and unexpected news. I had it first from Mrs Tomlin, at the post office; and although I always suspect anything from that source, it was soon afterwards confirmed by the vicar himself. It appeared that as soon as it was established that the will was of no effect, the vicar had enquiries made for the whereabouts of the son, and these enquiries had met with a speedy and most unhoped result. Charles Wheeler was no more! He had perished, very miserably, I am sorry to say, in some foreign town, quite soon after his last letter to his mother asking for assistance. The vicar had been shown that letter at the time, and he told me that in it he had stated that he was dangerously ill. It was the vicar who had counselled Mrs Wheeler not to reply to it, thinking that the statement of his condition was only a ruse to get more money from the mother who had cast him off; and he said, very generously as I thought at the time, that he now regretted that he had not allowed his aunt to take measures which might have prolonged the unfortunate man's life a little longer. But I told him that although the sentiment did him credit, it was much better as it was, and I remember that I went so far as to say that the death of Charles Wheeler might be accounted a providential event.

So after all the vicar, as the only living relative of his aunt, came into all her possessions, and we were all so pleased at this happy turn of events that I am afraid we had very little thought to spare for poor Miss Dalrymple, who, after all, was the person whom Mrs Wheeler had mainly had in mind. And the vicar was so popular in the village – except, of course, with old Judd and people of his stamp – that there was no one who did not rejoice in his good fortune. Indeed, and this is my great difficulty at the present moment, he is still just as popular as ever, simply because nobody, myself only excepted, knows the *truth*.

Just over a week ago I spent a night in London with my brother and sister-in-law, a thing I do very rarely, except when the summer sales are in progress. They took me to the theatre that evening, I remember – it was a most amusing piece, but I do not recollect the name – and invited to join the party a Mr Woodhouse, whom I had never met before. During the interval, between the acts, he asked me where I lived and, when I told him, said, 'Then I suppose you know Mr – ' (mentioning the vicar by name).

'Indeed I do,' I told him, and was about to go on to tell him something of the strange story of Mrs Wheeler's will when he interrupted me.

'I was up with him at Oxford,' he said. 'A very clever fellow, I thought him.'

'He is a very *good* man,' I answered with some emphasis, 'and I think that is more important.' One does not somehow like to hear one's vicar described as 'a very clever fellow', even if it is kindly meant.

'Oh, but he is clever too,' Mr Woodhouse persisted. 'I remember he took a first-class honours degree in Law the year I graduated.'

I was thunderstruck.

'In Law, Mr Woodhouse?' I said. 'Are you sure that you are not mistaken?'

'Quite sure,' he said. 'He was intended for the Bar, you know, but he changed his mind and went into the Church instead. Rather a waste of a good intellect, I thought.'

Luckily the curtain rose for the next act before I could ask him what he meant by his last very improper observation, and I took good care not to refer to the subject again.

All the way down in the train next day I could think of nothing but what Mr Woodhouse had told me. If the vicar had really studied the law at Oxford how was it possible that he had made such a mistake as he had done about witnessing the will? I tried to comfort myself by reflecting that he might have forgotten this particular point, but it seemed hardly possible, and indeed John has told me since that it is one of the 'first principles' of the Law of Wills – though why they should make a first principle of anything so unjust and cruel I do not in the least understand. But if he *knew* that by becoming a witness Miss Dalrymple was losing her right to Mrs Wheeler's property, however hostile to her he may have felt, why had he been content to destroy his own chances of getting a thousand pounds also? It was all most puzzling and mysterious, and I made up my mind, come what might, to speak to him at the very first opportunity. And that opportunity came last Sunday, after matins.

I still blush when I think of it – not for myself, for I feel that I only obeyed my conscience in saying what I did, but for him. His effrontery was so astonishing. I can recall – I do not think I shall every forget – exactly what passed between us.

I met him, as I said, just as he was coming out of the vestry door after the service. He said 'Good morning' to me, and I responded as politely as I could.

Then I said, 'I met an old acquaintance of yours in London, Vicar, a Mr Woodhouse.'

'Oh, yes, Woodhouse,' he replied. 'I haven't seen him for a very long time.'

I resolved not to beat about the bush.

'He told me,' I said, 'that you had studied the law at Oxford, and were awarded first-class honours for your proficiency.'

He did not show the least confusion, but merely said, 'It is pleasant to have one's little triumphs remembered.'

'Then did you not know,' I pressed him, 'that Miss Dalrymple ought not to have witnessed that will?'

'Ought not, Miss Burnside?' he asked. 'I should prefer to say that Mrs Wheeler ought not to have tried to dispose of her property in the way that she did.'

I could hardly speak for indignation.

'Then you deliberately so arranged matters that Miss Dalrymple should lose what Mrs Wheeler wished her to have?' I said.

'I did.'

'Even at the cost of losing your own legacy?'

'But you see, I have not lost it,' he answered with a smile, and then I suddenly saw the light.

'Vicar!' I said. 'You knew all the time that Charles Wheeler was dead!'

He nodded.

'I had a telegram from the British Consul informing me of his death some months ago,' he said. 'In view of my aunt's state of health I thought it wiser to keep the news from her. Do you blame me?'

I was so angry that I am afraid I lost all respect for his cloth.

'Blame you?' I said. 'I think you have behaved like a common thief!'

And then he used those awful words that I have already mentioned: 'Well, Miss Burnside, and what are you going to do about it?'

What indeed! Tomorrow it is Sunday again. I know that my absence from church would cause the most *undesirable* talk in the place, but yet I feel as if, so long as he is vicar, dear St Etheldreda's can never be the same place for me again. The Hall is up for sale and I hear dreadful rumours that it is to be bought by a *builder*. All our pleasant life in this village is at an end, so far as I am concerned. I wish somebody would answer that question for me: What am I going to do?

MR LEGGATT LEAVES HIS CARD

J. S. Fletcher

THE Reverend Francis Leggatt, Vicar of Meddersley, was one of those men whom it is not easy to excite or to disturb. Nature had blessed him with a well-balanced temperament, and he had seconded nature's beginnings, during his school days at Eton, and his undergraduate days at Cambridge, by a strict devotion to the study of mathematics; he was essentially a mathematical sort of person, precise, orderly, given to perfection of detail. His taste was for the straight line, but he was certainly thrown off it when, one fine spring morning, he hurried across from the vestry door of his fine old parish church to the study of the vicarage, into which peaceful retreat he immediately summoned the wife of his bosom. Mrs Leggatt, hastening thither, found him standing on the hearthrug, his hands thrust in the pockets of his trousers, his eyes bent to the toes of his well-polished shoes.

'Marian!' he said, looking up with an expression which his wife had never seen before. 'Prepare yourself for a shock. There's been a theft from the church. The Hislip Chalice is gone.'

Mrs Leggatt threw up her hands, and sank into the nearest chair with a stifled moan. Her husband's curt announcement took her breath away. She could not have been more horrified if he had said that the local bank had gone smash, or Government securities dropped to zero; either of these catastrophes would not have been exactly irretrievable. But the loss of the Hislip Chalice was another matter.

The Hislip Chalice was famous, unique; its value was – Mrs

Leggatt did not know what. What she did know was that it was
one of the very few pre-Reformation Chalices left in England; that
it dated from 1427 A.D., and that experts and archæologists regarded
it with a reverence such as that which devotees accord to the bones
of a saint. Dry-as-dust gentlemen came from far and near to look
at it; now and then, Leggatt, as custodian, allowed it to be photographed, standing guard over its sacredness while the man of the
camera was busy. And once a vandal from way over the Atlantic
had calmly offered the Vicar ten thousand dollars for it – and had
added insult to insult by an equally calm suggestion that perhaps
twenty thousand might do when Leggatt answered icily that ten
thousand would not.

Mrs Leggatt found words at last.

'Impossible, Francis,' she gasped. 'It – it must be mislaid!'

'No!' said Leggatt, with a snap of his lips which his wife knew
well enough. 'It's – gone. I had occasion to open the safe in the
vestry just now and, of course, I saw that the Hislip Chalice wasn't
there. I've always kept it in one place, ever since I came here, nine
years ago – in the far right-hand corner. Well – that corner's empty!'

'You have not misplaced it, yourself?' suggested Mrs Leggatt.

'I never misplace anything,' replied the Vicar, with a characteristic
sniff. 'As you are aware,' he added.

Mrs Leggatt was very well aware. She was not given to undue
tidiness herself, and her husband was somewhat trying. It pained
him to see a newspaper thrown on the floor, a book out of place
on its shelf, a picture one-hundredth of an inch out of line; no, she
couldn't conceive of Leggatt misplacing, mislaying anything; he was
the sort of man who can get up at midnight without a candle and
lay his hand on whatever he happens to want.

'When did you last see it, Francis?' she asked feebly.

'To-day is Thursday,' replied Leggatt. 'I last saw it on Monday.
To be precise, on Monday afternoon. We had better recall the
circumstances, Marian. You will, perhaps, remember that Monday
was a very wet day. During the afternoon, Sir Charles sent a note
across from the Hall saying that his guests were kept indoors by the
bad weather, and would I help him by showing them over the
church? They all came across – Sir Charles with them. I showed
them everything; they were in the church, with me, well over an

hour. An hour and twenty-five minutes to be exact. Of course, I showed them the church plate. I took it all out of the safe and set it on the vestry table. Naturally, I told them all about the Hislip Chalice – its history, its unique character, its immense value. I put it back in the safe with all the rest of the plate.'

'And, of course, locked up the safe?' said Mrs Leggatt.

Leggatt, who still stood on the hearthrug, shifted his position uneasily.

'Well,' he answered, 'I'm sorry to say I did not – just then, at any rate! I left the keys in the lock, though – I think I had some idea about taking one of the registers out before finally locking up the safe. No, we went out of the vestry, then, to examine the church. I regret to say – now – that the party didn't keep together. Some remained with me, listening to my description, some went off one way, some another – you know what people do in such circumstances. Eventually they all left. Then I locked up the safe – without reopening it – and came home. Marian – there's no doubt about it. The Hislip Chalice was stolen while those people were in the church.'

'You think somebody slipped into the church while you were showing Sir Charles and his guests round?' suggested Mrs Leggatt.

'No, I don't,' replied Leggatt, sardonically. 'Nobody could slip in! I locked the church door from the inside, so that we shouldn't be disturbed. No – I think that one of Sir Charles's guests stole the chalice.'

Mrs Leggatt let out an exclamation of horror.

'Francis!' she said. 'One of Sir Charles's guests! Impossible. Not to be thought of!'

'I think of it, anyway,' retorted Leggatt. 'And as to its being impossible, that's pure nonsense, Marian. What do we know of Sir Charles Leddingham's guests? Absolutely nothing – as regards their moral characters, anyhow!'

'But – but – people of that class – ' protested Mrs Leggatt.

'Oh, fudge!' said Leggatt. He laughed, contemptuously. 'That's all nonsense, too! But let's go through them. We'll rule out Sir Charles; he's nothing worse – and nothing better, for that matter – than a horse-racing squire. Well, there's old Lord Pelford and, of course, Lady Pelford. I don't suspect them – I mean, I don't see any reason for suspecting them. Old Pelford, of course, is a retired judge – I don't think he'd steal the Chalice. Nor would his wife.'

'I should think not!' said Mrs Leggatt, indignantly. 'Dear people – they were both extremely nice to me when we dined there the other night.'

'Then there's Sir Robert Sindall,' continued Leggatt. 'I know nothing about him except that his horse won the Derby last year.'

'And he's a very wealthy man, too,' observed Mrs Leggatt.

'That doesn't impress me,' said Leggatt. 'I've heard of millionaires who were afflicted with kleptomania. Then there's Colonel Belchanter.'

'And Mrs Belchanter,' added Mrs Leggatt. 'They're nice people, too, Francis!'

'I daresay they are all nice people, Marian,' answered Leggatt, freezingly. 'But one or other has appropriated the Hislip Chalice – I'm as sure of it as I am that I see you sitting there.'

'Well – there are four others. Captain Riversley – raffish sort, I should say. Horses – cards – that sort of thing. Mr Hawksfoot – I don't know anything about him, but I should imagine he's some sort of an adventurer – the sort of man you see at Monte Carlo, and at Deauville, and at Tattersall's, on a Monday morning.'

'How do you know, Francis?' suggested Mrs Leggatt. 'You've never been to any of those places.'

'I've read a good deal about them, anyway,' retorted Leggatt. 'And I keep my ears open. Well – two more. Women. Miss Field-Maple – '

'Such a very nice girl,' exclaimed Mrs Leggatt. 'You couldn't suspect . . .'

'And Mrs Peacock – '

'Mrs Peacock is a delightful woman!' said Mrs Leggatt. 'I took quite a liking to her! She was so awfully sympathetic about Bobby when I told her that I was uneasy about his cough.'

'I noticed that Mrs Peacock is remarkably fond of, and extremely proficient at Bridge!' remarked Leggatt cynically. 'And I should say, from her conversation, that she's like all the lot there – a devotee of horse-racing, and that sort of thing. Marian, you can't get away from two facts. First, the houseparty across there at the Hall is of the Turfy sort – gamblers, every man and woman of them, from old Pelford downward. Second, one or other of them has stolen the Hislip Chalice. No one else could steal it. It was stolen while I had those people in the church – I told you that the party split up and wandered about. You know how the vestry is situated – what easier, than for the thief, having learned the immense value of the Chalice from my lips, to slip in unobserved, open the door of the safe, and take the Chalice? It would easily be hidden. It's of no great size. As sure as I'm Vicar of Meddersley, one of Sir Charles Leddingham's guests has appropriated that Chalice, with a view to selling it! But – which?'

'What shall you do, Francis?' asked Mrs Leggatt, in a whisper. 'The police?'

'Not at present,' answered Leggatt. 'No – I'll think!'

At that Mrs Leggatt rose and departed, and her husband picked up his pipe, and after carefully filling it with tobacco, felt for his match-box.

Leggatt thought hard, and deep, and long. Of one thing he felt almost absolutely certain: nobody had entered the church from the time he left it on Monday afternoon to the moment in which he had gone into it that – Thursday – morning. There was no daily service at Meddersley; Leggatt's view of his duty was that two services on a Sunday were amply sufficient in a parish the scattered population of which did not exceed fifty souls, all told. There was, of course, just a possibility that Higson, the parish clerk and sexton, might have visited the sacred edifice for some reason during the intervening two days, but that could be ascertained presently – he had little doubt that Higson had not. No, the theft had taken place while he, himself, was acting as cicerone to the house-party from the Hall.

He had a very clear recollection of everything that had happened while he was in the church with the Squire and his guests. After admitting them to the church and locking the door from the inside, he had first taken them to the vestry and, opening the safe, had shown them the old plate, the parish registers, dating from 1547, and various other matters of interest that had accumulated during the last two or three centuries. He had left his keys in the lock of the safe when he and the others passed into the church to examine the architecture, the monuments, the inscriptions, the old brasses and mural paintings. He and old Lord Pelford had got into an argument over a certain recumbent figure – that of Sir Geoffrey de Meddersley, who lay in chain armour in a niche in the chancel; the argument had become so technical that most of the others had first yawned and then wandered off into other parts of the gloomy old building.

And while one was here and another there, the thief had quietly slipped into the vestry, opened the safe, and abstracted the Hislip Chalice. It was an article that could easily be hidden, reflected Leggatt – a gilt cup, standing about seven and a half inches high and measuring two and a half inches in diameter across the upper rim and the circular base – why it could be slipped into a pocket.

'And, of course, I'd told them all about it,' he mused regretfully, 'told them, I remember, about the American collector who offered first ten, and then twenty thousand dollars for it. That was dangling temptation before the needy. And some of these racing, card-playing people are often at their wits' end for ready money, I believe. No doubt whoever took the Chalice did so with the intention of selling it across the Atlantic – it's pretty well known that European treasures go across there, and that no questions are asked by men with a mania for collecting.

'However that's neither here nor there – the thing is, what's to be done? I don't want the Bishop to know, and as for the Archdeacon – whew! Last time he was here he said pretty plainly that, in his opinion, the Hislip Chalice, being what it is, ought to be removed to the Cathedral, or handed over to the Nation, and he'd row me no end if he heard that I'd left that safe unlocked while strangers were about. And I can't very well go across to the Hall and demand to search the boxes of every man and woman there. And as for the police – no, I do not want *that*!'

Eventually, knocking the ashes out of his pipe, Leggatt went down into the village and saw Higson. He soon discovered that the parish clerk had not been near the church since Sunday evening. And Higson was the only person in the parish who could have entered the church: Leggatt had one of the two keys that gave admission; Higson had the other. No, for the twentieth time Leggatt told himself that the Chalice had been taken during the inspection of Monday afternoon.

Now, who was the thief? And – how to bring the theft home to the thief?

He stayed talking with Higson some little time; an hour had passed before he went back to the Vicarage. Mrs Leggatt met him in the hall.

'Any news, Francis?' she asked anxiously.

'None,' he said. 'I've just been down to Higson's. Of course, I didn't tell him anything of this. Nobody must know, Marian. But Higson has never been in the church since he locked up after even-song on Sunday night. He's never lent his key to anyone, either, so . . .'

He paused at that, checked by the sight of a card which lay on the old oak side table in the hall. Mrs Leggatt followed his glance.

'Mrs Peacock called,' she said, indicating the card. 'She was so charming – called to ask after Bobby, and gave me some awfully good advice about some stuff that she says works wonders for a child's cough. Most sympathetic! She promised to call again in a day or two – she's staying at the Hall a few days longer.'

Leggatt was staring at the card. Suddenly he glanced sharply at his wife.

'You didn't tell her anything about – eh?' he asked.

Mrs Leggatt flushed.

'Francis!' she exclaimed indignantly. 'As if I should! Really – '

'Sorry, Marian – sorry. Of course, you wouldn't! I – it's so important, you see, that we should keep strict silence about it. If the Archdeacon knew . . .'

'As if I didn't know all that,' said Mrs Leggatt. She was still offended, and she turned and went off towards the nursery. 'Of course, I said nothing!' she flung over her shoulder. 'Nothing.'

Leggatt remained in the hall. He began, absent-mindedly, to finger Mrs Peacock's card. So Mrs Peacock had been to the Vicarage to inquire after Bobby, had she? Very kind of her, of course, but – supposing Mrs Peacock had – had had another idea in her mind? Supposing Mrs Peacock had come fishing – wanting to find out – if – if . . .

It was at that moment that Leggatt had a brain-wave. He had not the slightest notion then, or ever afterwards, where that brain-wave came from. But it swept him straight out of his front door, and down the path to the village.

Leggatt, as a man with a good deal of spare time on his hands, was a great reader, almost an omnivorous one. He had no special subject; he read anything that came to hand from his library. Recently he had been reading criminology; a chance-acquired volume on that fascinating subject had induced him to procure others of the same sort. And now, as he hurried away from his Vicarage for the second time that morning, he found himself repeating a sentence which he had read only a day or two before in a technical work on theft: 'The thief's first instinct, on securing a stolen object, is to "plant" it, i.e., to dispose of it, as quickly as possible, in some safe place, so that in the event of his immediate or speedy arrest, he may not be found to be in possession of it.'

That, no doubt, reflected Leggatt, applied to the procedure of the professional thief – but it had its origin in a certain attribute of human nature, and might be applied to the amateur wrongdoer as well as to the skilled expert. To get rid of the purloined article quickly – that was all of a piece with the instinct to hide, to get away, to secrete.

Well, in this case, his brain-wave had shown him how the purloiner of the Hislip Chalice could get it out of reach smartly and surely; he proposed to find out at once if the means he was imagining had been employed. And within five minutes he had turned into the village post-office, and there being nobody else there, was closeted with the woman who presided over it, Mrs Marsh.

Mrs Marsh was an elderly person, the widow of a former schoolmaster, who, on the death of her husband, had been given the postmistress's job to help her to eke out a living. In such a small place she had little to do, except when the Squire was in residence at the Hall; then, to be sure, she was fairly busy, especially of an afternoon, when racing telegrams flowed in from two o'clock to half-past five, Sir Charles being an inveterate betting man and keen about results as they materialized on the various race-courses. As became one holding her responsible position, Mrs Marsh was a woman of a reserved, not to say severe, temperament, and Leggatt, glancing at her as she received him in her neatly appointed little office, was doubtful whether he would get out of her what he wanted to get.

'Mrs Marsh,' he began, leaning confidentially across the counter, 'I've called to see you on a very important matter – so important that I can't tell you its nature. I daresay I ought really to have gone to the postmaster at Chilminster to get his permission to come to you, but the matter is of such pressing moment that I daren't waste the time. So – I've come straight to you.'

'What is it, sir?' asked Mrs Marsh.

Leggatt made sure that no one was in earshot. He had taken care to close the outer door as he entered; he now closed an inner one which communicated with Mrs Marsh's private parlour. He came back and leaned closer over the counter.

'This, Mrs Marsh,' he replied, his tone suggesting mystery as well as confidence. 'I want to see your registered letter book.'

Mrs Marsh let out an exclamation that was not encouraging.

'Oh, dear me, Mr Leggatt,' she said. 'I – I'm afraid I can't do that, sir. We're under strict instructions not to divulge any post-office business to anybody. It would be as much as my place was worth. . . .'

'Mrs Marsh,' interrupted Leggatt. 'If I went to the postmaster at Chilminster, and told him my reason, he'd come here with me himself and show me your book. But that would mean – the police. And I don't want to have the police dragged in. I have reasons for that – and reasons for asking you to show me the book. All I want is to see the entries made in that book since Monday last. And, Mrs Marsh – you know me. No one – no one – will ever know anything about this!'

But Mrs Marsh still hesitated. She looked right and left, evident distaste for the vicar's proposal strong in her expression.

I don't like it, Mr Leggatt!' she said. 'Irregularity. . . .'

'The circumstances are exceptional, Mrs Marsh,' interrupted Leggatt. 'Otherwise – you would not have had me here! Still, if you feel you can't, I must go at once to the postmaster at Chilminster.'

'You're sure he'd come back with you, sir?' asked Mrs Marsh.

'I am quite sure he would, Mrs Marsh,' replied Leggatt. 'But,' he added, significantly, 'he would bring the police-superintendent with him. And that I do not want – for the sake of the village.'

Mrs Marsh glanced at her curtained window; then at the parlour door. She suddenly pushed an oblong book across the counter, and opening it, showed Leggatt a page of counterfoils.

'There's only been three registered letters sent away from this office since Monday morning, Mr Leggatt,' she said hurriedly. 'Look for yourself. I know all about them, of course. That first one – that's for a weekly affair, from John Coates; he sends his widowed mother a pound every Monday and he always registers it. That's for a letter, in a registered envelope, from Sir Charles to his bankers in London. And the third is for a small parcel that was brought in here and registered, on Tuesday morning, by one of those ladies staying at the Hall.'

'Just so,' said Leggatt, keeping his voice as steady as possible. 'And – that's all?'

'That's all, sir,' affirmed Mrs Marsh. 'And I beg you'll not let anybody know, sir, that – '

'Make yourself quite easy, Mrs Marsh,' said Leggatt. 'Not a soul will ever know. It's a dead secret between you and me. And – I'm very much obliged to you.' Mrs Marsh put away her book.

'I hope you've found out what you wanted to know, sir?' she said, eyeing her caller inquisitively.

'I – I can't tell you,' replied Leggatt. 'At least – not yet. But. . . .' He hesitated a moment, seemed to reflect, then, nodding again, murmured another word of thanks, and forthwith left the office. Outside, at a place in the village street where there was none to see, he pulled out a note-book and pencil. 'Sent it to herself,' he muttered. 'Clever. And – she's going to stay at the Hall a few days longer, is she? And came to inquire about Bobby's cough, eh? And will be kind enough to come again. Um!'

Then he wrote down an address:

Mrs Guy Peacock,
23, Heatherfield Mansions,
W.1.

The first thing that Leggatt did on returning to the Vicarage was to pick up the card which Mrs Peacock had left on the hall table and put it carefully away in his pocket book; he had already thought out a plan of action in which that card was to be a highly useful factor. The second was to announce to Mrs Leggatt, over the luncheon table, that he was going up to town by the afternoon train. Mrs Leggatt looked her astonishment. She was country bred, and to her a visit to London, nearly two hundred miles away, was as much of an event as a journey from London to Yokohama would be to most people.

'Francis,' she exclaimed. Then light burst in upon her. 'You have some – idea?' she suggested. 'A – a clue?'

'An idea, yes,' assented Leggatt. 'A clue – well, I don't know. But – I'm going. And – it's to be kept secret – mentioned to – no one!'

'Of course,' said Mrs Leggatt. She glanced at the clock. 'You've not much time for packing,' she added. 'I suppose you'll get the London train at Chilminster? There's only one train from here to Chilminster, you know – the 3.15. I'd better hurry.'

'Don't hurry at all,' said Leggatt. 'I can pack all I want in a handbag in five minutes – I'm only going for the night. I shall be back here to-morrow afternoon.'

At three o'clock, looking very determined, his wife thought, he went off to catch the local train; at five minutes to four he was on the platform at Chilminster, awaiting the London express. And as he stood by the bookstall, whiling the time away by glancing at the various wares, he suddenly saw one of Sir Charles's guests – Hawksfoot, the man whom he had described to Mrs Leggatt as looking like an adventurer. Hawksfoot, who seemed to be in a hurry, did not see the vicar; Leggatt watched him snatch up some sporting papers and magazines and hasten off towards the express, just then steaming in. Presently he saw him enter a first-class smoking compartment. Leggatt passed its door; he travelled third-class. He had another glimpse of Hawksfoot when the train arrived at King's Cross four hours later; Hawksfoot was stepping into a taxi-cab. Once again there was no meeting between them.

Leggatt went off to a quiet, old-fashioned hotel in the neighbourhood of Bond Street, and after a belated dinner, got into a quiet corner of the smoking-room, and over two or three pipes of tobacco, reviewed his plan of campaign for the morrow.

Certain circumstances, he thought, were highly in his favour – in fact he was being extremely lucky. He knew Heatherfield Mansions extremely well; he had once had a small flat there himself, when, before his marriage, he had been curate at a West End church. Accordingly, he was acquainted with what was done there about letters. There were some thirty flats, of various sizes, in Heatherfield Mansions; if any flat-holder happened to go away and lock up his or her flat, all letters and parcels for that particular person were deposited with the hall porter at his office in the main entrance until the addressee returned.

And it was doubtless in the hall-porter's pigeon-holes that the registered parcel, sent off by Mrs Peacock from Meddersley on the previous Tuesday morning, was reposing. In that parcel Leggatt firmly believed the Hislip Chalice would be found. And – he was determined to get it.

At ten o'clock next morning, Leggatt walked into the main entrance of Heatherfield Mansions, and to his great joy recognized in the hall-porter the same man who had acted in that capacity when he himself was a tenant – an ex-Army man named Murphy. Murphy remembered the former curate well enough, and greeted him almost affectionately. Leggatt let him talk awhile before entering on his own business. At last he drew out Mrs Peacock's card – and prepared to tell the lies which he had just got to tell. They were lies, he knew, pure and simple lies, and Leggatt was no casuist; he treated them as lies and told them boldly.

'I don't know whether you're aware of it, Murphy,' he began. 'I have been Vicar of Meddersley, away in the North, for some years, since leaving here. There is one of your flat-holders, Mrs Guy Peacock, staying at Meddersley Hall just now, as a guest of Sir Charles Leddingham. Mrs Peacock is going to remain there rather longer than she intended, and knowing that I was coming to town last night and returning home this afternoon, she gave me her card, asked me to hand it to you, and to ask you for a small registered parcel which she sent here the other day and now wants – she said you'd have it.'

He knew before he had come to the end of his last hurried sentence that there was something wrong, that something had happened. Murphy was looking at him oddly.

'Well, bedad, that's the queer thing entirely, Mr Leggatt!' he said. 'You're the second gentleman that's called for that same parcel this morning, and with the same message. Mr Hawksfoot, that's a great chum of Mrs Peacock's when she's at home – sure, he was round here for that parcel at nine o'clock. And, of course, I gave it to him.'

Leggatt thanked his stars that he was able to keep his countenance.

'Oh, Mr Hawksfoot's got it, has he, Murphy?' he answered. 'Oh, that'll be all right. I know Mr Hawksfoot – he's staying at Sir Charles Leddingham's too. I see how the mistake arose. Of course, so long as he's got the parcel. . . . By-the-by, doesn't Mr Hawksfoot live somewhere round here?'

That was a chance cast, but Murphy swallowed the bait.

'Oh, he does, Mr Leggatt,' he answered. '231A, Half Moon Street. I often carry notes for him there from Mrs Peacock – mighty thick is them two, sir – and rale sports, both of them.'

Then he turned to attend to another caller, and Leggatt, with a nod, went out into the street. He was conscious of only one thing – Hawksfoot, without doubt, had got the Hislip Chalice.

And now Leggatt stood wondering what to do next. The solicitor he employed, whenever he had any legal business, had his office two streets away; should be go to him? Or should he go to the police, to Scotland Yard? That, perhaps, was what he ought to do. One of the two had stolen it; for anything he knew they might both have been in at the actual theft. And there was no doubt, could be no doubt, that it was now in Hawksfoot's possession – had been so since nine o'clock that morning. And it was now a quarter past ten.

Leggatt suddenly came to a decision. He would go round to Half Moon Street, call on Hawksfoot at his rooms and tell him his business, in plain words. If Hawksfoot blustered, equivocated, protested, he would not only threaten him with the police, but would immediately summon their assistance. That was surely the thing to do – and, as Half Moon Street was close by, in five minutes more Leggatt was at Hawksfoot's door.

A youthful valet answered his knock, and on hearing what he wanted, shook his head.

'Mr Hawksfoot's just gone out, sir,' he replied. 'Ten minutes since, sir. I couldn't say when he'll be back – might be some little time, sir. I know he's lunching at his club, sir.'

'But you're not sure he'll be there, now?' suggested Leggatt. 'Just so – might be about the town, eh? Um! I think I'll step in and leave Mr Hawksfoot a note, if I may?'

'Certainly, sir,' said the valet, standing politely aside. 'This way, sir.' He ushered Leggatt into a cosy sitting-room and pointed to an old bureau that stood in a recess. 'Notepaper and envelopes there, sir.'

'Thank you,' replied Leggatt. He drew a chair up to the bureau – and then, as the valet withdrew, closing the door behind him, he let out a sharp, sibilant breath of surprise and relief. For there, right before him, in an open compartment of the bureau, stood the Hislip Chalice! Close by, thrown away on the lid of the desk, were the various wrappings of soft paper from which Hawksfoot had disengaged it on opening the parcel.

Leggatt acted and moved with a determination and speed that surprised himself. The Hislip Chalice went straight into his pocket in one moment; within the next, he was out in the hall again, summoning the valet.

'On second thoughts,' said Leggatt, calmly, 'I won't write a note. I'll call round at Mr Hawksfoot's club instead. But,' he added, drawing out his card-case, 'in case I miss him there, will you please give him my card? Thank you. Good morning!'

A moment later Leggatt was downstairs and going swiftly away. At the corner of Clarges Street, he chanced on an empty taxi-cab, and plunged into it with a sharp order to the driver.

'King's Cross!'

At seven o'clock that evening Leggatt, tired but triumphant, let himself into his vicarage. He went straight to his study; took a bunch of keys from a certain hiding-place and stole out again into the adjacent churchyard. Presently he was in the church and in the vestry – and when he had done what he wanted there, he slammed the door of the safe viciously. Then he went home and summoned his wife.

'Marian,' he said, 'I've got it. It's back in the safe! And if ever I run any risk about it again, may I be . . . shot!'

Mrs Leggatt was clasping her hands in a paroxysm of delight – and of admiration at her husband's cleverness.

'Francis!' she exclaimed. 'But – where did you find it? And how?'

'I found it' – replied Leggatt, with a glance at the door – 'on Mr Hawksfoot's desk, in his flat in Half Moon Street. What d'you think of that, Marian? But – that's not all! Have we ten minutes before dinner? Then listen!'

Mrs Leggatt listened open-mouthed. When her husband had told her the whole horrible story, she threw up her hands.

'Then that accounts for it,' she exclaimed. 'That accounts for it!

'For – what?' asked Leggatt.

'For this!' replied his wife. 'This afternoon, about three o'clock, Mrs Peacock called here – to inquire about Bobby's cough, of course. While she was here, a footman came across from the Hall with a telegram which had just arrived there for her – Sir Charles thought it might be of importance. She opened it – and I saw at once that it gave her a shock. She gave me a very queer look – very queer! Then she jumped up and said she'd had news that necessitated her returning to town at once. She hurried away and, not long afterwards I saw one of Sir Charles's cars, setting off towards Chilminster. Of course, that telegram would be from Hawksfoot. He, no doubt, Francis, had found your card there when he went in. Francis, don't you wish we'd been there to see his face when he found it?'

The dinner bell rang before Leggatt could answer. But before he had twice put his spoon in his soup, he looked up and smiled at his wife across the table.

'I wish we had, Marian,' he said. 'However, you had the pleasure of seeing Mrs Peacock open her telegram. I hadn't. But it gave me an absolutely fiendish pleasure to leave Hawksfoot my card!'

SANCTUARY

Agatha Christie

THE vicar's wife came round the corner of the vicarage with her arms full of chrysanthemums. A good deal of rich garden soil was attached to her strong brogue shoes and a few fragments of earth were adhering to her nose, but of that fact she was perfectly unconscious.

She had a slight struggle in opening the vicarage gate which hung, rustily, half off its hinges. A puff of wind caught at her battered felt hat, causing it to sit even more rakishly than it had done before. 'Bother!' said Bunch.

Christened by her optimistic parents Diana, Mrs Harmon had become Bunch at an early age for somewhat obvious reasons and the name had stuck to her ever since. Clutching the chrysanthemums, she made her way through the gate to the churchyard, and so to the church door.

The November air was mild and damp. Clouds scudded across the sky with patches of blue here and there. Inside, the church was dark and cold; it was unheated except at service times.

'Brrrrrh!' said Bunch expressively. 'I'd better get on with this quickly. I don't want to die of cold.'

With the quickness born of practice she collected the necessary paraphernalia: vases, water, flower-holders. 'I wish we had lilies,' thought Bunch to herself. 'I get so tired of these scraggy chrysanthemums.' Her nimble fingers arranged the blooms in their holders.

There was nothing particularly original or artistic about the decorations, for Bunch Harmon herself was neither original nor artistic, but it was a homely and pleasant arrangement. Carrying the vases carefully, Bunch stepped up the aisle and made her way towards the altar. As she did so the sun came out.

It shone through the east window of somewhat crude coloured glass, mostly blue and red – the gift of a wealthy Victorian church-goer. The effect was almost startling in its sudden opulence. 'Like jewels,' thought Bunch. Suddenly she stopped, staring ahead of her. On the chancel steps was a huddled dark form.

Putting down the flowers carefully, Bunch went up to it and bent over it. It was a man lying there, huddled over on himself. Bunch knelt down by him and slowly, carefully, she turned him over. Her fingers went to his pulse – a pulse so feeble and fluttering that it told its own story, as did the almost greenish pallor of his face. There was no doubt, Bunch thought, that the man was dying.

He was a man of about forty-five, dressed in a dark, shabby suit. She laid down the limp hand she had picked up and looked at his other hand. This seemed clenched like a fist on his breast. Looking more closely she saw that the fingers were closed over what seemed to be a large wad or handkerchief which he was holding tightly to his chest. All round the clenched hand there were splashes of a dry brown fluid which, Bunch guessed, was dry blood. Bunch sat back on her heels, frowning.

Up till now the man's eyes had been closed but at this point they suddenly opened and fixed themselves on Bunch's face. They were neither dazed nor wandering. They seemed fully alive and intelligent. His lips moved, and Bunch bent forward to catch the words, or rather the word. It was only one word that he said:

'*Sanctuary.*'

There was, she thought, just a very faint smile as he breathed out this word. There was no mistaking it, for after a moment he said it again, 'Sanctuary . . .'

Then, with a faint, long-drawn-out sigh, his eyes closed again. Once more Bunch's fingers went to his pulse. It was still there, but fainter now and more intermittent. She got up with decision.

'Don't move,' she said, 'or try to move. I'm going for help.'

The man's eyes opened again but he seemed now to be fixing his attention on the coloured light that came through the east window. He murmured something that Bunch could not quite catch. She thought, startled, that it might have been her husband's name.

'Julian?' she said. 'Did you come here to find Julian?' But there was no answer. The man lay with eyes closed, his breathing coming in slow, shallow fashion.

Bunch turned and left the church rapidly. She glanced at her watch and nodded with some satisfaction. Dr Griffiths would still be in his surgery. It was only a couple of minutes' walk from the church. She went in, without waiting to knock or ring, passing through the waiting-room and into the doctor's surgery.

'You must come at once,' said Bunch. 'There's a man dying in the church.'

Some minutes later Dr Griffiths rose from his knees after a brief examination.

'Can we move him from here into the vicarage? I can attend to him better there – not that it's any use.'

'Of course,' said Bunch. 'I'll go along and get things ready. I'll get Harper and Jones, shall I? To help you carry him.'

'Thanks. I can telephone from the vicarage for an ambulance, but I'm afraid – by the time it comes . . .' He left the remark unfinished.

Bunch said, 'Internal bleeding?'

Dr Griffiths nodded. He said, 'How on earth did he come here?'

'I think he must have been here all night,' said Bunch, considering. 'Harper unlocks the church in the morning as he goes to work, but he doesn't usually come in.'

It was about five minutes later when Dr Griffiths put down the telephone receiver and came back into the morning-room where the injured man was lying on quickly arranged blankets on the sofa. Bunch was moving a basin of water and clearing up after the doctor's examination.

'Well, that's that,' said Griffiths. 'I've sent for an ambulance and I've notified the police.' He stood, frowning, looking down on the patient who lay with closed eyes. His left hand was plucking in a nervous, spasmodic way at his side.

'He was shot,' said Griffiths. 'Shot at fairly close quarters. He rolled his handkerchief up into a ball and plugged the wound with it so as to stop the bleeding.'

'Could he have gone far after that happened?' Bunch asked.

'Oh yes, it's quite possible. A mortally wounded man has been known to pick himself up and walk along a street as though nothing had happened, and then suddenly collapse five or ten minutes later. So he needn't have been shot in the church. Oh no. He may have been shot some distance away. Of course, he may have shot himself and then dropped the revolver and staggered blindly towards the church. I don't quite know why he made for the church and not for the vicarage.'

'Oh, I know *that*,' said Bunch. 'He said it: "Sanctuary." '

The doctor stared at her. 'Sanctuary?'

'Here's Julian,' said Bunch, turning her head as she heard her husband's steps in the hall. 'Julian! Come here.'

The Reverend Julian Harmon entered the room. His vague. scholarly manner always made him appear much older than he really was. 'Dear me!' said Julian Harmon, staring in a mild, puzzled manner at the surgical appliances and the prone figure on the sofa.

Bunch explained with her usual economy of words. 'He was in the church, dying. He'd been shot. Do you know him, Julian? I thought he said your name.'

The vicar came up to the sofa and looked down at the dying man. 'Poor fellow,' he said, and shook his head. 'No, I don't know him. I'm almost sure I've never seen him before.'

At that moment the dying man's eyes opened once more. They went from the doctor to Julian Harmon and from him to his wife. The eyes stayed there, staring into Bunch's face. Griffiths stepped forward.

'If you could tell us,' he said urgently.

But with his eyes fixed on Bunch, the man said in a weak voice, 'Please – *please* – ' and then, with a slight tremor, he died . . .

Sergeant Hayes licked his pencil and turned the page of his notebook.

'So that's all you can tell me, Mrs Harmon?'

'That's all,' said Bunch. 'These are the things out of his coat pockets.'

On a table at Sergeant Hayes's elbow was a wallet, a rather battered old watch with the initials W. S. and the return half of a ticket to London. Nothing more.

'You've found out who he is?' asked Bunch.

'A Mr And Mrs Eccles phoned up the station. He's her brother, it seems. Name of Sandbourne. Been in a low state of health and nerves for some time. He's been getting worse lately. The day before yesterday he walked out and didn't come back. He took a revolver with him.

'And he came out here and shot himself with it?' said Bunch. 'Why?'

'Well, you see, he'd been depressed . . .'

Bunch interrupted him. 'I don't mean *that*. I mean, why here?'

Since Sergeant Hayes obviously did not know the answer to that one, he replied in an oblique fashion, 'Come out here, he did, on the five-ten bus.'

'Yes,' said Bunch again. 'But *why*?'

'I don't know, Mrs Harmon,' said Sergeant Hayes. 'There's no accounting. If the balance of the mind is disturbed – '

Bunch finished for him. 'They may do it anywhere. But it still seems to me unnecessary to take a bus out to a small country place like this. He didn't know anyone here, did he?'

'Not so far as can be ascertained,' said Sergeant Hayes. He coughed in an apologetic manner and said, as he rose to his feet, 'It may be as Mr and Mrs Eccles will come out and see you, ma'am – if you don't mind, that is.'

'Of course I don't mind,' said Bunch. 'It's very natural. I only wish I had something to tell them.'

'I'll be getting along,' said Sergeant Hayes.

'I'm only so thankful,' said Bunch, going with him to the front door, 'that it wasn't murder.'

A car had drawn up at the vicarage gate. Sergeant Hayes, glancing at it, remarked: 'Looks as though that's Mr and Mrs Eccles come here now, ma'am, to talk with you.'

Bunch braced herself to endure what, she felt, might be rather a difficult ordeal. 'However,' she thought, 'I can always call Julian in to help me. A clergyman's a great help when people are bereaved.'

Exactly what she had expected Mr and Mrs Eccles to be like, Bunch could not have said, but she was conscious, as she greeted them, of a feeling of surprise. Mr Eccles was a stout florid man whose natural manner would have been cheerful and facetious. Mrs Eccles had a vaguely flashy look about her. She had a small, mean, pursed-up mouth. Her voice was thin and reedy.

'It's been a terrible shock, Mrs Harmon, as you can imagine,' she said.

'Oh, I know,' said Bunch. 'It must have been. Do sit down. Can I offer you – well, perhaps it's a little early for tea – '

Mr Eccles waved a pudgy hand. 'No, no, nothing for us,' he said. 'It's very kind of you, I'm sure. Just wanted to . . . well . . . what poor William said and all that, you know?'

'He's been abroad a long time,' said Mrs Eccles, 'and I think he must have had some very nasty experiences. Very quiet and depressed he's been, ever since he came home. Said the world wasn't fit to live in and there was nothing to look forward to. Poor Bill, he was always moody.'

Bunch stared at them both for a moment or two without speaking.

'Pinched my husband's revolver, he did,' went on Mrs Eccles. 'Without our knowing. Then it seems he come out here by bus. I suppose that was nice feeling on his part. He wouldn't have liked to do it in our house.

'Poor fellow, poor fellow,' said Mr Eccles, with a sigh. 'It doesn't do to judge.'

There was another short pause, and Mr Eccles said, 'Did he leave a message? Any last words, nothing like that?'

His bright, rather pig-like eyes watched Bunch closely. Mrs Eccles, too, leaned forward as though anxious for the reply.

'No,' said Bunch quietly. 'He came into the church when he was dying, for sanctuary.'

Mrs Eccles said in a puzzled voice, 'Sanctuary? I don't think I quite . . .'

Mr Eccles interrupted. 'Holy place, my dear,' he said impatiently. 'That's what the vicar's wife means. It's a sin – suicide, you know. I expect he wanted to make amends.'

'He tried to say something just before he died,' said Bunch. 'He began, "Please," but that's as far as he got.'

Mrs Eccles put her handkerchief to her eyes and sniffed. 'Oh, dear,' she said. 'It's terribly upsetting, isn't it?'

'There, there, Pam,' said her husband. 'Don't take on. These things can't be helped. Poor Willie. Still, he's at peace now. Well, thank you very much, Mrs Harmon. I hope we haven't interrupted you. A vicar's wife is a busy lady, we know that.'

They shook hands with her. Then Eccles turned back suddenly to say, 'Oh yes, there's just one other thing. I think you've got his coat here, haven't you?'

'His coat?' Bunch frowned.

Mrs Eccles said, 'We'd like all his things, you know. Sentimental-like.'

'He had a watch and a wallet and a railway ticket in the pockets,' said Bunch. 'I gave them to Sergeant Hayes.'

'That's all right, then,' said Mr Eccles. 'He'll hand them over to us, I expect. His private papers would be in the wallet.'

'There was a pound note in the wallet,' said Bunch. 'Nothing else.'

'No letters? Nothing like that?'

Bunch shook her head.

'Well, thank you again, Mrs Harmon. The coat he was wearing – perhaps the sergeant's got that too, has he?'

Bunch frowned in an effort of remembrance.

'No,' she said. 'I don't think . . . let me see. The doctor and I took his coat off to examine his wound.' She looked round the room vaguely. 'I must have taken it upstairs with the towels and basin.'

'I wonder now, Mrs Harmon, if you don't mind . . . We'd like his coat, you know, the last thing he wore. Well the wife feels rather sentimental about it.'

'Of course,' said Bunch. 'Would you like me to have it cleaned first? I'm afraid it's rather – well – stained.'

'Oh, no, no, no, that doesn't matter.'

Bunch frowned. 'Now I wonder where . . . excuse me a moment.' She went upstairs and it was some few minutes before she returned.

'I'm so sorry,' she said breathlessly, 'my daily woman must have put it aside with other clothes that were going to the cleaners. It's taken me quite a long time to find it. Here it is. I'll do it up for you in brown paper.'

Disclaiming their protests she did so; then once more effusively bidding her farewell the Eccles departed.

Bunch went slowly back across the hall and entered the study.

The Reverend Julian Harmon looked up and his brow cleared. He was composing a sermon and was fearing that he'd been led astray by the interest of the political relations between Judaea and Persia, in the reign of Cyrus.

'Yes, dear?' he said hopefully.

'Julian,' said Bunch. 'What's *Sanctuary* exactly?'

Julian Harmon gratefully put aside his sermon paper.

'Well,' he said. 'Sanctuary in Roman and Greek temples applied to the *cella* in which stood the statue of a god. The Latin word for altar "*ara*" also means protection.' He continued learnedly: 'In A.D. three hundred and ninety-nine the right of sanctuary in Christian churches was finally and definitely recognized. The earliest mention of the right of sanctuary in England is in the Code of Laws issued by Ethelbert in A.D. six hundred . . .'

He continued for some time with his exposition but was, as often, disconcerted by his wife's reception of his erudite pronouncement.

'Darling,' she said. 'You *are* sweet.'

Bending over, she kissed him on the tip of his nose. Julian felt rather like a dog who has been congratulated on performing a clever trick.

'The Eccles have been here,' said Bunch.

The vicar frowned. 'The Eccles? I don't seem to remember . . .'

'You don't know them. They're the sister and her husband of the man in the church.'

'My dear, you ought to have called me.'

'There wasn't any need,' said Bunch. 'They were not in need of consolation. I wonder now . . .' She frowned. 'If I put a casserole in the oven tomorrow, can you manage, Julian? I think I shall go up to London for the sales.'

'The sails?' Her husband looked at her blankly. 'Do you mean a yacht or a boat or something?'

Bunch laughed. 'No, darling. There's a special white sale at Burrows and Portman's. You know, sheets, table-cloths and towels and glass-cloths. I don't know what we do with our glass-cloths, the way they wear through. Besides,' she added thoughtfully, 'I think I ought to go and see Aunt Jane.'

★

That sweet old lady, Miss Jane Marple, was enjoying the delights of the metropolis for a fortnight, comfortably installed in her nephew's studio flat.

'So kind of dear Raymond,' she murmured. 'He and Joan have gone to America for a fortnight and they insisted I should come up here and enjoy myself. And now, dear Bunch, do tell me what it is that's worrying you.'

Bunch was Miss Marple's favourite godchild, and the old lady looked at her with great affection as Bunch, thrusting her best felt hat farther on the back of her head, started on her story.

Bunch's recital was concise and clear. Miss Marple nodded her head as Bunch finished. 'I see,' she said. 'Yes, I see.'

'That's why I felt I had to see you,' said Bunch. 'You see, not being clever – '

'But you *are* clever, my dear.'

'No, I'm not. Not clever like Julian.'

'Julian, of course, has a very solid intellect,' said Miss Marple.

'That's it,' said Bunch. 'Julian's got the intellect, but on the other hand, I've got the *sense*.'

'You have a lot of common sense, Bunch, and you're very intelligent.'

'You see, I don't really know what I ought to do. I can't ask Julian because – well, I mean, Julian's so full of rectitude . . .'

This statement appeared to be perfectly understood by Miss Marple, who said, 'I know what you mean, dear. We women – well, it's different.' She went on, 'You told me what happened, Bunch, but I'd like to know first exactly what you think.'

'It's all wrong,' said Bunch. 'The man who was there in the church, dying, knew all about Sanctuary. He said it just the way Julian would have said it. I mean, he was a well-read, educated man. And if he'd shot himself, he wouldn't drag himself into a church afterwards and say "sanctuary". Sanctuary means that you're pursued, and when you get into a church you're safe. Your pursuers can't touch you. At one time even the law couldn't get at you.'

She looked questioningly at Miss Marple. The latter nodded. Bunch went on, 'Those people, the Eccles, were quite different. Ignorant and coarse. And there's another thing. That watch – the dead man's watch. It had the initials W. S. on the back of it. But inside – I opened it – in very small lettering there was "To Walter from his father" and a date. *Walter*. But the Eccles kept talking of him as William or Bill.'

Miss Marple seemed about to speak but Bunch rushed on, 'Oh, I know you're not always called the name you're baptized by. I mean, I can understand that you might be christened William and called "Porky" or "Carrots" or something. But your sister wouldn't call you William or Bill if your name was Walter.'

'You mean that she wasn't his sister?'

'I'm quite sure she wasn't his sister. They were horrid – both of them. They came to the vicarage to get his things and to find out if he'd said anything before he died. When I said he hadn't I saw it in their faces – relief. I think myself,' finished Bunch, 'it was Eccles who shot him.'

'Murder?' said Miss Marple.

'Yes,' said Bunch. 'Murder. That's why I came to you, darling.'

Bunch's remark might have seemed incongruous to an ignorant listener, but in certain spheres Miss Marple had a reputation for dealing with murder.

'He said "please" to me before he died,' said Bunch. 'He wanted me to do something for him. The awful thing is I've no idea what.'

Miss Marple considered for a moment or two, and then pounced on the point that had already occurred to Bunch. 'But why was he there at all?' she asked.

'You mean,' said Bunch, 'if you wanted sanctuary you might pop into a church anywhere. There's no need to take a bus that only goes four times a day and come out to a lonely spot like ours for it.'

'He must have come there for a purpose,' Miss Marple thought. 'He must have come to see someone. Chipping Cleghorn's not a big place, Bunch. Surely you must have some idea of who it was he came to see?'

Bunch reviewed the inhabitants of her village in her mind before rather doubtfully shaking her head. 'In a way,' she said, 'it could be anybody.'

'He never mentioned a name?'

'He said Julian, or I thought he said Julian. It might have been

Julia, I suppose. As far as I know, there isn't any Julia living in Chipping Cleghorn.'

She screwed up her eyes as she thought back to the scene. The man lying there on the chancel steps, the light coming through the window with its jewels of red and blue light.

'Jewels,' said Bunch suddenly. 'Perhaps that's what he said. The light coming through the east window looked like jewels.'

'Jewels,' said Miss Marple thoughtfully.

'I'm coming now,' said Bunch, 'to the most important thing of all. The reason why I've really come here today. You see, the Eccles made a great fuss about having his coat. We took it off when the doctor was seeing to him. It was an old, shabby sort of coat – there was no reason they should have wanted it. They pretended it was sentimental, but that was nonsense.

'Anyway, I went up to find it, and as I was just going up the stairs I remembered how he'd made a kind of picking gesture with his hand, as though he was fumbling with the coat. So when I got hold of the coat I looked at it very carefully and I saw that in one place the lining had been sewn up again with a different thread. So I unpicked it and I found a little piece of paper inside. I took it out and I sewed it up again properly with thread that matched. I was careful and I don't really think that the Eccles would know I've done it. I don't *think* so, but I can't be sure. And I took the coat down to them and made some excuse for the delay.'

'The piece of paper?' asked Miss Marple.

Bunch opened her handbag. 'I didn't show it to Julian,' she said, 'because he would have said that I ought to have given it to the Eccles. But I thought I'd rather bring it to you instead.'

'A cloakroom ticket,' said Miss Marple, looking at it. 'Paddington Station.'

'He had a return ticket to Paddington in his pocket,' said Bunch.

The eyes of the two women met.

'This calls for action,' said Miss Marple briskly. 'But it would be advisable, I think, to be careful. Would you have noticed at all, Bunch dear, whether you were followed when you came to London today?'

'Followed!' exclaimed Bunch. 'You don't think – '

'Well, I think it's *possible*,' said Miss Marple. 'When anything is possible, I think we ought to take precautions.' She rose with a brisk movement. 'You came up here ostensibly, my dear, to go to the sales. I think the right thing to do, therefore, would be for us to *go* to the sales. But before we set out, we might put one or two little arrangements in hand. I don't suppose,' Miss Marple added obscurely, 'that I shall need the old speckled tweed with the beaver collar just at present.'

It was about an hour and a half later that the two ladies, rather the worse for wear and battered in appearance, and both clasping parcels of hardly-won household linen, sat down at a small and sequestered hostelry called the Apple Bough to restore their forces with steak and kidney pudding followed by apple tart and custard.

'Really a prewar quality face towel, gasped Miss Marple, slightly out of breath. 'With a J on it, too. So fortunate that Raymond's wife's name is Joan. I shall put them aside until I really need them and then they will do for her if I pass on sooner than I expect.'

'I really did need the glass-cloths,' said Bunch. 'And they were very cheap, though not as cheap as the ones that woman with the ginger hair managed to snatch from me.'

A smart young woman with a lavish application of rouge and lipstick entered the Apple Bough at that moment. After looking round vaguely for a moment or two, she hurried to their table. She laid down an envelope by Miss Marple's elbow.

'There you are, miss,' she said briskly.

'Oh, thank you, Gladys,' said Miss Marple. 'Thank you very much. So kind of you.'

'Always pleased to oblige, I'm sure,' said Gladys. 'Ernie always says to me, "Everything what's good you learned from that Miss Marple of yours that you were in service with," and I'm sure I'm always glad to oblige you, miss.'

'Such a dear girl,' said Miss Marple as Gladys departed again. 'Always so willing and so kind.'

She looked inside the envelope and then passed it on to Bunch. 'Now be very careful, dear,' she said. 'By the way, is there still that nice young inspector at Melchester that I remember?'

'I don't know,' said Bunch. 'I expect so.'

'Well, if not,' said Miss Marple thoughtfully, 'I can always ring up the Chief Constable. I *think* he would remember me.'

'Of course he'd remember you,' said Bunch. 'Everybody would remember *you*. You're quite unique.' She rose.

Arrived at Paddington, Bunch went to the luggage office and produced the cloakroom ticket. A moment or two later a rather shabby old suitcase was passed across to her, and carrying this she made her way to the platform.

The journey home was uneventful. Bunch rose as the train approached Chipping Cleghorn and picked up the old suitcase. She had just left her carriage when a man, sprinting along the platform, suddenly seized the suitcase from her hand and rushed off with it.

'Stop!' Bunch yelled. 'Stop him, stop him. He's taken my suitcase.'

The ticket collector who, at this rural station, was a man of somewhat slow processes, had just begun to say, 'Now, look here, you can't do that – ' when a smart blow in the chest pushed him aside, and the man with the suitcase rushed out from the station. He made his way towards a waiting car. Tossing the suitcase in, he was about to climb after it, but before he could move a hand fell on his shoulder, and the voice of Police Constable Abel said, 'Now then, what's all this?'

Bunch arrived, panting, from the station. 'He snatched my suitcase,' she said.

'Nonsense,' said the man. 'I don't know what this lady means. It's my suitcase. I just got out of the train with it.'

'Now, let's get this clear,' said Police Constable Abel.

He looked at Bunch with a bovine and impartial stare. Nobody would have guessed that Police Constable Abel and Mrs Harmon spent long half-hours in Police Constable Abel's off-time discussing the respective merits of manure and bone meal for rose bushes.

'You say, madam, that this is your suitcase?' said Police Constable Abel.

'Yes,' said Bunch. 'Definitely.'

'And you, sir?'

'I say this suitcase is mine.'

The man was tall, dark and well dressed, with a drawling voice and a superior manner. A feminine voice from inside the car, said, 'Of course it's your suitcase, Edwin. I don't know what this woman means.'

'We'll have to get this clear,' said Police Constable Abel. 'If it's your suitcase, madam, what do you say is inside it?'

'Clothes' said Bunch. 'A long speckled coat with a beaver collar, two wool jumpers and a pair of shoes.'

'Well, that's clear enough,' said Police Constable Abel. He turned to the other.

'I am a theatrical costumer,' said the dark man importantly. 'This suitcase contains theatrical properties which I brought down here for an amateur performance.'

'Right, sir,' said Police Constable Abel. 'Well, we'll just look inside, shall we, and see? We can go along to the police station, or if you're in a hurry we'll take the suitcase back to the station and open it there.'

'It'll suit me,' said the dark man. 'My name is Moss, by the way. Edwin Moss.'

The police constable, holding the suitcase, went back into the station. 'Just taking this into the parcels office, George,' he said to the ticket collector.

Police Constable Abel laid the suitcase on the counter of the parcels office and pushed back the clasp. The case was not locked. Bunch and Mr Edwin Moss stood on either side of him, their eyes regarding each other vengefully.

'Ah!' said Police Constable Abel, as he pushed up the lid.

Inside, neatly folded, was a long rather shabby tweed coat with a beaver fur collar. There were also two wool jumpers and a pair of country shoes.

'Exactly as you say, madam,' said Police Constable Abel, turning to Bunch.

Nobody could have said that Mr Edwin Moss under-did things. His dismay and compunction were magnificent.

'I do apologize,' he said. 'I really *do* apologize. Please believe me, dear lady, when I tell you how very, very sorry I am. Unpardonable – quite unpardonable – my behaviour has been.' He looked at his watch. 'I must rush now. Probably my suitcase has gone on the train.' Raising his hat once more, he said meltingly to Bunch. 'Do, *do* forgive me,' and rushed hurriedly out of the parcels office.

'Are you going to let him get away?' asked Bunch in a conspiratorial whisper of Police Constable Abel.

The latter slowly closed a bovine eye in a wink.

'He won't get too far, ma'am,' he said. 'That's to say he won't get far unobserved, if you take my meaning.'

'Oh,' said Bunch, relieved.

'That old lady's been on the phone,' said Police Constable Abel, 'the one as was down here a few years ago. Bright she is, isn't she? But there's been a lot cooking up all today. Shouldn't wonder if the inspector or sergeant was out to see you about it tomorrow morning.'

It was the inspector who came, the Inspector Craddock whom Miss Marple remembered. He greeted Bunch with a smile as an old friend.

'Crime in Chipping Cleghorn again,' he said cheerfully. 'You don't lack for sensation here, do you, Mrs Harmon?'

I could do with rather less,' said Bunch. 'Have you come to ask me questions or are you going to tell me things for a change?'

'I'll tell you some things first,' said the inspector. 'To begin with, Mr and Mrs Eccles have been having an eye kept on them for some time. There's reason to believe they've been connected with several robberies in this part of the world. For another thing, although Mrs Eccles *has* a brother called Sandbourne who has recently come back from abroad, the man you found dying in the church yesterday was definitely not Sandbourne.'

'I knew that he wasn't,' said Bunch. 'His name was Walter, to begin with, not William.'

The inspector nodded. 'His name was Walter St John, and he escaped forty-eight hours ago from Charrington Prison.'

'Of course,' said Bunch softly to herself, 'he was being hunted down by the law, and he took sanctuary.' Then she asked, 'What had he done?'

'I'll have to go back rather a long way. It's a complicated story. Several years ago there was a certain dancer doing turns at the music halls. I don't expect you'll have ever heard of her, but she specialized in an Arabian Night turn, "Aladdin in the Cave of Jewels" it was called. She wore bits of rhinestone and not much else.

'She wasn't much of a dancer, I believe, but she was – well – attractive. Anyway, a certain Asiatic royalty fell for her in a big way. Amongst other things he gave her a very magnificent emerald necklace.'

'The historic jewels of a Rajah?' murmured Bunch ecstatically.

Inspector Craddock coughed. 'Well, a rather more modern version, Mrs Harmon. The affair didn't last very long, broke up when our potentate's attention was captured by a certain film star whose demands were not quite so modest.

'Zobeida, to give the dancer her stage name, hung on to the necklace, and in due course it was stolen. It disappeared from her dressing-room at the theatre, and there was a lingering suspicion in the minds of the authorities that she herself might have engineered its disappearance. Such things have been known as a publicity stunt, or indeed from more dishonest motives.

'The necklace was never recovered, but during the course of the investigation the attention of the police was drawn to this man, Walter St John. He was a man of education and breeding who had come down in the world, and who was employed as a working jeweller with a rather obscure firm which was suspected of acting as a fence for jewel robberies.

'There was evidence that this necklace had passed through his hands. It was, however, in connection with the theft of some other jewellery that he was finally brought to trial and convicted and sent to prison. He had not very much longer to serve, so his escape was rather a surprise.'

'But why did he come here?' asked Bunch.

'We'd like to know that very much, Mrs Harmon. Following up his trail, it seems that he went first to London. He didn't visit any of his old associates but he visited an elderly woman, a Mrs Jacobs who had formerly been a theatrical dresser. She won't say a word of what he came for, but according to other lodgers in the house he left carrying a suitcase.'

'I see,' said Bunch. 'He left it in the cloakroom at Paddington and then he came down here.'

'By that time,' said Inspector Craddock, 'Eccles and the man who calls himself Edwin Moss were on his trail. They wanted that suitcase. They saw him get on the bus. They must have driven out in a car ahead of him and been waiting for him when he left the bus.'

'And he was murdered?' said Bunch.

'Yes,' said Craddock. 'He was shot. It was Eccles's revolver, but I rather fancy it was Moss who did the shooting. Now, Mrs Harmon, what we want to know is, where is the suitcase that Walter St John actually deposited at Paddington Station?'

Bunch grinned. 'I expect Aunt Jane's got it by now,' she said. 'Miss Marple, I mean. That was her plan. She sent a former maid of hers with a suitcase packed with her things to the cloakroom at Paddington and we exchanged tickets. I collected her suitcase and brought it down by train. She seemed to expect that an attempt would be made to get it from me.'

It was Inspector Craddock's turn to grin. 'So she said when she rang up. I'm driving up to London to see her. Do you want to come, too, Mrs Harmon?'

'Wel-l,' said Bunch, considering. 'Wel-l, as a matter of fact, it's very fortunate. I had a toothache last night so I really ought to go to London to see the dentist, oughtn't I?'

'Definitely,' said Inspector Craddock . . .

Miss Marple looked from Inspector Craddock's face to the eager face of Bunch Harmon. The suitcase lay on the table. 'Of course, I haven't opened it,' the old lady said. 'I wouldn't dream of doing such a thing till somebody official arrived. Besides,' she added, with a demurely mischievous Victorian smile, 'it's locked.'

'Like to make a guess at what's inside, Miss Marple?' asked the inspector.

'I should imagine, you know,' said Miss Marple, 'that it would be Zobeida's theatrical costumes. Would you like a chisel, Inspector?'

The chisel soon did its work. Both women gave a slight gasp as the lid flew up. The sunlight coming through the window lit up what seemed like an inexhaustible treasure of sparkling jewels, red, blue, green, orange.

'Aladdin's Cave,' said Miss Marple. 'The flashing jewels the girl wore to dance.'

'Ah,' said Inspector Craddock. 'Now, what's so precious about it, do you think, that a man was murdered to get hold of it?'

'She was a shrewd girl, I expect,' said Miss Marple thoughtfully. 'She's dead, isn't she, Inspector?'

'Yes, died three years ago.'

'She had this valuable emerald necklace,' said Miss Marple, musingly. 'Had the stones taken out of their setting and fastened here and there on her theatrical costume, where everyone would take them for merely coloured rhinestones. Then she had a replica made of the real necklace, and that, of course, was what was stolen. No wonder it never came on the market. The thief soon discovered the stones were false.'

'Here is an envelope,' said Bunch, pulling aside some of the glittering stones.

Inspector Craddock took it from her and extracted two official-looking papers from it. He read aloud, "Marriage certificate between Walter Edmund St John and Mary Moss." That was Zobeida's real name.'

'So they were married,' said Miss Marple. 'I see.'

'What's the other?' asked Bunch.

'A birth certificate of a daughter, Jewel.'

'Jewel?' cried Bunch. 'Why of course. Jewel! *Jill!* That's it. I see now why he came to Chipping Cleghorn. *That's* what he was trying to say to me. Jewel. The Mundys, you know. Laburnum Cottage. They look after a little girl for someone. They're devoted to her. She's been like their own granddaughter. Yes, I remember now, her name *was* Jewel, only, of course, they call her Jill.

'Mrs Mundy had a stroke about a week ago, and the old man's been very ill with pneumonia. They were both going to go to the infirmary. I've been trying hard to find a good home for Jill somewhere. I didn't want her taken away to an institution.

'I suppose her father heard about it in prison and he managed to break away and get hold of this suitcase from the old dresser he or his wife left it with. I suppose if the jewels really belonged to her mother, they can be used for the child now.'

'I should imagine so, Mrs Harmon. *If* they're here.'

'Oh, they'll be here all right,' said Miss Marple cheerfully . . .

'Thank goodness you're back, dear,' said the Reverend Julian Harmon, greeting his wife with affection and a sigh of content. 'Mrs Burt always tries to do her best when you're away, but she really gave me some *very* peculiar fishcakes for lunch. I didn't want to hurt her feelings so I gave then to Tiglath Pileser, but even *he* wouldn't eat them so I had to throw them out of the window.'

'Tiglath Pileser,' said Bunch, stroking the vicarage cat, who was purring against her knee, 'is *very* particular about what fish he eats. I often tell him he's got a proud stomach!'

'And your tooth, dear? Did you have it seen to?'

'Yes,' said Bunch. 'It didn't hurt much, and I went to see Aunt Jane again, too . . .'

'Dear old thing,' said Julian. 'I hope she's not failing at all.'

'Not in the least,' said Bunch, with a grin.

The following morning Bunch took a fresh supply of chrysanthemums to the church. The sun was once more pouring through the east window, and Bunch stood in the jewelled light on the chancel steps. She said very softly under her breath, 'Your little girl will be all right. *I'll* see that she is. I promise.'

Then she tidied up the church, slipped into a pew and knelt for a few moments to say her prayers before returning to the vicarage to attack the piled-up chores of two neglected days.

THE LION'S TOOTH

E. Crispin

IT lay embedded in crudely wrought silver, with a surround of big lusterless semiprecious stones; graven on the reverse of the silver was an outline which Fen recognized as the ichthys, pass-sign of primitive Christianity.

'Naturally, one thinks of Androcles,' said the reverend mother. 'Or if not of him specially, then of the many other early Christians who faced the lions in the arena.' She paused, then added: 'This, you know, is the convent's only relic. Apparently it is also our only clue.'

She stooped to replace it in the sacristy cupboard; and Fen, while he waited, thought of frail old Sister St Jude, whose only intelligible words since they had found her had been 'The tooth of a lion!,' and again – urgently, repeatedly – 'The tooth of a lion!'

He thought, too, of the eleven-year-old girl who had been kid-napped and of her father, who had obstinately refused to divulge to the police the medium through which the ransom was to be paid, for fear that in trying to catch the kidnapper they would blunder and bring about the death of his only child. He would rather pay, he had said; and from this decision he was in no way to be moved . . .

It had been the reverend mother who had insisted on consulting Fen; but following her now, as she led the way back to her office, he doubted if there was much he could do. The available facts were altogether too arid and too few. Thus: Francis Merrill was middle-aged, a widower and a wealthy businessman. Two weeks ago, immediately after Christmas, he had gone off to the Continent, leaving his daughter Mary, at her own special request, to the care of the sisters. During the mornings Mary had helped the sisters with their chores. But in the afternoons, with the reverend mother's encouragement, she would usually go out and ramble round the countryside.

On most of these outings, Mary Merrill was accompanied, for a short distance, by Sister St Jude. Sister St Jude was ailing; the doctors, however, had decreed that she must get plenty of fresh air, so even through the recent long weeks of frost and ice she had continued to issue forth, well wrapped up, and spend an hour or two each afternoon on a sheltered seat near the summit of the small hill at the convent's back. It had been Mary Merrill's habit to see her settled there and then to wander off on her own.

Until, this last Tuesday, a search-party of the sisters had come upon Sister St Jude sprawled near her accustomed seat with concussion of the brain.

Mary Merrill had not come home that night. The reverend mother had, of course, immediately notified the police; and Francis Merrill, hastening back from Italy, had found a ransom note awaiting him.

To all intents and purposes, that was all; the police, it seemed, had so far achieved precisely nothing. If only – Fen reflected – if *only* one knew more about the *girl herself*: for instance, where she was likely to have gone, and what she was likely to have done, on these rambles of hers. But Francis Merrill had refused even to meet Fen; and the reverend mother had been unable to produce any information about Mary more specific and instructive than the statement that she had been a friendly, trusting, *ordinary* sort of child . . .

'I suppose,' said Fen, collapsing into a chair, 'that it's quite certain Sister St Jude has never said anything comprehensible *other* than this phrase about the lion's tooth?'

'Absolutely certain, I am afraid,' the reverend mother replied. 'Apart from a few – a few sounds which may conceivably have been French words, she has not yet been able – '

'*French* words?'

'Yes. I should have mentioned, perhaps, that Sister St Jude is a Frenchwoman.'

'I see,' said Fen slowly. 'I see . . . Tell me, did she – does she, I mean – speak English at all fluently?'

'Not very fluently, no. She had only been over here a matter of nine months or so. Her vocabulary, for instance, is still rather

limited . . .' The reverend mother hesitated. 'Perhaps you are thinking that the phrase about the lion's tooth may have been misheard.
But she had used it many times, in the presence of many of us –
including Sister Bartholomew, who is another Frenchwoman – and
we have none of us ever had the least doubt about what the words
were.'

'Not misheard,' said Fen pensively. 'But misinterpreted,
perhaps . . .' Looking up, the reverend mother saw that he was on
his feet again. 'Reverend Mother, I have an idea,' he went on. 'Or
an inkling, rather. At present I don't at all see how it *applies*. But
nonetheless, I think that if you'll excuse me, I'll go now and take a
look at the place where Sister St Jude was attacked. There's a certain
object to be looked for there, which the police may well have found,
but decided to ignore.'

'What kind of object?' the reverend mother asked.

And Fen smiled at her. 'Yellow', he said. 'Something yellow.'

No prolonged search was needed; there the thing lay, in full view
of everyone, as plain as the nose on a policeman's face. In a mood
of complacency which the reverend mother could hardly have
approved, Fen pocketed it, climbed the remaining distance to the
top of the little hill, and looked around him. The complacency
waned somewhat; from this vantagepoint he could see buildings
galore. Still, with any luck at all . . .

The gods were with him that day; within three hours – three
hours of peering over hedges, and of surreptitious trespassing in
other people's gardens – he located the particular house he sought.
A glance at the local directory, a rapid but rewarding contact with
the child population of a neighbouring village, and by six o'clock
he was ready for action.

The man who answered the knock on the front door was grey-
haired, weedy, nervous-seeming; while not unprepossessing, he yet
had something of a hungry look. 'Mr Jones?' said Fen, pushing him
back into his own hall before he had time to realize what was
happening, and without waiting for a reply, added: 'I've come for
the child.'"

'The child?' Mr Jones looked blank. 'There's no child here. I'm
afraid you've got the wrong house.'

'Indeed I haven't,' said Fen confidently. And even as he spoke, the thin, high scream of a young girl welled up from somewhere on the premises, followed by incoherent, sobbing appeals for help. Fen noted the particular door to which pallid Mr Jones's eyes immediately turned: an interesting door, in that it lay well away from the direction whence the scream had come . . .

'Yes, we'll go through there, I think,' said Fen pleasantly; and now there was an automatic pistol in his hand. 'It leads to the cellar, I expect. And since I'm not fond of men who try to smash in the skulls of helpless old nuns, you may rely on my shooting you without the slightest hesitation or compunction if you make a single false move.'

Later, when Mr Jones had been taken away by the police, and Mary Merrill, hysterical but otherwise not much harmed, restored to her father, Fen went round to the back garden, where he found an engaging female urchin wandering about eating a large bar of chocolate cream.

'That was jolly good,' he told her, handing over the promised ten-shilling note. 'When you grow up, you ought to go on stage.'

She grinned at him. 'Some scream, mister, eh?'' she said.

'Some scream,' Fen agreed.

And: 'It's obvious,' he said to the reverend mother over lunch the next day, 'that Mary Merrill made friends with Jones soon after she came here, and got into the way of visiting him pretty well every afternoon. No harm in that. But then he found out who her father was and began envisaging the possibility of making some easy money.

'What actually *happened*, I understand, is that Mary, on that last visit, took fright at something odd and constrained in his attitude to her, and succeeded in slipping away while his back was turned. Whereupon he very stupidly followed her (in his car, except for the last bit) and tried to grab her when she was already quite close to home.

'She eluded him again, and ran to Sister St Jude for protection. But by that time Jones had gone too far for retreat to be practicable or safe; so he ran after her, struck Sister St Jude down with his stick, and this time really did succeed in capturing Mary, knocking her out, and so getting her back to his house.

'Whether the dandelion part of it belongs to that particular afternoon, or to some previous one, one doesn't know, but whichever it was, Sister St Jude clearly *noticed* the flower and equally clearly realized, even in her illness and delirium, that it provided a clue to –'

'Wait, please,' the reverend mother implored him faintly. 'Did I here you say "dandelion"?'

And Fen nodded. 'Yes, dandelion. English corruption of the French *dent-de-lion* – which of course means a lion's tooth. But Sister St. Jude's vocabulary was limited: *she* didn't know the English name for it. Therefore, she translated it literally, forgetting altogether the existence of that confusing, but irrelevant, relic of yours –

'Well, I ask you: a dandelion, in January, after weeks of hard frost! But Mary Merrill had managed to find one; had picked it and then perhaps pushed it into a buttonhole of her frock. As every gardener knows, dandelions are prolific and hardy brutes; but in view of the recent wheather, this particular dandelion could really *only* have come from a weed in a hot-house within an hour's walk from here. As soon as I saw Jones's, I was certain it was the right one.'

The reverend mother looked at him. 'You were, were you?' she said.

'Well no actually I wasn't certain at all,' Fen admitted. 'But I thought that the luck I'd had up to then would probably hold, and I was tired of tramping about, and anyway I haven't the slightest objection to terrorizing innocent householders so long as it's in a good cause . . . may I smoke?'